LADY OF RAVENSMERE

RAVENSMERE BOOK 1

MARY MCKENNA

MARBLE EGRET PRESS

For more by Mary McKenna, visit her at mary-mckenna.com. Sign up for notice of new releases and receive a short story.

❀ Created with Vellum

For E and E:
I hope this is enough of a 'real book' for you.

And for J
I love you.

CHAPTER ONE

The carriage rumbled over the hard-packed dirt of the road. Jenevra, wrapped in her wool cloak, her feet tucked up underneath her since the warming stones had long since gone cold, looked out the curtain-covered window occasionally. She could only see the road and a little of the area beyond the road, where grass faded from green into brown.

Someone - a nearby lord who took his road-keeping duties seriously - had mended the road in the past, but the dirt and rocks that filled in the ruts wore away with every wheel that passed over it, especially as the ground grew colder, until he might as well have not bothered.

She would have liked to see more of where they were going, but one of her father's guardsmen rode to the side of the carriage, always keeping approximately level with her. Another rode on the other side of the carriage, outside her mother's window. On other occasions, she might have talked with them - she had always known the guards and they her - but her father and the captain of the guard considered this a dangerous area. The northern border lay a bare twenty miles away, and attacks were not uncommon. As well, the king's law had only recently been reestablished in the area, and bandits roamed too freely in the woods nearby.

If she could look out the window properly, she would see her father riding in front of the wagon, his captain riding beside him. Other guards rode in front of and beside him, with outriders a mile ahead. Behind the carriage were wagons, one with the new members of her household - her companion, three maids, a confessor - and the other containing all her household goods, her linens and plate, her clothing, and in a hidden place, the portion of her dowry that came in gold, with more guards flanking and following the wagons.

A discreet throat-clearing reminded her to drop the curtain, and she did. The inside of the carriage bored her, though, as she had been in it for near a fortnight. The seats were hard, despite thin cushions, and she felt every bump in the road through them. The wood of the carriage had been polished to a high finish, so that she could rest her head against the side and feel only smoothness, but nothing decorated the ceiling or the sides, nothing drew her attention.

Nothing kept out the cold. The curtains on the windows kept the wind out, and they had warm stones in the morning when they set out, and blankets and cloaks aplenty. But by midday, she had chilled. It seemed too early in the year for this kind of cold; the late autumn harvests had not even been gathered in yet. At her home, she could still walk out to enjoy the last flowers. Here, frost coated the grass every morning.

Conversation had become scarce as the days wore on. Her mother, who she loved dearly, had been her only companion for the journey. They had played at cards a bit, and she had read the book her father had given her before leaving, but those had paled too, leaving her with too many hours to listen to horses' hooves and wheels on the road and think. She tired of both.

Despite her mother's disapproval, she drew the curtain aside again. Just beyond the guard, she could see the start of the great hills that lay just nearer the border. They were large, at least to her, though she'd been told that the mountains in the north were higher yet. She could just make out the outline of a keep, the square shape distinguishing it from the land around it. A long afternoon and evening to reach it, but they would reach it before moonrise.

They would be expected. Ravensmere Keep commanded a view of miles around, and their wagon train would have been spotted easily by now. Jenevra supposed that at some point, the keep would send out riders to guide them up the mountain to the gates.

She dropped the curtain again now that the endpoint of her journey sat in view and sank back into her cloak.

In the late spring, not long past her thirteenth birthday, the Northern invaders had been beat back from this land for the first time in decades. The victory, as the bard told it, had rested on a small and determined force led by a young knight whose father had been friends of long standing with the king. After the battle, the king had awarded this knight, Sir Conoc Torval, Ravensmere and the land around it. Sir Conoc would guard the border he had won.

Soon thereafter, her father, Lord Oswin had received a message under the king's seal suggesting in strong terms that she be wed to this knight. She had not seen the letter herself - her father would not include a mere girl in such a discussion - but from her father's temper over it, she could only conclude that the king's suggestion had been tantamount to a decree.

Her father had never taken decrees well. Especially not from the king, to whom he was kin, albeit distantly. But royal decrees, howsoever unwelcome, could not be gainsaid, and so her father's brother had spent the summer here, negotiating with Sir Conoc the terms of their betrothal, with their marriage to follow after she reached her sixteenth year.

She, along with her parents, now traveled to Ravensmere for

the formal betrothal ceremony. They would then return home. She would remain, for the now as bride-to-be and in three years as bride in truth.

She would miss her home. Ravensmere might be a fine place, but it would take time before she could love it. In her heart, where no one knew her feelings, she wondered if she would ever come to love Conoc. As a husband, as a companion, as a lover, as anything... She knew it was not required for marriage, but she could not help but believe it would be a fine thing.

She heard voices outside, near the front of the procession. Though she could not make out words, the tone was friendly, and she presumed that this was some knight or other from Ravensmere. Indeed, after the voices ceased - at least to her ears - the carriage began moving upward, taking the hill road.

The bumps in the road grew worse. Whatever Sir Conoc did or did not do as Lord of Ravensmere, tending the road did not appear to have been one of those tasks. She supposed that he had other more urgent tasks to occupy his mind.

Her uncle Lewin, when he had returned from Ravensmere to Allandale to bring her father the marriage articles, had taken time to sit with her and tell her somewhat of her to-be-home. He had assured her that she could find nothing wanting in the land, that the small lake from which the keep took its name brought life aplenty to trees and plants. He did not speak as much on her new lord, other than to reassure her that he was a good man, one who took his duties seriously. And of the keep itself he had said even less.

She understood his reasons when they drew through the outer wall and into the courtyard.

The keep could not be described as lovely. The walls were barren, dark with the natural color of the stone. The outer wall stood strong, but the wooden gates born testimony to the fighting that had been done here. The courtyard, the same hard-packed dirt as the road, barely seemed to fit her father's guards and the wagon, along with the few guards who belonged to Ravensmere.

The tall walls of the inner keep rose high above them, and Jenevra could see few windows to allow light inside. A place of war, and she shivered.

Few normal sounds greeted her ears. Some animals, horses in the stables, some others in proper enclosures, but not many. Men trained but made little noise. She had never heard her father's castle so silent; hundreds of people lived there and no one could make that many people still. This silence felt empty.

She heard her father swing down from his horse - the otherwise placid gray jennet always tossed his head when her father dismounted, causing the harness to jingle - heard him offered a greeting by the man waiting for them on the steps, a man she had seen for only a moment when they came through the gates.

"My lord Earl," Conoc said, "You are most welcome to Ravensmere."

"Lord Conoc," her father replied, "I have brought you your bride."

The carriage door opened, and she blinked in the sudden light filling the space. For a moment, she could see little but her father's hand, reaching in to hand her out. She took it and stepped out of the carriage into the courtyard of her new home.

Conoc looked at her, and for the space of a heartbeat, she looked at him. He stood on the steps into the keep, which added to his already considerable height. Black hair, cut short, shorter than the fashion at court, and dark blue eyes focused intensely on her. His face was narrow, with faint lines that made him look unyielding. He wore a mail shirt and a sword at his side, and both shirt and scabbard showed signs of use. He did not smile.

Her father let go her hand. "My daughter, Jenevra Louvet of Allandale."

She curtseyed, aware of her appearance in that moment. She could not help that her kirtle had become travel-stained, or that her hair escaped the chaplet that held it away from her face and now wisps blew in the breeze. "My lord," she murmured.

"My lady," her replied, bowing in turn. Then he offered her his arm, so that she joined him on the step. Standing beside him, she could not but notice that he still stood tall above her. His hand under hers had the calluses of a swordsman, and his arm, despite the mail between them, held very firm.

He looked to two men standing near. "Kenan, get the Earl's men settled in the barracks. Lorent, have someone arrange for the Lady Jenevra's belongings to be moved into the keep; my mother will have seen someone to arrange it all." Both men nodded and went off in different directions.

"I had thought that proper welcomes could be done indoors," he said, as her lead her inside the keep, her parents following close behind. His voice, neither high nor low, had a faint hint of an accent she did not recognize. "The weather remains unpredictable, other than the cold at this time of year. My mother awaits us in the great hall."

The great hall, when they entered in, was very grand in its stark and imposing way. No banners softened the walls, no tapestries, nothing everywhere but hard stone. The rushes on the floor had been changed recently, today perhaps, but the floor underneath had not been scrubbed in some time. Jenevra thought that the lady of the castle had not done her duties properly, then realized with a moment of horror that she would be the lady of the castle. This would be her duty soon. True, Lord Conoc's mother lived here and was chatelaine for the time, but Lewin had said she was often too ill to leave her rooms. Jenevra would be expected to assume those duties, and her throat tightened.

A beautiful, if tired looking, woman, waited at the table on the dais for them. She had the same black hair as Conoc, worn in two long plaits bound about with ribbons. Her skin was paler than his, and her eyes a brighter blue, but shape of their faces and their eyes matched perfectly.

She rose, and Conoc brought Jenevra forward. "My mother, Lady Mellyn."

Despite fatigue, those blue eyes observed Jenevra keenly. She held herself, back straight, head up, expression unflinching, her own eyes meeting those of her husband-to-be's mother. Her throat tightened again, and her stomach knotted up, but she would not let such feelings show. After a heartbeat, Mellyn's eyes softened slightly, and she gestured for Jenevra to take the carved chair next to hers.

Conoc made a slight motion of his head, and someone brought mulled wine over to them. Jenevra let her fingers warm while holding the metal cup. Conoc had taken the seat on her other side, with her father beyond him and her mother even farther away. The two men fell into a discussion of the roads and the bandit activity, some of which lay within the Ravensmere lands. Her only conversational partner was Lady Mellyn, and she could not decide what she felt for her husband's mother.

When her fingers had warmed sufficiently, she did turn to Mellyn, to find the other woman observing her again.

"My lady?" Jenevra asked.

Mellyn shook her head once. "You are full young," she said, her voice betraying the same accent as Conoc's, though far more pronounced. She flattened her vowels oddly. "Among my own people, you are too young to even consider a betrothal."

"Your people?" Jenevra did not say anything about her youth; she could do nothing to alter that.

Her smile thinned for a moment. "Did no one tell you of 't? I came to your people to marry my beloved. I am from the North."

Jenevra blinked, startled enough that she could not react. She had known that Conoc was not full Merembrian. Nor was she; her own mother came from Gallrech as one of the old Queen's ladies and had stayed to marry. But a Northerner... The very people Conoc fought against. Her fingers tightened on her cup. "Then Lord Conoc..."

"Fights his own, aye. And they hate him the more for it, for he is one of them. But he loves your land more." Mellyn's eyes stared off into some world that only she could see. "As I loved his father more than my own people, and my family never forgave me for 't."

The silence stretched between them, Jenevra uncertain what she ought to think or speak. She had not known this, nor did she think her father knew, for he would have used it to avoid any agreement, despite the king's will. Although, perhaps he did know, and that had been one source of his anger.

Mellyn seemed content as well to let the silence be now. Lines of pain now showed in her face, as though the revelations had cost her what little reserves she possessed. On her other side, Conoc and her father rose to attend to their own matters, and Jenevra offered Mellyn her arm. "You ought to rest," she said.

"So ought you," Mellyn replied, but she accepted Jenevra's help to rise. "You have a very long day tomorrow, and you spent the day traveling. Warm water will be waiting in the solar for you."

Jenevra, when she reached the solar, found herself too tired to do more than crawl into the pallet her maids had prepared, wishing for a moment that she were in her own comfortable bed far away from this strange place.

CHAPTER TWO

From the moment the king's letter had come with his suggestion of a bride, Sir Conoc, newly Lord of Ravensmere, had understood that he would not be able to make his parents' choice and marry for love. The king commanded - if in softer language - and he obeyed as he had always done.

Jenevra Louvet of Allandale had seemed, by all accounts, to be an excellent match - well-bred, well-dowreyed, both pretty and intelligent. Her father the Earl, a magnate of the Council, controlled much of the south and, as a cousin of the king, had an influence even greater than his lands and title alone. His brother Lewin, when he came to negotiate the betrothal agreement, had subtly and not-so-subtly emphasized that. Her mother, Lady Carelia de Moy, had come from Gallrech to be lady-in-waiting to the late queen, and the queen had expected much in that position. Her ladies had been, to a one, beautiful, intelligent, modest, and well-born, and she had arranged their marriages herself.

Conoc had understood this. And he had understood that he needed this kind of arrangement. He might have a title and a castle, but that was all he had. The castle stood on the northern border and had been back in the king's hands for less than a year, since he himself had beaten the Northerners back.

No one had lived in the keep for a score of years. The wooden gates were bent and warped, the glass in most windows long since broken and taken by scavengers. Ravens had taken one tower and had fought loudly and vociferously against the men who would take it back. Little furnishings had remained, and those were broken more than not.

He had found pride in it, though. This belonged to him, as both power and responsibility.

With what little income he had, he had repaired the barracks and made places for his men. With them, he had begun to make repairs, even working with his own hands as necessary. Their wives became the support inside the keep, under his mother's direction, such as she had been able to provide. To do more would take years and would require the dowry his wife would bring with her.

All this he had understood.

Seeing the wagon train from Allandale as it arrived, he realized that he'd no idea the bargain he was making.

The guards alone equaled nearly half the size of his garrison, and they rode easily, hands unencumbered and swords comfortably loose in scabbards worn from use. Though they had talked and laughed among themselves as they approached the keep, as they rode through the gates they had fallen silent, alert to their surroundings. Compared to them, his own men looked like what they were: ragtag and undisciplined levies, not soldiers.

The Earl rode a gray horse of fine and graceful lines that moved easily. Conoc could only imagine the fortune that had been spent on it. Two equally fine, if less beautiful, working horses pulled the carriage behind him. For a moment, he wished his wife-to-be's dowry had come in horses, if these were examples of what her father owned.

He tried not to let any of it show on his face as he moved down the steps to greet the dismounting Earl. He had the king's favor, and that counted for something, though not as much as he had thought. "My lord Earl," he said, "You are most welcome to Ravensmere."

"Lord Conoc," the Earl replied, "I have brought you your bride." His lips twisted slightly before he turned to hand out his daughter, and Conoc understood the meaning of that too.

She was nothing that he had envisioned when he had bothered to picture his bride at all.

A delicate girl-child, only just beginning to show a hint of the woman she would grow to. She was slim, like a willow, and tall for her age. Silky strands of red-brown hair blew across her face, and soft blue eyes large in her face met his for a moment. The queen herself could not have stood with a spine so straight nor held herself with such confidence.

She curtseyed and murmured a greeting, and he bowed and took her hand in his. Small and delicate, like the rest of her. How the king must have laughed as he arranged this pairing.

Hours later, long after his guests had retired, Conoc leaned on the tower parapet by himself and looked out over the land. If he looked north, he could see the mountains that his mother had grown up among. To the south, his father's homeland. And he and his castle sitting in the middle.

The stone under his arms, cool despite the sun's warmth not that long ago, had been dug from the mountain to his back and carved and shaped to suit a king who had cared neither for the mountains nor the people within them. He'd sought to impose his will on them and had built the castle and installed one of his own men there to see it done. A hundred years later, nothing much had changed.

The evening air carried a hint of moisture, though too little for rain, and the faint cloud cover concurred. The stars shown brightly, and he could pick out the constellations his father had taught him long ago: the Archer, the Wolf, the Huntress...

Faint splashes from the lake outside the walls could just be heard. Inside the walls, the bailey had more activity than usual tonight, with all the guardsmen from Allandale sharing the space. They'd been there only a matter of hours, and already a few men had been disciplined for the brangling that would precede a fight.

Allandale had made his opinion clear in everything he had said: he wanted better for his daughter than a jumped up knight with nothing to show for himself. Conoc could understand that. Jenevra came with a dowry of one thousand gold dragons as well as a small property nearly the size of Ravensmere and far more valuable that would be her dower. She was fair, and she had a lineage that would not shame a prince.

For a woman such as she, he was little enough. He had castle and lands, true enough, but they would need some years to be truly profitable. He had a reputation as a warrior and the acclaim that went along with it. But otherwise... His father had been little better than a mercenary, knighted for service to the king in a battle but otherwise without anything to his name. His mother had been a captive, taken when an attack had captured a village. His father had loved her from the first moment; she had resisted at the first, but had come to love him. He had spent what little coin he had to ransom her, and she had stayed with him instead of returning to her own.

They had never had a great deal, and he had never had a home until he became a squire, but he had been surrounded always by his parents' love for each other and their love for him. His father's death had shattered something within his mother, something that would never heal. He suspected that the decline in her health dated from the same time, but she had kept it from him until after they arrived at Ravensmere and she could hide it no longer. Or perhaps, coming here had changed something in her, as he sometimes found her staring out to the north with longing in her eyes.

Footsteps behind him, but he didn't turn, and in a moment, a man leaned on the wall to his side looking out as he did. On the other side, another man leaned back against the wall. Had they meant him harm, he would have been in a bad way, but they were his oldest friends, trusted before any others, as close as brothers.

Kenan Halacre on his left leaned back, to look across the castle to the mountains. That also gave him the better opportunity to see Conoc and for Conoc to observe him. Like himself, Kenan was half-Northerner, and they shared the same dark hair and eyes as a result. His mother had been taken the same time as Conoc's own. But she had lived unhappily with a man who had not loved her, always longing to return to her home and to bring her son and daughter. She had died before that could happen. Kenan longed for the north, for their people, and viewed his time in Merembria as a period of exile.

He had known Kenan - and his sister Eseld - from his childhood. They had been together often, for their fathers were the same sort of landless knight and their mothers friends of longstanding. He had few memories of any sort that did not also involve his friend.

Lorent Smithson, on his other side, had joined them during their years as squires. He had foiled them perfectly, with his brown hair and open brown eyes, like the farm boy he was. Always quick to smile or laugh, not as weighed down with past hurts and far more grateful for any opportunities that came his way. He had no name of note, no story but that his father had rescued his lord and by way of repayment had asked for his son to have a better chance than his own.

Together they had been three set apart from the other squires, all of whom had noble parents and an inbred superiority that they could never match and had not long tried to.

He did not say anything to them as they stood there. For some time, neither did they. Finally Kenan spoke, which did not surprise Conoc at all.

"The Earl was..."

"Yes," Conoc agreed without looking over. "He was. He does not like this at all." Neither did Kenan, who had argued against it most strenuously during the entire negotiations. Conoc had never fully understood his friend's objections, since his stated reasons had been flimsy.

"Then why did he agree? If he did not want this, he ought to have taken it up with the king, rather than come here and insult you."

Kenan's words cheered Conoc immensely. Friends did that, supported you no matter the situation, even against their own interests at times. Allandale would be gone in a few days, and he could bear the sly insults easier with his friends.

"The king's will prevails," Lorent commented. "Even over the Earl of Allandale. Conoc is just the nearest target for his anger."

"His anger won't last." Conoc shrugged. "He'll have something else to draw his attention soon enough. The king will not be satisfied with this for long." The king and Council had wrangled for on and off for two years over their wars, and now that he held the northern border secure, they were free to turn their eyes in other directions. Gallrech would need look to its borders.

That would be some other lord's problem. The king, with the advice of the Council, would appoint someone as commander over the armies there, who would try and retake the land they'd traditionally held there. A fool's errand, Conoc believed and was glad and grateful that he would be here at Ravensmere and not there with that force.

"You think he'll push the war in Gallrech?" Lorent asked.

"Probably. He's still smarting from losing Ranais and Vantes, and the Earl of Heraglind is left holding only the edge of the province." The king had raged over that loss - Conoc had still been serving near the king at the time and had heard it himself. But nothing else could have been done. The Earl of Heraglind had had neither the men nor the supplies to hold all the cities. He'd done well to hold what he had.

"The Council will not like it," Kenan said. "They want the war to end, if the rumors are true. But they've a fine line to tread. The prince was banished for speaking against it, or so I heard."

He didn't know the truth of that, but Conoc could almost believe it. The king had grown old and had become more set in his opinions and less willing to accept any sort of challenge, even from his son. But if the prince had truly been banished, it would be for more cause. The prince was the king's only child and the only clear heir to the throne. Banishing him would open the succession to a variety of cousins and risk a war.

"The Council can't actually force the king to anything. They can refuse to cooperate, they can make his choices more difficult, but they cannot force him. He'll have his war in Gallrech."

Lorent and Kenan exchanged looks, which Conoc saw. "You do realize you're marrying into that?" Lorent said. "Your father by marriage spends a great deal of time opposing the king, if rumor is to be believed."

"I know," Conoc said sourly. Allandale would not have been his choice for alliance, had he a choice. But the king had commanded, and while Allandale might have had the power to object and hold that line, he didn't. Besides, he was the king's man, and he owed the king his loyalty.

For a long moment, all three were silent. The evening deepened into night, and the chill of autumn nipped at him. Still Conoc stood, his eyes fixed on a distant spot, his mind elsewhere. Finally, he shook his head and extended a hand to each of his friends, which they clasped in their own.

"Inside," he said, his voice hollow. "Tomorrow will be a long day."

CHAPTER THREE

The formal betrothing ceremony took place early in the morning. Tradition dictated that such ceremonies, for it would be a religious ceremony as well as a legal one, took place when the sun's light touched the chapel. Jenevra felt as though she had barely time to sleep before she'd been woken and hustled into a bath.

She had a new formal gown, the kind that girls did not often have chances to wear. A soft kirtle of green wool came first, with a scooped neckline and tight, fitted sleeves. The top half had subtle laces to fit it snug to her body, then from her hips it fell looser. Over that went another gown, in a lighter green velvet. These sleeves laced tight along the back of her arms to her elbow, then fell open with a contrasting inner lining. The dress itself laced along her sides, again to keep everything smooth, and the skirt opened up to show off the kirtle underneath. It finished with a belt of fine soft leather at her waist.

Then she sat while her maids brushed her hair until it shone, then carefully plaited two plaits, which were then wrapped in ribbon and coiled up over her ears. Finally, the chaplet on her head that she always wore, polished until it gleamed.

She felt a doll or a puppet, something for others to play with rather than a person of her own. She had chosen the gown, and it had seemed very exciting at the time, to be accorded the privilege of having an adult gown of her own choosing. Now she could not feel that same excitement.

Indeed, as her parents escorted her to the chapel, she felt more nerves than excitement. In a matter of minutes, she would be bound to Lord Conoc in all but the finalities, for breaking a betrothal was rarely done and only in cases of great cause.

The chapel, she noted, was the only room she had seen thus far where the stone walls were softened by anything. Religious hangings covered the walls, depicting great miracles and saints. Behind the alter, a stained glass window, as tall as she, filled the wall, with images of the God in icy white and Goddess in golden yellow so real to life that she half-expected them to step out and join the assembly.

The room blazed with light. Multiple windows in the ceiling had been opened so that the light streamed down. Warm light filled the space behind the great stained glass, so that vivid colors were thrown everywhere by the light.

Every person in Ravensmere stood in rows, and many from the town below the castle. Though she knew the betrothal to be very important, she had not expected so many for a ceremony that was, in essence, only a promise for a future ceremony.

Every single head turned to look at her as her parents, one on each side of her, walked her down the aisle. The chapel was not large; the aisle could not have been more than fifty or so steps, though she did not count. But that walk, before all those people of whom she knew none, took more heartbeats than it ought. Or perhaps her heart beat too fast, as the weight of everyone's expectations settled on her.

Conoc waited for her beside the priest. Today he did not wear his mail so openly, though she caught a flash of metal off the links when he turned. Instead he wore black, with a surcoat of deep blue over it, and on the surcoat a crest embroidered in black, his crest - an eagle, wings outspread. He took her hands in his and faced her, face serious and composed, while the priest began a lengthy blessing on the day and the promises about to be made.

She did not actually pay much attention to the priest, though he had a rich baritone voice well-suited to the chanted prayer he did. Her participation in this consisted of assenting to the terms stated and agreeing to the marriage after her sixteenth birthday.

Conoc pledged his assent in a deep voice, never breaking his solemn observation of her. Her own voice shook only slightly as she assented and gave her pledge in return. After another interminably long prayer, this one asking a future blessing upon them, the ceremony itself ended. Entire weddings had taken less time than this betrothal ceremony.

They turned, hand-in-hand, to face the assembled people, who gave a less than fully enthusiastic cheer, though Jenevra couldn't tell if they disapproved the match or had simply missed the moment after being stupefied by prayer. Conoc took her hand, slid it through the crook of his arm, and began to walk back down the aisle. Her fingers tightened where they rested on his arm; she felt very small and very young beside him. But she drew her spine straight and walked at his side; she would give no one the satisfaction of seeing her tremble. Not even her promised husband.

They would celebrate soon with a feast, but for now, the most involved parties gathered in the great hall to sign the contract. Jenevra herself did not sign, as she was not old enough to make the contract by her own will. Her father did, and he seemed not displeased with the final version. Instead, she sat in the carved chair by Conoc's side, a chair that was not truly hers until they wed in three years. But Lady Mellyn had made it clear the night before that she was ceding the place to Jenevra now.

After Conoc and her father signed, the required three witnesses signed next. Her father's guard captain for his side, Conoc's friend and captain Sir Lorent for his side, and the priest, Father Andreu, as the neutral witness, all very correct and formal. Then one copy went to her father, along with a copy to be sent to the king for his formal approval, and Conoc kept one copy for himself.

Then, "A toast," her father proposed. "To Lord Conoc and Lady Jenevra." He had his own man hand round glasses of a Gallreian vintage he had brought for the occasion. Jenevra, sipping from her own glass, thought it a rather subtle insult and knew her father did not actually approve. He would, in his own way, show his son-to-be that his daughter was marrying down.

Conoc didn't give any sign that he'd seen the insult; he showed very little reaction to anything. But he didn't return the toast, simply nodded his head and raised his glass to accept it. She wondered if he meant the return insult or simply didn't know how he ought behave.

THE FEAST itself lasted from midday to near sunset. Servants brought out course after course, including the wild deer so plentiful near Ravensmere and a fantastic bread sculpture of the keep. Game pies, fish pies, eel, which she didn't care for at all. The servants from Allandale had provided multiple types of sweets, all of her favorites, using several months' worth of sugar. Jenevra detected her mother's hand in that, for good and ill. A great deal of dancing had taken place as well, though she had not participated, since Lord Conoc did not ask her, and no one else would with him sitting beside her sternly.

By the time she could leave with the other women, leaving the men to drink more and louder, she was tired and, more than that, drained. She had done her best to play her part as lady of the keep, and though she thought it successful, the effort had left her weary.

Her mother, along with her companion Sess, escorted her up to her new room. Last night she had slept with her parents in the solar, the room best fit for guests though it would be put to her purposes during the day. Tonight she would sleep in the room that would be hers from hereafter, a room near the back of the keep, looking out over the lake. Conoc's room lay beside, separated from hers by only a door.

If she were a bride, she would be escorted by more than her mother. A bride needed a great deal of company and advice before her husband saw her on her wedding night.

She, though, had no such needs. And her mother did not speak as they walked through the silent halls until they reached the door to her room.

"I had your maids work on this," her mother said. She held the door closed for a moment. "I hope it will help you feel more comfortable as you settle in. The castle may be unfamiliar, but this room should not ever be." Then she opened the door.

Jenevra stepped in and smiled through the tears that threatened to block her sight. Not all of the furniture had come with her, but old and new pieces had been rearranged to suit her preferences. Her linen chest, with the covering cushion she'd embroidered with unicorns, sat under the window opening - now shuttered - where she could sit and look out. Her bed, a great wooden one that must have weighed as much as a horse, stood where the sun would fall on it in the morning through the tiny glass-paned mullion window. The comb for her hair and the ties she used lay waiting for her on the table by the wall. Hangings covered the stone walls, on one side a family tapestry that showed her lineage for generations back, on the other a scene of a famous queen and the knights who had served at her side.

"Thank you, Mother," she whispered as she hugged her mother.

"The rest of your things will be in the solar, for you to distribute as you decide," she replied, holding Jenevra tight. "But this is a small gift I can give to you." She had reverted to her native language, a language that Jenevra alone of her siblings had learned.

"There is so much I would tell you, if we had time," her mother went on. "You are as well-prepared as any young woman, and I have no fear that you'll manage your new home as featly as you managed your old. I will miss you though." Her mother kissed her forehead. "I love you, my daughter. Do not forget that, whatever may come. Your mother loves you."

"I love you as well," Jenevra replied.

Another kiss to her forehead, and her mother left the room, leaving Jenevra feeling bereft. She and her mother had always been close, and in her mother's leaving, she saw the beginning of the ending of that closeness. Her own attentions and focus must, of necessity, someday align with her husband's, as her mother's did with her father's.

Sess, who had been standing off to one side of the room, now came over and began unlacing the sides of her gown, without saying anything. Since Sess's silences often meant that she felt she couldn't say anything, despite what she thought, Jenevra waited a few minutes, until the gown had been unlaced and she stood in her inner kirtle.

"What have you to say, Sess?"

Sess urged her to sit and began unwinding her long plaits of hair. "I think," she began, then pressed her lips together. "I should not say anything. My loyalty is to you, but I will live here too." Cecilie had been her companion since she was seven, a cousin on her father's side whose family fortunes had decayed until she and her brother had nothing, and who, despite being five years older, had been as much friend as waiting woman.

"Sess…" A shiver ran through Jenevra's body.

After picking up a comb, Sess began to brush out her hair. "I think some - your lady mother for one - believe this not in your best interest," she said softly. "And some on Lord Conoc's side as well."

Jenevra huffed impatiently. "That is not a surprise, nor a shock. I knew my mother had reservations, though she would not discuss them with me." She paused. "Who of Lord Conoc's men has said anything?"

"Some of the guardsmen alluded to an argument Lord Conoc had had, and one of his captains said something, but I could not catch all the words. He referred to another woman. And some did not like a long betrothal." Sess finished brushing and tied her hair so that it would not tangle during her sleep. "Do you want my help with your kirtle?"

Jenevra shook her head, just wanting to be alone, to feel the shape of her own self for a while. "I can manage to unlace a kirtle on my own. Go; I will see you in the morning." She heard the door open and close without Sess saying anything else and regretted her tone. She rarely had been so abrupt with her.

She went to the window. The narrow opening was shuttered and barred, but she could, with effort, lift the bar enough to open the shutter and, kneeling on her chest, see out. She could look out over the lake, which came almost to the feet of the castle. Nature protected this side of the castle.

The lake itself stretched out, perhaps a mile at its widest point. The sun hadn't completely set, and she could spot water-birds poking in the reeds. Curlews had begun their lonesome calls already. The ravens the lake was named for were visible everywhere, dozens of them. St. Something-or-other claimed that so many ravens were called an unkindness, but she half-suspected him of making up such a thing to suit his own purposes.

From here she could not hear the noise from the great hall.

That lay in a more central location. She could almost pretend that none of that existed in this moment. Not Lord Conoc, not Lady Mellyn, not her almost marriage, not even her father. Just the land and the water, the birds and her.

She sat long enough to watch the sun finish setting and the purple dusk fade into dark. She could no longer see much, and even most of the calls had ended, save one early owl faintly in the distance. Past time she re-barred the shutters and finished readying for sleep.

With regret, she closed the window. Her window at home - her old home - had larger glass panes so that she could see out as she willed, and the weather there was mild enough that only in winter had she needed to close the shutters for warmth. Here she knew it was not merely a matter of warmth that required the windows closed and barred. She traced the window frame - this window had once held glass as well, but probably not for some years. It was not her home, not the safe, warm place she knew. She laid her head down on her knees, just for a moment, to mourn the end of her life as she had known it.

At the sound of footsteps on the stone, she picked her head up. No one should come to her room, not since she'd sent Sess away. Her maids would never... But the steps were too heavy to be a woman's. Lord Conoc's, then, or one of his men. No hurry to it, just a firm steady step.

She ran to her bedroom door and pressed her ear to the wood. The steps passed her door without pause but stopped in front of the door beside hers, and that door opened.

The door between their rooms did not have any locks or bars, but the footsteps did not move towards it. She could not tell what he did, but he made no attempt to come near her. He had very heavy footsteps, which she had not noticed earlier in the day. And such noise could hardly work in his favor if he needed to approach an enemy in silence.

With all the silence she possessed, she went to that door and stood beside it, listening to him moving around, still making enough noise to startle birds off their perches. Then she opened the door and stood there watching him.

His room did not appear much different to hers. A bed, a chest for linens against one wall. A large window closed as hers was. A stand for mail and weapons. It smelled different, however. It lacked the musty, damp smell that lingered in hers, and instead she smelled leather and metal and oil and something else, something masculine that she could not identify.

He didn't see her as he paced. He had removed both surcoat, thrown over the chest with no care, and the mail coat, hung with precise care, and now walked about in shirt and hose.

She didn't speak, just watched him. His steps continued to be firm, and his attention focused inward, as though he paced to work his thoughts out. Until he turned at just the right angle and saw her.

"My lady," he said, inclining his head. "Can I help you?"

"I heard you," Jenevra replied. She did not back up, but his sudden focus on her had her wishing to flee.

"I meant you to. I wanted you to hear that I did not go near you."

She tilted her head. "I did not expect that you would. Ought I have?"

Conoc barked out a laugh. "Oh, my lady... They were taking bets, you see, my men and your father's, on whether I would be able to resist you tonight. I did not know if you had heard any of such talk."

Jenevra did not have an answer to that. She had not hear anything of the sort, and her father would have been furious if any man had breathed a word of such a thing near her. But Sess's discomfort meant that she must have heard and not wanted to admit to it.

"You need not worry, my lady. I had no intention of such.

You are my bride-to-be, you are not my wife yet. And you are too young."

She bristled. "Too young for what, my lord? I sat beside you at table, in a seat I have no right to. I sleep in the room beside yours, where I also do not belong as yet. You give every indication that I am your wife in all but name."

"Name matters." His eyes looked at her seriously, the dark blue almost black. "And I believe you know that, my lady."

"I do." Jenevra shook her head. "I should not have come in here; I will not bother you further, my lord."

He crossed to her and laid his hand on the door, trapping her in place. "Conoc," he said. "My name is Conoc."

"I know that, my lord." Jenevra stared him, unblinking and utterly confused by this turn of the conversation. She had pledged to wed him only that morning; she knew his name.

"Then say it, my lady. You are my bride-to-be, surely you can call me by my name."

"As you say, my lord, names matter." She ducked under his arm and into her room. Then she made him a formal curtsey. "I give you good e'en, my lord."

"Good evening, Jenevra," Conoc replied, with the first smile she had seen from him.

She smiled back, then, as silently as she'd entered, she closed the door.

CHAPTER FOUR

Conoc slept badly. His conversation with Jenevra had kept him awake far longer than it should have, given the fatigues of the day. Saying her name, with no title, had given the conversation an intimacy he had not intended. The smile she had given him in return had felt like a gift, something she did not share with many.

Still, she was a girl of thirteen, a child. He had no business to think of a girl her age as anything but a girl. Except that she was his bride-to-be, and unless he wanted a cold marriage and a cold bed in the future, he would need to find some common ground between them.

He went down to the chapel far before either his bride or his guests would be awake. He had no wish to see Jenevra yet and even less interest in speaking with her father. But in the chapel was one he could speak to.

The chapel, in the dim light before the sun reached it and illuminated the windows here, looked dull and dreary. The stone floor absorbed what little light there was, and the stained glass windows - blazing with color when the sun shone - simply looked black. Andreu, already awake and at work as Conoc had expected, in his simple black cassock, seemed to blend in to the shadows.

A faint hint of incense still hung in the air from yesterday's betrothal ceremony, but the air otherwise was cold and crisp. He shivered once; the chapel rarely grew fully warm.

"Have you come looking for me, Conoc?" Andreu asked without ever looking up from the metal work he polished. Conoc did not know how he had even been noticed. "It is too early for morning services, not," now the priest did look up, "that you are one to be present at them."

Conoc smiled, but his heart wasn't in it. Andreu had been his teacher and a surrogate father for many years, and he managed still to make him feel like a recalcitrant boy. He did not know Andreu's history, except that Andreu had been his father's friend long before his own birth, even before Andreu had become a priest. He had never found anyone who gave better counsel, and he knew that Andreu would never give him bad advice.

Instead he sat down and picked up a goblet and a cloth to polish it with. "Did they need cleaning?" he asked, indicating the four goblets sitting there.

"You have guests," Andreu replied. "Should they choose to attend this morning's service, I did not want anything to be amiss."

Conoc rubbed at a spot. "You could have one of the women do this, you know."

"I prefer to do it myself." They polished in silence for several minutes before Andreu opened the conversation again. "You're troubled, Conoc, or you would not have come. What can I do for you?"

"I don't even know what I want to ask," Conoc said. "But I could not sleep, and I did not wish to see my lady or her family this morning." Andreu didn't speak, and Conoc found himself talking on without thinking.

"I do not know what to do with her. She is not what I expected. I expected a woman, hearty and ready to work to rebuild this," he waved a hand at the walls of the keep, "and instead, I am presented with a lady, a girl-child with no discernible skills."

"You knew she would be thirteen when you agreed to this," Andreu said, no judgment in his voice.

"Aye, I did, but I was never so young as she by that age. And I am to wed her in two years. Will she be a woman by then? And what am I to do with her in the mean?"

Andreu set his polishing aside. "Conoc, you had a different life than she. No doubt she is more sheltered than you were at that age. Most women of this station are. I doubt she is as useless as you imagine, for she has undoubtedly been learning the skills of a wife while you learned those of a warrior. But if you cannot live with this bargain, you must say so today so that the contract can be broken before the king approves it."

"That I cannot do, even if I wished it. The king may not have sealed it, but he would not take it well if I changed my mind. And," he sighed, "I do not exactly want to. She is pretty, and if her mother is anything to go by, she will be more so when she is grown. When you can get her to speak, she is quick and spirited. But she is thirteen."

"And if she were not, Conoc? What if she were sixteen or seventeen?"

"I would woo her," Conoc said frankly. "I would try, at any rate. My parents..." Had been a love match that had crossed borders. His mother had left her own people to live among those she had hated all her life.

Andreu resumed his polishing. "Your parents were an exception. But if that is your end, I would not wait too long to begin."

. . .

JENEVRA'S PARENTS stayed only two more days, and those were two days more than Conoc thought he could bear. The Earl did not bother to hide his disdain for Conoc, Ravensmere and everything contained therein. Conoc found himself wondering why the Earl had agreed to this match if he held such opinions, but no opportunity to ask presented itself. The Earl kept all the conversations to neutral topics: road care, bandits, the state of hostilities with the Northerners.

Conoc found them to be informative. Unquestionably, Oswin knew a great deal about these subjects, and Conoc would have been only too happy to learn from him had the situation been different. As it was, he stored up information to be considered and implemented later.

Lady Carelia he saw only at dinner. She spent her time with Jenevra, who he also did not see. Nor could he get her to speak to him in company, beyond bland greetings and commonplace remarks. Not once in those two days did he see a smile, even when she came to the door of his room to say good night.

Seeing them off brought him a sense of relief. The Earl mounted his horse, Lady Carelia was handed into the carriage, and the guards set forth. Once the gates closed behind them, he expected a sense of the familiar to descend again upon the castle.

He turned to Jenevra, who stood beside him upon the steps. Her posture remained perfectly straight, but he thought he detected a hint of a slump to her shoulders. "My lady?" he asked gently, trying to draw her attention.

"My lord?" She looked to him, and he saw the lost girl-child behind her mask of self-control. He had not expected that; she had been so perfect in all her behavior, she had simply fooled them all with it.

"I need to train with my men; it has been put off these last few days. You have the run of the castle; nothing here is forbidden you. If you need me, send someone for me."

She nodded once and slipped away inside. He had seen that spark in her, but something had utterly quenched it, and he wondered how he might bring it to the surface again.

Kenan fell into step beside him as he walked to the training area. For the time that Jenevra' parents had been here, they'd no time to talk as they usually did. He might have enjoyed Kenan's thoughts, but he suspected that Allandale would not have, not would Kenan have enjoyed Allandale's company. The two men, each so proud of their own heritage, would only have moved to insult each other.

"Will you admit it now?" Kenan asked lowly enough that no one else would hear. "She is too young, too gently bred for life here."

"You have been arguing that since the beginning. It is done; the contracts are signed pending His Majesty's approval. I cannot change now." Never mind that Conoc had argued this in his own mind more than once and did not like that he had. The slip of a girl he'd pledged to marry meant more than just her own person.

"Contracts can be broken, even betrothals." Kenan stopped, laid on hand on Conoc's arm, his eyes as serious as ever, but more urgent. His voice lowered even more. "She could be returned to her parents no worse for the trip. My sister -"

"Your sister brings no alliance and not much dowry," Conoc replied. "Besides, isn't she happy with her own man? She's to marry him in a week if I mind rightly."

"She would give him up for you an' you ask her. You know 't to be true. She has always loved you."

Conoc could not dispute that, nor would he try. That Eseld cared for him had been no surprise. She saw him as everything she could hope for, a man who shared her heritage and yet had risen far above their birth, a childhood friend turned hero. When he left to be a squire, she'd been a girl, younger even than Jenevra, and she had hero-worshipped him. Coming back, she had been a woman and he a man grown. If nothing had changed, he might have married her; their mothers would have been pleased enough at that. But Ravensmere had changed that.

"Neither of us is free now. And this is the path I must take, for the good of everyone." Conoc saw the flash of frustration on Kenan's face. His old friend did not settle into this harness easily, and he did not want Conoc to settle either. But in time, he would see this had been the right choice, and he would accept it. Eventually.

CHAPTER FIVE

Not quite a full month after her arrival, Jenevra sat in the solar when the afternoon sun streamed through the windows. Her confessor, Father Bardin sat in a chair across the room, reading aloud from a philosophical text that she supposed was to be educational.

This room was her favorite in the keep. It had a row of windows, so even though they were not very wide, they allowed in a great deal of light. A long bench ran along the wall under the windows, giving her and Sess places to sit and look out over the bailey while they worked. A carpet that had been part of her dowry, brought from thousands of miles away, covered the floor. Along one wall, she had set up her tapestry loom and her spinning wheel sat not far away.

She could hear, faintly, the sounds of Lord Conoc and his men training in the yard as they did every day and that familiar sound relaxed her. She had often listened to her father's men train the same way.

With a sigh, she put down the embroidery in her lap. She did not feel much like concentrating today. She had spent the morning delivering Lady Mellyn's instructions around the keep, as Lady Mellyn had kept to her bed since the betrothal ceremony. She did this most days, except when Mellyn left a matter entirely in her hands, but today had involved a great deal of running up and down stairs before everyone had been quite satisfied.

Satisfaction was perhaps too strong a word. The cook, a gruff man who never smiled, had never done as she'd asked, even with Lady's Mellyn's support and instructions as well. He grunted when she asked him almost anything and argued about everything he did not grunt about. Today had been a perfect example, for she had simply asked about a special dish for dinner, and he had gone on a tirade about the spices necessary and how everyone would end up ill from it, never giving her a moment to speak, until she had fled the kitchen in tears.

Father Bardin stopped reading. "Is everything well, my lady?" he asked. He would not have been her first choice for her household, but he had volunteered and his preceptor had approved. On the surface, he appeared to be everything a priest ought to be: modest, humble, ascetic to a degree. He wore his light hair shorter even than most of the soldiers, and she had never seen him in anything but his cassock. But he had the eyes of a fanatic; they lit up when he spoke about any issue of faith. His tone as well; he did not allow for differences in thought. Only one way was ever right.

"Yes, everything is -" She glanced out the window and stopped. A pair of couriers were riding through the gate, and the banner... It was the king's.

She scrambled out of the seat, her embroidery falling unheeded to the floor, and ran out the door. She ran down the stairs as quickly as she dared, down the corridor, and reached the Great hall before the courier had finished dismounting.

Jenevra gestured to one of the women and asked her to bring in warm drinks and some sort of pastry - she thought she had smelled pie earlier. The courier would have to be offered food and drink before he delivered his message. She didn't know what the king could want, but his messenger was owed every courtesy in his name.

A few minutes later, Conoc escorted the messenger in. He looked travel-worn and cold, as Jenevra had expected. But she had a goblet of mulled wine in hand to offer him when he sat down. His clothing, stained with mud and horse, had been of good quality, and the badge he wore, besides indicating a rank higher than that of a mere messenger, belonged to the Rennes family.

"My lady, Jenevra," Conoc introduced. He lifted one eyebrow slightly at her preparations, which she took as a faint gesture of surprise.

The courier bowed, then saluted her with the cup. "My lady. I bear messages for you as well."

She didn't say anything, but served him a small hand-held pie. Then she offered as much to Conoc, who saluted her in turn.

"So what is the king's will, Sir Wyeth?" Conoc asked, after the messenger had a chance to eat and drink a little. "It must be urgent to send you so close the winter."

Sir Wyeth shook his head and swallowed. "I admit, I don't know his majesty's mind. He gave me several written messages for you, although some messages come from others, including those for Lady Jenevra. But he charged me to wait for the replies he knew you would send." He handed over the satchel that hung at his side. "This contains all of them."

Conoc took it. "Thank you, Sir Wyeth. For now, I'll have someone escort you to a room where you can rest, and we'll speak at dinner, after I've read his majesty's mind."

Jenevra gestured for one of the serving women and hurriedly whispered instructions for a room and bath for Sir Wyeth before Conoc took her by the elbow and pulled her away.

"I expect I'll need to speak to my lady before I've a return message to send."

When they had reached a small room where they would not be overheard, a room that held nothing except dust, he looked at her. "Sir Wyeth. What do you know of him?"

She closed her eyes while she thought. "Wyeth of Rennes… Lord Elger Rennes is Earl of Thordal; he's one of the less powerful magnates, but no magnate is without power. They're allied to the Courcys. Lord Wilstan Courcy is a duke, of Gilshire in the west midlands. All told, he has one of the two or three largest holdings in the country. I think his sister or niece married a Rennes lord." Now she opened them again. "Lord Wilstan and my father oppose each other openly. He would not be a friend to you, though I cannot say where Sir Wyeth would fall."

Conoc sighed heavily, then nodded. He touched her shoulder. "I'll let you see to the welfare of our guest."

EVENTUALLY JENEVRA RETURNED to the solar and her embroidery. She did not know why the king had sent Sir Wyeth, but she couldn't shake the feeling that there had been a reason. Not that she said that to either Lady Mellyn or to Sess, both of whom she told about their unexpected visitor.

Her embroidery suffered her lack of attention, for she kept her mind busy wondering, rather than following the pattern she'd sketched on the linen. Something did not sit right, and clearly Conoc had felt the same way. But she had little to go on, and no answers came to her that afternoon.

Conoc met her in the solar to walk her to dinner. When she raised her eyebrows in question, he shook his head once. "Later," he said softly, which did nothing to assuage her curiosity, either about their visitor and what messages he had brought or about his own uncharacteristic behavior.

Neither did she learn much at dinner. Sir Wyeth sat at her side, while Lady Mellyn sat beside Conoc.

Sir Wyeth talked more at the table than he had earlier. Rested and bathed and dressed in clean clothes, he presented more the image of a knight than he had. To Jenevra, he spoke predominantly about his adventures fighting Northerners - a subject on which she knew little, though she resolved to ask Conoc for the truth of the tales later. He also told tales from Court, which interested Jenevra far more. She had been to Court only once, some months before the subject of her betrothal had come up, but her parents had gone regularly, and she had a friend or two nearby.

"And so the king ordered that Isabelle Courcy be married to Danel Pevren as an end to *that* feud. He deeded them the land that had been at the center of the dispute, though they will have no home until one is built, and even with a Courcy dowry, that will not happen quickly. Although Danel remains in the king's service, and they can stay at court for the time."

"And what of my family?" Jenevra asked, when Wyeth finally did not launch into another story. "Have they been at Court of late?" They ought to have been, if only to deliver the betrothal contract into the king's hands.

"Your family, my lady?" Wyeth frowned. "Lord Conoc did not mention your family..."

"My father is Lord Oswin Louvet, the Earl of Allandale." Wyeth, for all his gossip, seemed less informed than she would have thought. She knew of no other Jenevras among the nobility.

He blanched. She had never see a grown man pale so quickly before. "My lady, your parents were at Court just before I left. The Earl had a private audience with the king - not even any of the Privy Council present - and whatever passed between them, the Earl was seen stomping off and the king was in a temper after. The next day, he summoned me and sent me here."

Jenevra nodded and let the subject drop, to Sir Wyeth's obvious relief. Whatever had happened between her father and the king had clearly been upsetting, and equally clearly, Wyeth knew more than he said. Rumor would have run rampant around the court after an encounter as he described. She did not think her father and the king had ever argued; her father tailored his opinions to match the king's. Something had gone very wrong.

The rest of the meal passed uneventfully, though she felt Conoc on her left shift impatiently more than once. Dinners at Ravensmere were rarely formal affairs, and she'd had to argue with the cook to make this one more so, given their guest. She did not think the cook would forgive her too quickly.

When the meal had ended, Conoc offered her a hand to help her up. "Take my mother to her room, if you would, before retiring to your own room."

JENEVRA PACED IN HER ROOM, a fact made more difficult by the lack of room to pace. Sess had helped her out of her gown, leaving her as usual in her kirtle, and brushed her hair out and bound it for bed. She had offered to stay and keep Jenevra company, but a half-hour of Jenevra's restless energy had finally caused even the loyal Sess to leave.

If the floor were not stone, she was certain she would wear a hole in it. From the door to the window then to the other door and back, stopping every second or third time to peer out the window at the stars emerging, marking time by the appearance of the constellations. Her personal favorite was Emery, the Huntress; she had always liked the story of the young woman who had stalked a deer, only to find it had been the god in disguise.

She picked up her embroidery and just as quickly put it back. She would not focus in her current mood, and to sit and even pretend required more control than she had at this moment. She would not have believed that time moved at all, had not the candle on her table kept burning.

Finally she dropped onto the bench by the window. She let the night breeze wash over her, bringing a sense of patience, if not exactly calm. She loved to listen to the curlews in the evening and the owls as night progressed.

When she thought, despite the beautiful evening outside, that she might go mad if she had to wait much longer, she heard Conoc's footsteps in the hall. In the weeks she had been listening, she had come to identify his step. Neither Kenan nor Lorent walked with such firm purpose, and everyone else hesitated when approaching their respective doors.

He did not seem surprised when she immediately opened the door between the rooms.

"I was expecting you, my lady," he said. He indicated the pile of letters on the chest and turned his back to unlace and strip off his surcoat.

Only five tentative steps to the chest, but they might as well have been five miles. She had not yet actually crossed the threshold of his room, nor had she actually thought she had the right before.

She picked up the letters and saw that two were addressed to her, one in her mother's hand. But she suspected that Lord Conoc intended for her to see the topmost letter, a formal letter written in a scribe's perfect hand with the Royal Seal at the bottom.

From Renier, King of Merembria, Prince of Ladinor, and Lord Protector of Ralais, to Conoc Torval, Knight of the Order of St. Firman, Lord of Ravensmere

Sir,

It is in my mind that you have been misled by others, who shall not be named, in the matter of your alliance with Allandale. I had no thought that you would enter into a lengthy betrothal, leaving a girl-child destined to be your wife as your ward. I had intended that you should marry and seal such an alliance precipitously, both for your own benefit and that of the realm.

It is my wish, then, that the enclosed contract be revised as a marriage contract and that all rites of such be completed upon the earliest occasion.

As witness thereof, I am sending a most worthy knight, Sir Wyeth Rennes, with this message. It is my expectation that he will bring back word of your nuptials.

By my seal,

Renier

OH. She understood her father's fury now. "He was outmaneuvered," she said aloud. Sending Rennes had not been coincidence.

"My lady?" Lord Conoc asked. He had come to stand behind her, now wearing only shirt and hose, while she read.

"My father. Sir Wyeth said he had a private meeting with the king, and both were angry after. My father was angry because the king outmaneuvered him." She handed Conoc the letter. "I think he did not intend that we should marry, or at least not without something else he wanted, and now the king has forced his hand. That would make him very angry."

Something did not sit right. Her father had planned this alliance at the king's instigation, and her uncle Lewin had never once gone against her father in her memory. If the king had wanted a marriage, a marriage would have happened. Yet they had planned a betrothal of more than two years length; they had not misunderstood the king.

"The king usually sends such letters by his own hand," Lord Conoc mused. "Not written by a scribe and sealed by him." He shook his head. "Can you be ready to wed in the morning, my lady?"

"I do not think the king gave us a choice, my lord, unless we plan to keep Sir Wyeth here all winter."

Conoc smiled more than her weak jest called for. "I meant you, my lady. Father Andreu will be ready to perform the ceremony, though we cannot prepare a feast on such short notice."

"I... Yes." She drew the word out. Her gown lay carefully in her chest, and Sess would be able to help her. She had no real option; she must be ready.

"Jenevra." Conoc touched her arm. She could not ignore the tone or the touch. "This changes nothing between us."

She looked down at his hand, too full of emotion to take even a little more on. "An you say so, my lord."

CHAPTER SIX

Jenevra had not slept much, and, well before any errant sunbeam could find her window, she was awake. Cecilie, who had slept even less, had arrived with hot water before even the curlews had started calling.

She sat without fidgeting as Sess carefully twisted her hair into a net of twined gold. She already wore a gown made of some white material, softer and more delicate than she was used to. Her mother and her grandmother had been married in this dress; it had been part of her mother's dowry when she left Gallrech to serve the queen and later marry her father. In her mother's country, women married in white and gold to shine with the goddess' own light.

When Sess had finished with her hair, she stood up and let her put on her other accouterments: a belt of gold that sat awkwardly on her hips, a gold necklace set with gems that had also come from her mother's dowry, and finally her own gold chaplet.

"I feel overdone," she said softly. Her fingers trembled, and she clasped them together to hide that.

"You are," Sess replied. "At least for Ravensmere. I suspect in Allandale, with proper ceremony, you would not feel so." She laid her hand over Jenevra's. "You do not need to be afraid."

"But I am. Very."

"Before tonight, we will talk. But I think - and I think you know this also - Lord Conoc is not a man to hurt those under his protection, whether they be crofter or wife."

Cecilie had a certain streak of practicality that Jenevra occasionally envied, and as her friend hurried her down to the chapel, she concluded that Sess was almost certainly correct. Though that did nothing to steady her nerves.

Compared to the betrothal ceremony, they had few witnesses. The people of the castle were there in large part, but other than that, only Sir Wyeth stood in the front with Lady Mellyn. Sess attended her, and Lorent stood with Conoc. Perhaps one-third the number of people as had been at the betrothal. Though in truth, the betrothal had been more important, making the alliance. This just finished it.

There ceremony itself was very short. They had no choir, no music as she had heard of at other weddings. Father Andreu did not even preach for more than a few minutes. Then he asked Conoc to take her by the hand, which he did, her left hand in his.

His hand was very large and callused, as a swordsman's, but he did not squeeze hers too hard while he made his vows to her. "I, Conoc, offer you my pledge, that I will be your husband, with my strength to support you, my sword to protect you and my shield to guard you from all storms."

Her fingers and her voice shook, but she could only control one and decided it must be her voice. "I, Jenevra, accept your pledge, that I will be your wife, to comfort you with my love, bear your children and keep your home."

"As the god takes the goddess each year, let Conoc take Jenevra as his wife, and she him as her husband," Father Andreu prayed. "Let them know joy and love, with the blessings of god and goddess over them."

THEY DID NOT HAVE MUCH CELEBRATING. It had not been a month since the betrothal, and winter came too soon to spend necessary store on frivolities. Or so Jenevra had been told, although in nicer words, when she had inquired about something else. As well, with only overnight to prepare, nothing fancy could be readied in time.

A small feast, with enough courses that Sir Wyeth would take back a good report to the king and others. Plenty of game, as this was the time of year for it. Jenevra barely picked at most of the dishes, none of which were her favorites. She missed her mother, missed having someone to think of her. Sess was a dear, and did her best, but she had no authority to arrange anything. And Lord Conoc... she did not think he even noticed such things yet. If there had been more time, perhaps things might have been different, but she felt very much like a barely-needed accessory rather than a bride.

She did not care for the feeling.

Though feasts could - and did, especially at court - last all day if the celebration called for it, this one did not. By just after the noon hour, the men were bored and drunk enough to say exactly what they were thinking, not all of which was either complementary or appropriate. The toasting grew out of hand, and, though Jenevra did not understand everything the men said, she understood very well what they meant.

Lady Mellyn, from Conoc's other side, gestured slightly with her head. Jenevra blushed; she now outranked even her husband's mother, and none of the other women could leave without her lead.

She rose from her chair, and silence ran like a wave outward from the high table. "My lord," she said, voice low, and curt-seyed, "the ladies beg leave to retire now."

He took her hand and kissed her fingertips. "Granted. And if my lady will take a word of advice, I would suggest she keep to her room today. I do not think there will be trouble, but I would not want it to find her by mistake."

The other women followed her out, and Jenevra smiled. All the women had come, no matter how low their rank, and she wondered how many men would be taken to task by their wives later.

In her room, with only Sess for company and one maid tidying up, Sess tried to talk.

"I know the mechanics, Sess," Jenevra said in frustration. "I am not a simpleton, and I have heard plenty of talk."

"I know you have." Sess carefully unlaced one sleeve of the gown, then the other. "I'm simply trying to make sure you have accurate information. Women gossip, and gossip isn't truth."

"And what do you know about it?" Jenevra's voice was muffled as she lifted the dress over her head and off. "You aren't wed."

Sess shrugged. "I'm not. But I was your age when my father lost everything. He had less than your father, but if you think he didn't try to sell me off in a last attempt to save what little he had, you are mistaken. And, since I have lived with you, though the Earl would have been angry, I have had my share of offers."

Jenevra didn't reply. She had known, vaguely, that such things happened. Her father allowed no man to harass a woman on his lands, no matter their respective ranks, which had less to do with concern for the women than it did for his own image as a model of chivalry. But it happened sometimes, all the same. And tales were full of such things, though always worded in very delicate terms. But that her Sess should have dealt with it!

"I do not think you have much to be concerned about," Sess went on eventually. She had finished folding the wedding gown and now unlaced the white kirtle underneath it. "Lord Conoc appears to know what he is about, and he will not hurt you."

There seemed to be nothing to say to that, or at least, Jenevra could think of nothing. Sess's practicality did not sit well at the moment, but she was all too aware that Sess was, in all likelihood, again correct. Lord Conoc, whatever else might be true or not, would never hurt her intentionally.

After she had put on a fresh green kirtle, and Sess had put the white one away, she sat down on the chest by the window and picked up her embroidery, Lord Conoc's full crest lying beside her own. Sess took up a book, one they had read many times before, and began to read.

They had often sat like this in Allandale, usually with her mother and some of the other women. Everyone's hands occupied, for idleness displeased her mother, but they could talk and listen. Sometimes someone would play music on the harp or lute. If she closed her eyes, she could almost imagine herself back there, the comforting presences surrounding her.

The smells brought her back. Her room here still smelled faintly of damp and disuse, despite a month's occupancy, and she noticed it more when her eyes were closed. From the open window, she could smell the lake and the water plants. At Allandale, she could always smell the gardens, the green hedges freshly cut, and the roses blooming. She wanted to be home.

As dusk fell and the sky turned to lavender, she heard the curlews come out. The little birds had become her favorites, and she heard their calls most often at dusk and dawn. She put down her embroidery and knelt to look out. No matter how she tried, she could not imitate the calls, but she tried anyway. Sometimes she thought the birds listened.

. . .

CONOC HAD KEPT himself busy through the forenoon. Sir Wyeth had been sent on his way, with a re-signed marriage contract and a letter to the king to assure him that all was as he had wished.

After that, he had trained with his men, ignoring the wide variety of ribald comments. Andreu had told him more than once that he was too close to his men, and he began to see what the priest had meant. Such barracks comments might have been appropriate among themselves, but were certainly not when directed at him or when regarding his lady.

Kenan and Lorent did not say anything, and the silence, coming from men he had grown up with, disturbed him the more. Kenan, he knew, had not wanted the marriage to go through and had refused to attend the ceremony for that reason. Lorent's feelings were less on display.

As the sun finally began to set, and he dismissed the men, some to dinner and some to night watch under Kenan, he turned to Lorent beside him. "Well?" he asked.

Lorent raised an eyebrow. "Well what?"

"You haven't said anything all day. Or any other day, if it comes to that, since she arrived."

"I didn't much think there was anything to say," Lorent replied, his own common accent broad to tease his lord. "Even less now, since all is done. Besides, seems like Kenan and the others have been doing plenty of speaking already."

Conoc didn't deny that, nor that it had been pleasant to have someone not commenting on the situation endlessly. Still, if a man could not rely on his oldest friends for counsel, friends as close as brothers, who could he rely on?

"I don't know what you want me to say, Conoc. She is a pretty girl, with a pleasant temper. You could have done better perhaps, but you could certainly have done worse. But I have to live with your choice only indirectly. Are you content with it? If yes, then ignore all the comments." Lorent looked at him shrewdly. "Now, my lord, I must seek my bed - new levies are arriving tomorrow and I'll be up early to meet them and begin their training. You should seek your own."

CONOC ENTERED HIS ROOM, surprised and grateful that Jenevra was not already there waiting. He had worried that she would feel pushed to be there, by her own expectations of what would happen, or by others' expectations of her. Mostly the latter, since he knew that her father and the king would both expect it despite her youth.

He had no interest in a child, and, while he did not find her as useless as he had the first day he had met her, she was still a child. Among his mother's people, a girl would not be old enough to wed until she had more than sixteen years. Even a betrothal before then might not stand.

He unlaced the sides of his surcoat, pulled it off and tossed it in the direction of the linen chest. His mail, a constant companion, he removed more carefully; though the Northerners had not attacked - nor did he expect an attack so soon - he could not be complacent. They had been beaten back for less than a year.

With his back to the door as he adjusted the mail on its rack, he didn't see the door open, and he never heard it. But he felt the difference all the same and turned to see his child-bride standing there in the doorway.

He could find little different about her appearance from most evenings when she came to say goodnight. The gold net she had worn at the ceremony still held her hair, where most nights she had a single long plait. But otherwise, her attire remained identical.

Something had changed though. She held herself even more hesitantly than usual, and he disliked it immensely. The first night, she had almost teased him, and he'd hoped for more of that and less of the sober, serious-eyed child before him.

"My lady," he said with a slight bow. "You may come in; you have the right to enter my room at your convenience."

"My lord Conoc," she replied, taking two small steps in. "I did not wish to overstep. My mother... Sess..." She seemed lost for words.

His mother, when he was a child, had told him stories about the Northerners and their traditions. Though she had chosen to leave that life for love of his father, she had always wanted him to know her people's ways, to hang on to them in small ways. He was reminded, looking at Jenevra now, of a tradition where a newly married couple were put to bed by their friends and relations with a great deal of teasing and laughter.

Such a thing would save her the awkwardness of presenting herself to him, and he wondered if he shouldn't have gone to her room this once.

"I will not bite, my lady." He removed his belt and the dagger that hung on it, then his boots, and put them away.

"I did not think you would." Jenevra pulled a chain out from her dress, a key dangling from it. She lifted it over her head and extended it to him. "This is for you."

He raised an eyebrow in question. The chain consisted of delicate gold links, fit for a lady's neck, certainly. The key, however, was cold iron and almost as long as her fingers. He could not think of any lock that such a key would fit.

"It is the key for the lock my father put on my dowry," she said. "You were not to have it until we were properly wed."

"Are those your words or his?"

She looked away, chewed her lower lip, then looked back at him. "He said you could have it when you could take it off me."

In his head, Conoc cursed Oswin. Aye, when she was sixteen and ready for it, that might have been clever enough, though he'd never call it fair to her. But now he had simply given her more reason to be afraid.

He grabbed her arms, loosening his fingers when she gasped.

"I will not hurt you, Jenevra. Not tonight or any other night. And I wish you would not think it of me."

"I do not!" she cried. "But I have ears. I know the men talk, that they have talked since I arrived. The women are no better. My mother's letter... She tried to not worry me, as did Sess, but it is all anyone can speak of. Most girls, if they marry so young, live with their parents for a few years yet, but the king's own cousin Gobelin married Keina Belet four years ago, and she was but eleven and she bore her first child before she was twelve."

The words tumbled out from her, as though she could not hold them in any longer, and Conoc grinned despite the seriousness of the situation. Those might have been the most words he'd heard out of her at a single time since she arrived.

"Aye, and is that what you'd have me do? I will not."

"If you did..." Jenevra huffed. "I do know my duty, and it is not to argue with my husband."

He laughed. "Argue with me, please, lady. I'd rather that than the unsmiling silent girl of this last month. I would not have you ever come to me out of duty." He let her go and turned away, ostensibly putting away the key, but really giving her time to leave if she wanted.

When he turned back, she still stood there, watching him.

"Do you intend to stay, my lady? It would satisfy one kind of rumor and create another if they find you still here in the morning." Still in his shirt and breeches, he blew out the candle and climbed into his bed. He ought to insist, for a night in a shared bed would ensure the marriage was legal in all ways, but he would not force her, and even if she joined him, it would be for sleep alone.

In the dim light of the fire, he watched her unlace her outer dress and slither out of it. Then she also climbed into the bed, carefully not touching him.

In response, he slid an arm under her and drew her closer to him. "You are safe, my lady," he whispered. Slowly, her stiff muscles relaxed and she began to breathe normally. He was amazed such a slight body could hold so much tension as she'd had.

"Why did you marry me?" she asked, when her calm breathing had convinced him she'd fallen asleep.

"Because my king commanded it. Because you are all that I could hope for in a wife, and I do not expect I could find another woman thus. Because marry I must." A pause, while he listened to the stillness of the room. "Why did you accept me?"

"I did not," was the soft response. "My father did, after some swearing and temper. I didn't have a choice."

"No one dragged you into the chapel today," he said. Her hair tickled his nose, but he liked the scent that clung, something faintly floral. "You could have refused."

"That was my duty." She yawned. "I could no more have refused than I could have flown."

He smiled. "I will try to make your duty not too onerous for you. The he kissed her head and whispered, "Go to sleep, Jenevra."

CHAPTER SEVEN

Morning had happened approximately as he'd expected. Dawn had barely broken when a pounding at his door pulled him out of sleep. Jenevra had jerked up to a sitting position, then, as the door began to open, she had scrambled out of the bed, grabbed her dress off the floor and run for the open door to her own room. That door slammed shut just as Kenan and Lorent came in the room.

He had met their eyes unabashedly. He had done nothing of which to be ashamed. His wife - his wife! - had spent the night sleeping in his bed. And neither Kenan's stony expression or Lorent's half-smile would induce any sort of confidence from him.

Both had declined to actually say anything. At least, to him. He expected the story would be heard around the castle before long.

Father Andreu had certainly heard it before he reached the chapel. The old priest busied himself carefully mending altar linens when Conoc slipped in. Conoc did not think he had ever seen Father Andreu when his hands were not busy doing some kind of chore. He wondered if the priest were so overworked that he could not rest for everything that needed doing or if this were something about Andreu personally.

He sat down beside Andreu, but said nothing. He was not a religious man, he gave little thought to the problems of god and goddess. Such things were for men like Andreu to concern themselves with. But the chapel still gave him a feeling of comfort, of peace. Some of it must be attributed to Andreu, he knew, but not all. Some must come from the deities who watched over them.

"Most newly married men are in bed with their wives the morning after their wedding," Andreu said. "Of course, their friends usually have the sense not to startle new brides like frightened deer."

"They did not expect to find her there," Conoc replied. Or so both men had said. "She probably shouldn't have been."

"That is for you and your lady to decide." Andreu tied off a stitch. "I do not necessarily think it a bad thing, myself. You are, in fact, wed. If it gives either of you comfort to be together, then that is enough for me."

"She is a child," Conoc reminded him.

"Not according to the law," Andreu replied, mimicking Conoc's tone exactly. He remembered why he did not argue with Andreu. He never won; the priest always had a response, and a well reasoned one. "When will you let her be your wife in truth?"

Conoc shrugged. "I don't know. The betrothal... It was meant, on my side, to give her time to mature. The difference between a girl of thirteen and a young woman of sixteen are significant. Now I do not know where the line is. Or ought to be."

"I suspect that she will let you know when she is ready."

"If that be so," Conoc said, "I can say for certain she is not. Or else she would not have run like the deer you alluded to."

Andreu laughed. "No, I imagine not. But would you have

been better pleased to have her stay with them in the room? Or would that have violated her modesty and your comfort?"

"Oh, you are right, I know. She would have been uncomfortable either way." Conoc carefully folded the linen Andreu had finished mending. Here, in Andreu's domain, he always found himself working alongside the priest, and he'd noticed others did as well, though Andreu never asked nor suggested such a thing. He simply worked and listened and sooner or later, others joined in while they spoke of their concerns.

"She was scared of me," Conoc said, after a moment. That had been the concern that drove him here, though he had not realized it when he first came. He had frightened his wife, and he did not know what he had done.

Andreu set another seam. "She was not."

Conoc glared at him, but the priest did not look up. "You did not see her standing there, stiff as a board and afraid to enter my room, nor feel the stiffness in her body when I tried to simply hold her. She was scared."

"That was she was frightened, I do not doubt, but not of you." Andreu now looked at Conoc. "She does not behave as if she is frightened when she is near you. Quiet and hesitant, yes, but not scared, and I suspect the hesitancy will fade as she knows you and this castle better."

Andreu's certainty soothed Conoc's fears. "She said she had heard the men speak, and the women too. And she knew of other couples..."

"She knows too much, and that can be as terrifying as not knowing enough." He paused, then went back to his stitching. "She has not spoken to me, and I would not repeat anything she said in confidence. But she is a child, who has never felt any hint of desire, and her knowledge gives her no comfort. You did well not to push her."

CHAPTER EIGHT

Jenevra walked through the edge of the forest, swinging a basket in her hand, Sess a few steps away and two guards following along.

Oak trees towered over her, and the spaces between them were filled with ash and beech. Dead leaves covered much of the ground, but bright green moss anchored itself where trees roots pushed out from the ground. In between, little flowers began to poke out, little splashes of color against an otherwise dull ground.

Today was the first day she had been allowed out of the castle since her arrival in the autumn. The winter snows had been so heavy that no one had left. Inside the bailey, the snow had drifted to four or five feet deep in places. Outside, it had been above her head. The only choice for anyone had been to stay indoors when possible and keep warm. She had done nothing outside but go for short walks in the bailey for a bit of air now and then.

She breathed in the fresh spring breeze, closing her eyes to identify the plants she could smell. Heather, harebells, a faint hint of mint. From farther away, the scent of some flowering tree.

If she turned around, she would see the castle through the trees. As a condition of her walk today, she could not go beyond sight of the castle. Though that did not give her much room to walk or to look for flowers and herbs that did not grow within the castle walls, she had agreed after a long conversation with Conoc.

The winter had been a tense one. Though Conoc had expected an attack by Northerners at some point, no attack had ever come, and he had grown more edgy as the winter went on. As soon as a south wind had brought the hint of spring two weeks ago, he and his men had begun leaving the castle on increasingly wide scouting expeditions.

They had found nothing, which had made him more tense, if possible. But he had finally conceded that he had no reason to not allow her out if she were careful and agreed to his conditions. She had been so happy to see some place besides the stone walls of the keep and the flat space of the bailey that she had agreed without question.

So she kept to within sight of the walls, and two guards, Finn and Jamys, accompanied her and Sess.

She paused in her walk to listen to the birds who had returned. The little birds, the sparrows and the finches, twittered from sheltered spots, while the ravens cawed from more exposed places. She had promised herself that they would return to the castle by way of the lakeshore, and she would check if the curlews had come back yet. She missed their sad calls in the evening.

A hint of fresh green caught the corner of her eye, and she darted down the slope away from the road, a small cry of pleasure escaping.

"Jenevra," Sess called after her, following more slowly. The guards moved faster, one hurrying to catch up to Jenevra, the other staying closer to Sess.

"I'm well," she replied. She knelt down and began digging with her fingers to loosen the little green onions she'd spotted. Beyond them, now that she was on the ground, she could see mint and watercress. She put the onions in her basket, and moved over to begin gathering the mint.

Sess stayed on her feet and picked willow buds off a nearby tree. Jenevra supposed there must be a small stream that she didn't see for the willow and watercress to be happy here. She started to say as much when the birds abruptly stopped all their noises.

Her head went up to see what disturbed them, and she heard the metallic rattle of weapons and mail up on the road. She drew in a deep breath to steady herself against the sudden pounding of her heart and found herself shoved down into the leaves and bracken.

"Shh," her guard whispered.

Her heartbeats were no accurate measure of time, but she counted a hundred of them lying there, unable to see much beyond the dirt. At some point, Sess's fingers found hers and she held on tightly.

When the last bit of noise stopped, her guard helped her to sit up. "It's Northerners," he said, looking to the other guard.

"Aye, a hundred and perhaps a score more," the other guard replied, still watching the road above them. "Too many for a raiding party, too few for a serious attack."

"Lady, we can't get you back to the castle afore they get there," Finn said seriously. "Our best option is to find a safe place for you, where you can hide. Someplace closer to the castle." He cleared a patch of ground and rough sketched the area. "We're exposed here. If they came this way, they'll go back the same way, and our luck won't hold a second time for them to miss us. If we move straight it, we'll be between them and retreat. If we follow the slope around, we can move in close to the castle and still be away from them."

All three of them looked at her, and she stared back. "That sounds a sensible plan," she managed, when she realized that some response was needed.

The guard pulled her to her feet. "Stay on the downward side of the slope, and make no noise."

They began to walk in silence, Finn staying always at her side and Jamys near Sess. Walking along the slope, rather than at the top or going straight up or down, required watching where she went, and before many minutes, Jenevra's feet and back began to tire. Her shoes had not been meant for more than a casual stroll. The monotony of the walk tired her mind the same way, and she tried to hang on to the more pleasant sights and smells around her, but she had no time to stop and notice them.

Some of the noises of the forest had begun again. The birds called, especially the small ones, as if nothing had disturbed them. Perhaps they did not remember the men who had marched through. The ravens called louder, and flew in short spurts ahead of them, back to the castle.

Though they had not walked long out from the castle, they walked much further back following the curve of the slope. The guards seemed to have a location in mind, for they walked with more purpose than Jenevra or Sess and always kept the castle to their right.

"This is as close as we can get," Finn said. "Now we'll go downslope and find a rocky overhang or tree roots -"

A loud thunk cut off his words, and she turned to see Jamys slump to the ground, an arrow protruding from his back. A second arrow hit the tree above her head, and Jenevra ducked in spite of herself.

"Run!" Finn ordered and shoved her down the slope as he

turned and drew his sword to meet the bowman running at them.

Jenevra ran.

She didn't know if she pulled Sess or Sess pulled her, but they ran down the slope, away from the castle and away from the attackers. She could not think of anything but to get away, the image of the arrow protruding from Jamys's chest foremost in her mind. She did not choose a careful path, just ran as fast as she could.

They crashed through bushes that pulled at her skirts. A low-hanging tree branch caught her hair and she shrieked, thinking someone had caught up to them, and Sess had to untangle her, both of them wide-eyed and breathless every second. Once Sess tripped and Jenevra, sobbing, pulled her up and they continued to run down the hill. A stream soaked her feet and splashed water and mud over both of them. That was the stream the willow must have been growing near, she thought, her feet carrying her on even when her mind went in another direction.

Finally, after the stream, the ground leveled off.

"I can't run anymore," Sess gasped, dropping to the ground. Jenevra's own breath came hard and loud, and she tried to stifle it lest anyone hear them. But she couldn't hear anyone else, just the too-loud sounds of their own breathing.

"We cannot stay here." Jenevra sat against a tree and laid her head on her knees, her eyes closed, to try and catch her breath. Now that her feet stopped moving, her thoughts could catch up. She did not want to stand, but she knew if Conoc came looking for them, and he would, they needed to be somewhere they could be found.

Sess pushed herself to sitting. "Do you even know where we are?"

"The stream." Jenevra stood up. She depended on Sess; she did not know how to handle a situation when Sess depended on her. "The stream must flow from the lake. If we follow it, we'll find the lake, and from there, the castle cannot be far away."

They made poor time. Their feet hurt, and they both had scratches and bruises from their flight through the forest. More, Jenevra's nerves stayed on edge. Every sound had her starting and bracing to run again. She also had to support Sess, who was even more exhausted and who stumbled along lost.

By the stream, the underbrush was less. Only smaller plants and ferns clustered there, making for easier walking, though the ground squished under their feet, causing them to slip. They trudged on upstream and uphill, using trees as support when the hill grew too steep in places. Over and over, the normal noises of the forest had Jenevra's heart racing and her breath catching in her throat until she felt so numb she couldn't react any longer.

Finally a noise penetrated the fog she had slipped into. A little low cry, that of a bird, repeated over and over. She picked up her head; she knew that call. Her curlews were back! She dropped Sess's arm, picked up her skirt and began to run through the last of the forest. If she could hear the curlews, then they must be home!

She broke through the edge of the trees and stopped so short that Sess ran into her back. Her heart dropped like a stone, and tears clogged her throat. They had nearly reached the castle, only a short walk along the shore to go, but the attackers still stood between them.

One deep shuddering breath, and she forced herself to calm. They would just have to find their safe place and wait.

WHEN THE ATTACKERS finally broke at sunset and retreated back along the road, Conoc felt the exhaustion in every muscle of his being. Since late morning, when the guards on the wall had spotted the force coming along the road, he'd been on the wall, in full mail, with a sword, beating back men who had no real possibility of winning.

He'd watched them himself, since he'd been in the bailey when they'd first been sighted. Something had been different about them. Usually these attackers had little cohesion as a group and less discipline. They fought as rabble, not trained soldiers. This time, they had moved as a trained group, with order among them. They'd sought out the weak points of the castle, and they shouldn't even have known them.

Something had changed among them; someone new was leading or training them. But the changes hadn't fully taken affect; when his men had shot arrows back at the attackers, the attackers had broken ranks. And they still had little weaponry.

If they hadn't retreated at sunset, he'd have opened the gates for a sortie just to clear them away. The castle could withstand a siege if it had to, and a hundred men could not have held much of a siege. But he did not want to get cornered so easily or so early in the year.

The whole situation bothered him. A hundred men couldn't have taken the castle if he'd been the only man guarding it. A raiding party would not have even come to the castle; he would have seen the smoke from the fires in the village below the castle. They were testing him, what he would do, and he did not like the implications of that.

For now, he sent most of the men off the wall. The night watch had not been in the fighting, and they would take over soon. The others would need rest and food once the rest of the chores were seen to. Only a few had been injured, and they'd been carried off already.

Lorent joined him. "There are a few injured outside the gates."

"Open the gate," Conoc replied. "Tend to them and send them on their way. If we intend to kill them, we ought to do it on purpose and not just leave them there." His conscience could not allow him any other course, even if it would be wiser to let enemy soldiers die.

He kept his back resolutely turned though. He would not watch it, would not allow his own emotions to become engaged by this. If he remained loyal to his king, he could not care about those who opposed him.

A shout behind him had him whirling, his hand on his sword. Two of his men carried between them a third man. That man had a wound in his side that had bled through his clothing and mail, as well as cuts on arm and legs.

Conoc ran over as someone went for bandages. "What happened?" There had been no fighting that close; no one of his men should have been so hurt.

"Too many," the guard gasped. "Held 'em off... while I could."

"Why were you out there?"

"Guard... on Lady Jenevra..."

A chill ran down Conoc's spine, and he looked at Lorent, kneeling on the other side of the guard, and saw the same horror there. "Where is my wife? Why weren't you all inside the castle?" Too late he remembered that he had given in to her wish to go out for a little while, to stretch her legs and gather some of the early spring plants.

"Too late to go back... Told her... to run... She did..."

"Where?" He took the guard's hand. "Where did she go?"

"Don't know... Ran... down hill."

He stood up to let Father Andreu in to care for the guard, who was losing blood rapidly. His own heart sank. If she'd gone downhill, she'd run to the thickest part of the forest. Safer that way, since pursuit would be difficult. But also hard to find her without some kind of clue.

He gestured to Kenan, who had joined the group. "I want a group assembled, as many as can be spared. We'll go out searching for her."

"We won't find much," Kenan replied softly. "The sun is

down. We won't see any tracks."

Conoc stared up at the darkening sky. Kenan was correct in that; they wouldn't see tracks in the dark. They might even miss a girl completely if she were unconscious or unable to call for help. But he would not leave Jenevra alone in the dark and cold overnight; she would freeze.

The edge of the rising moon caught his eye. "No, we'll have light enough. We've a full moon tonight." He looked back at Kenan. "I want a search party formed. Now. I'll be with them."

The search party made ready in minutes. Conoc did not stop moving during that span of time, nor did several of the others. He had not realized that his wife had started to make an impact on the other men in the castle, particularly some of the younger ones.

They split up, some moving along the road while he took others towards the downhill slope. The men spread out in a line, sweeping down the hill, looking for any sign of his lady. Conoc tried to look, but his attention wandered, thinking of her and how she was feeling. Did she know that he would come for her or did she think she had been forgotten?

"Sir!" one of the men cried. "We've found something!"

He sprinted up to where three men gathered together. "What is it?

A young man pointed. Tangled in the low-hanging branch of a tree was a ribbon, a green one, similar to the ones Jenevra used to bind her hair. He started to reach for it, but one of the other men stopped him.

"Look, Sir, at the ground." He pointed to marks. "Those're small footprints, right enough. Too small for a man. She was getting dragged, and then she gets away and starts running."

"Where though?" Conoc asked. "Where did she go next?"

"Towards the castle," the third man said, examining more marks on the ground a few feet away. "But after here she's on to moss and leaving no trace."

"She ran towards the castle, but she didn't make it there." He looked back at the castle. It could not be above a half-mile in a straight line. Although there had been attackers in her way at the time, so she could not have gone straight if she'd wanted to. It was unlikely she'd have used the postern gate; he didn't even know if she knew where it was.

"We'll start from here and try and follow her steps." They hadn't come in straight; they'd followed the slope. Going back would be the straighter line. But that made assumptions about her movements, with no basis in truth. He didn't know how to follow her, which way would bring him closest to her.

They walked on, in the direction her footprints had led. Conoc looked at every broken branch, every bent leaf or blade of grass, as though they could tell him where she had gone.

"Another footprint!" The lead guard pointed. "Two, actually, and both women by the size and shape."

He breathed a sigh. Jenevra wasn't alone then. He hadn't known Sess had gone with her, but she must have. There were no other women Jenevra would take, and the footprints had the same dainty shape as Jenevra's own. No commoners shoes, those.

"Still moving towards the castle?"

"No. They're bearing west a bit. Hard to tell, the tracks are muddled."

Nothing much lay west of them. Just the curve of the lake... "Could the tracks lead to the lake?"

The men looked at each other, then at him. "Aye, they could. But she'd have to cross open space with the attackers there. A risk, as she'd be exposed through that stretch. They might have seen her, taken her with them."

"No," Conoc said firmly. "They didn't have any prisoners when they began their retreat. They wouldn't have found her after that if she went this way."

He was certain. She knew the lake better than any other

place, she had mentioned to him how often she looked out at it in the evening. She would have gone that way.

Now he led the men, not looking for traces, just moving towards the shore. She would be there, she and Sess both. He would not allow any other possibility.

The little shore birds picked around in the water grasses, calling lowly 'cur-looo' as the men drew closer to the shore. It was a bad omen, so sad did they sound. But the birds scattered as he grew closer.

Rocks and pebbles marked the edge of the lake, with larger piles of rock scattered around, as if a giant hand had scooped the lake out of the mountain. Dozens of places that could hide her if she wanted to stay hidden or conceal her if she were hurt, and nothing to give him a trail. Behind him, the men exchanged glances he pretended not to see.

"Jenevra!" he shouted and waited. "Jenevra!"

Three heartbeats passed, heartbeats that echoed in his ears and felt more like three lifetimes, before a dark head, her hair unbound and tangled, peered up over one of the rock piles. "Conoc!"

THE ROCK PILE stood tall enough that Conoc didn't see how a slim girl could lift herself up, even with another's help. He was taller and stronger than she and he didn't believe he could haul himself up there. Getting her down was, by far, the simpler task. She half-slid half-jumped down into his arms, with the other men looking away to preserve her modesty.

Her gown was wet through and had tears and rips in a variety of places, and she had worn one shoe down to almost nothing. She could not walk back in such a state, and he did not give her the chance for an argument, just swung her up - even wet, she weighed so little - and began to carry her.

"What happened that you became so wet?" he asked.

She laid her head down on his shoulder. "We swam. A man chased us, and we had nowhere to go, so we went into the lake. The rocks were not so high from the water side, and they were warm. Sess could not go any further, and I thought that would be a safe place to wait."

He looked over where two of his men carried Cecilie in a basket hold. She had hurt her ankle, and she showed signs of a fever, and he could not but resent her. Jenevra would have come back to the castle sooner, but she would not leave Sess. She had kept Jenevra in peril by being there. Jenevra would not see thus for she considered Sess as more an elder sister than a simple companion, which he understood only too well.

Kenan waited for them at the open gate, sword out, and Conoc's heart felt too full for words. His own brother of the heart had held his castle safe for him.

"Is she...?" Kenan asked softly.

"She is safe enough, but tired. I'll bring her to her room. Once everyone is inside, bar the gates and see the night watch is posted. I'm not certain that all is over yet."

CONOC CARRIED her up to her room without speaking. His always stern expression seemed more so. He set her down inside the open door and left before she could thank him, closing the door behind him.

Lady Mellyn sat on a chair, directing one maid in adding more water to a tub that steamed already and the other in finding fresh linens. She rose, took Jenevra's hand and pulled her over to the fireplace.

"Child, you are wet through. Off with those things." And fitting action to her words, she began to unlace Jenevra's gown herself. The maids joined in and before long, she was soaking in the tub with one maid scrubbing her hair.

"I don't need help," she protested. In response, another jug of warm water was poured over her hair to rinse out the soap.

"What you need..." Mellyn let her breath out in a huff. "Jenevra, you may be my son's wife, but if you ever scare everyone that way again, I will forget that. You terrified everyone."

"It was not my idea." Jenevra stood and wrapped a towel around herself. "I had no intention of being trapped in such a way." A maid handed her a clean chemise, and Jenevra put it on.

"But you were." Lady Mellyn sent the maids away with the bath water and took Jenevra's brush to untangle her hair.

Jenevra reluctantly felt her shoulders relax. Mellyn did not speak more, just hummed softly while she finished brushing and turned to plait the full length of her hair. She now felt a thread of guilt, that Mellyn should be caring for her when nothing was wrong.

"That is finished," Mellyn said finally. "I'll have some dinner sent to you, and Mally can keep you company while you eat. But you are to stay in bed. We do not need you getting ill."

LATER THAT NIGHT, Jenevra lay in her bed, wrapped up in more layers of blankets than she usually preferred. No one had asked her how she felt, however, and making everyone leave her had required submitting to a level of smothering care that vexed her.

She wanted Sess, who always knew the right way to care for her, if she needed any caring. But Sess had been carried off to her own room and her own care, and Jenevra only hoped that Sess was no worse than she had appeared.

She climbed out of her bed and wrapped one of the blankets around her. Then, walking as softly as she could manage, she sat down on the window seat and pushed open one shutter.

The night air blew coolly, more winter than spring in it, but she didn't mind. She was not cold, and despite what everyone seemed to think, she was in no danger of being ill. She needed to move. Lying in bed with nothing to do would only make her feel worse.

A low cry had her leaning out the window a little in an attempt to see the curlews, who were out in the full moon's light.

"I shall have to get new glass for that window, my lady, if you intend to open it at all hours," a voice said behind her. Conoc stood at the door between their rooms, a door she had not heard him open. She had not even heard him enter his own room, which she had not missed in all the months she had been here. "I do not believe this was what my mother meant when she bade you stay in bed."

"I expect that is true," she agreed, unmoving. "But I was not tired, and I did not wish to lay abed with nothing to do."

"While I can understand that, my lady, the fact remains that you ought to be resting. You had a difficult day." He indicated the bed with a gesture of his head.

Tears welled up in her eyes, and, though she tried to hold them back, after a moment they spilled out down her cheeks. She buried her face in her hands and let the tears fall. All the terror and helplessness of the day crashed in upon her and she could do nothing but let it out through her tears.

Conoc rushed over to kneel beside her and place a gentle hand on her shoulder. "My brave Jenevra, why do you cry now? You are safe and well. I did not mean to upset you."

She could not stop the tears long enough to answer him, and after a moment, he gathered her into his arms as if she were a child, holding her close until the tears came to their own natural end.

Then she took a breath, one that shuddered through her, and a second, more even. "I am well enough."

"An you say so, my lady." But Conoc did not let her go for a span of minutes, and Jenevra could feel his heart beating. "Never again, lady. I do not wish to govern your every move, but I will have my say in this: you will not leave the castle again without me or Lorent or Kenan with you."

"I am sorry," she whispered, making herself even smaller in his arms. A note of anger threaded through his words, and she felt again the weight of what had happened. She had been self-ish, and half the castle had been turned out to search for her, after they had fought a skirmish.

He looked down at her in surprise. "Did you think me seeking an apology, lady? If anything, I ought to offer one to you. Had I taken proper care... But I did not want to be pulled away from what I considered important, did not want to waste Lorent or Kenan's time. As a result, you were in very grave danger. I failed you as a husband; I am sorry."

She shuddered once, and his arms tightened around her.

"I will not make the same mistake twice. Ones of us must accompany you, no matter what." He kissed her forehead. "We do not wish to lose you, lady. You have won more hearts than mine."

Conoc again indicated the bed, and this time, she climbed back into it, though she did not pull on all the blankets that had been left. He shook his head with half a smile. "As you are now where you were supposed to be, I will close your shutter and take up my position again at the door."

Jenevra tilted her head to give him opportunity to explain himself.

"That is the boundary you have drawn for now, lady, and I will respect it until you invite me in." He smiled once more at her. "Until then, my place is no farther than the door. And with that, I will bid you good e'en."

After he closed the door, Jenevra stayed awake only long enough for her bed to warm.

CHAPTER NINE

Jenevra sat in the sun in the small garden that Conoc had given over to her. Low walls, high as her waist, marked it off from other areas, especially from the kitchen garden that lay beside. In this space, only two or three times the size of her own room, she had complete control.

Many things had changed since the spring attack. Such attacks came often as Conoc had predicted. Always small, always trying something new. Looking for weaknesses, Conoc said. The guard had grown in size, half again as many, mostly new levies from Caermor, the land that had made up her dowry. A few were wandering knights as Conoc's father had been. Conoc, Sir Kenan and Sir Lorent worked harder to train them as a group.

She would not be allowed out again, not unless she went with an entire party of armed guards. Conoc would not permit a repetition of the spring events. She found this hard, because the castle walls enclosed so little land. Ravensmere had been built for border defense. Allandale perhaps had been once the same, but it had been a generation at least that the wall had come down and the land around the keep itself allowed to flourish.

The garden had been Conoc's attempt to compromise. He'd had a few of the levies clear some of the land, and she was free to grow what she pleased within this space. More land between the garden and the wall still lay overgrown, and he had promised it would be cleared in the autumn or next spring when the men had time again.

She liked the location. Tucked on the back side of the keep, only the wide castle wall separated her from the lake. She'd been delighted, on her first day, to discover that she could hear the curlews during the day, even if she couldn't see them. Now every day when she paused, she listened to them calling and felt herself finally at home.

The scent of the various herbs filled the air. She had planted them first, before any flowers. Rosemary, mint, thyme, lavender, peppermint... She could walk through her garden with her eyes closed, simply by the scent. In another area, she had plants simply for their beauty, roses and lilies-of-the-valley and others. Some determined heather had sprouted there too, to her delight.

Here she could be alone, at least in her thoughts. Finn, now healed and returned to his duty guarding her, remained always at the edge of the garden, but he did not interfere. Sess accompanied her only rarely, and Father Bardin, who seemed to feel that any moment she was reasonably stationary should be spent in instruction, did not risk his books out of doors. For a few hours, she could have herself to herself.

In the mornings, at any rate. The afternoons were dedicated to the keep's business and spending time with Mellyn. Though she rallied from time to time, Lady Mellyn lost a little more every day, and, every day, Jenevra assumed more of the duties of running the keep, duties she ought to have taken up sooner, but had not because Mellyn had wanted her to have her bridal time.

But she did not worry about that. She rarely did when a matter concerned her husband.

A flicker of motion caught her eye, and she turned to see an inquisitive curlew peeking through the open postern gate. The postern gate, a small gate in the side wall of the castle, marked the diving line between the open area of the bailey and the gardens at the back. She had never seen it open before.

She stood and approached the gate slowly, wanting to shoo the bird back out so she could close the gate. A frisson of cold slid down her spine. No one was near the gate, and she had been the closest one for nearly an hour. The next closest was Sir Kenan, who stood some distance away working with the guards. But someone had opened the gate and left it open.

Jenevra pushed the heavy gate closed and fumbled with the bar until she had it in place. She had to tell someone, because that just wasn't safe. Sir Kenan would be best, since he was outside and nominally in charge of the ground at the moment. But he did not seem to care much for her, or so it seemed to her. She did not think she could trust him to listen to her now.

Finn touched her shoulder lightly. "My lady?"

She smiled absently, still wrestling with the problem. "Did you see the gate open?"

"Only after you were shutting it, my lady," he replied. "I admit, I wasn't watching that direction."

No one had been. She'd been turned toward her garden, her guard had his back that way because the wall was safe, and Sir Kenan had been focused forward, to his men and the front of the castle. "I need to see my husband."

"He's not here, my lady. He rode out more than an hour ago with a contingent of men, checking the small villages. He's not expected back until nightfall."

She began walking quickly, then picked up her skirt with one hand to allow her to walk even faster. That cold feeling had settled in her stomach. That Conoc was gone and the gate open at the same time could not be coincidental. "Sir Lorent, then. Immediately."

SIR LORENT LISTENED to her without reaction as she told what she had seen and what she though. His brown eyes, so often dancing with good humor and mischief, held no glimpse of that today. But he betrayed no other emotion as she spoke.

Her story, such as it was, sounded silly as she told it. Girlish fears, not governed by sense or reason. She had probably left some guard stranded outside who then had to come round to the main gate. She could not put into words the feeling she'd had, the sense of wrongness.

"You think I am imagining things," she said, when no reaction had come.

"Not at all, my lady," Lorent said. "I know you are not. Even if Finn had not confirmed the truth of what you saw, I would not believe it to be your imagination." She waited, staring at him, and he met her gaze unflinchingly. "I cannot tell you more now, lady. If you would know, you may ask your husband. But answer me this: why did you not tell Sir Kenan?"

The question threw Jenevra and startled the undiplomatic truth from her. "I - I did not think he would listen. He does not like me much."

"He does not like anyone much, my lady. You should not take it to heart." Lorent rose. "I'll mount an extra guard on the postern gate for now, so you need not worry, and I'll inform Lord Conoc when he returns. But if you see the gate open again, be careful! Don't approach it on your own."

She nodded once, and he smiled, though the humor failed to reach his eyes. He had not told her all that he thought, not even all that hat he knew, and Conoc would not either. She would have to keep her own eyes open.

. . .

"JENEVRA?" Conoc asked, when Lorent had finished telling the story.

Lorent had caught him almost as soon as he'd dismounted when he returned to the castle. He'd insisted on a private talk, and once Conoc understood the topic, he'd agreed. They settled in the small room where he usually met with his men, the door locked behind them.

The story had come out in one quick telling, but then Conoc had made Lorent go back over it in detail until he was certain he understood every bit of it.

Now he paced back and forth in the small confines of the room, with nothing to impede his stride but the chair Lorent sat in. The other furniture, mostly stools for the men to sit on while he spoke, sat stacked against the walls.

He had been gone only a matter of hours. His castle and his wife had been in danger and he not there to protect either.

"Aye, but I do not think she realizes it. She thought of danger to the castle, but if her observations are correct - and Finn agreed with her - she was the most vulnerable person."

"But you think she was the target?"

Lorent shrugged. "Perhaps. But twice she has been exposed to danger, without you or I or even Kenan near to protect her. Both times, she was the only person in real danger beyond a common guard."

Conoc did not like it, and he liked it less the more he thought. Though it could have been coincidence, that seemed too unlikely. But to imagine his wife as the focus of these attacks seemed incredible. She had less than nothing to do with the castle defense, and she had not even lived in the castle a year.

"Who knew where you were?" Lorent asked.

"You and Kenan. Jorin, since he came asking my help. Eseld, I suppose, by extension, for she came with him and stayed to visit with Kenan. I meant to introduce her to Jenevra, but I did not actually see her." Nor had he much wished to, when all was said. That subject felt too fraught still. "Jenevra's guard and one or two others knew I left, but nothing more."

"Not Lady Jenevra though." Lorent's voice carried a hint of censure, which Conoc felt. For a moment, both were silent. "What will you tell her?" he asked finally.

"I don't know," Conoc said. "I do not want to scare her, but I want her to be prepared. I do not know."

CONOC STILL DID NOT KNOW what to tell her when she came to the door between their rooms to say goodnight.

Her dark hair had been pulled into one long plait, neatly tied off, and she wore a kirtle that almost matched the blue of her eyes. She was, he thought not for the first time, an exceptionally pretty girl.

"Did Sir Lorent tell you?" she asked.

He nodded. "And I am grateful that you were so alert, though I wish you would be more careful with your own well-being. Someone could have been standing on the other side of the open gate."

"A curlew walked in, Lord Conoc," she replied. "I do not think it would have done so if someone had been standing there."

"Did you think that through then?"

With a shrug and downcast eyes, she admitted she had not. "I only thought to close it. But that does not mean that I was wrong."

"My lady, if I admit that you can out-argue me, will you listen to me?" Conoc took her hand in his. He rarely stood this close to her when she came to his door, not wanting her to feel any pressure. "I do not wish any harm to come to you. Please, take more care." He kissed her fingers. "Please."

Jenevra looked down at their joined hands. "I will try."

CHAPTER TEN

Midsummer dawned a brilliant beautiful blue. Jenevra did not think she had ever seen a sky so perfectly blue and cloud free, as if nature itself celebrated the longest day of the year. It did not matter that dawn had come too early. The birds sang, a light breeze blew.

She paused at the top of the steps to the keep to look out over the bailey, today not being used for any act of war. The villagers from the town below the castle had begun arriving almost before the sun had risen to prepare the castle for a grand festival. They had already erected a low stage for the musicians, and several sat there tuning instruments. A too-loose string plucked made her skin crawl until the player tightened it.

In another area, a great fire pit had been dug out, and two spits turned over the fire, one holding the most massive pig she had ever seen - she had to believe it weighed twice as much as she did - and the other a bull from Ravensmere's stock. She could not smell them yet, but she could well-imagine how good they would be in a few hours.

Jenevra loved the twin festivals at Midwinter and Midsummer. Midwinter and the longest night meant her birthday, but she also loved the god handing over the rule of the world to the goddess as she brought the light back. But on Midsummer, the god and goddess danced together before he resumed his rule, and married couples were honored.

Last year, it was on the feast of Midsummer that her father had announced her imminent betrothal. This year, she would celebrate as a married woman.

"You look well-suited for a summer fest, my lady," Conoc said, coming from behind to join her on the steps. "I hope the festival pleases you."

"I do not see how it could not." Her cheeks colored faintly at the quick once-over he gave her. She wore a new dress that she and Sess had sewn frantically on over the last few days after discovering that her dresses from last summer were too small and too short. She hadn't realized she had grown so much.

He looked fine himself, foregoing any mail that she could see and even his usual dark colors for a tunic and surcoat in light blue. He wore no sword, and she thought it the first time, outside his own room, that she had seen him not under arms.

Conoc produced a wreath of flowers, including little rosebuds and sweet-smelling lavender, which he settled on her head. "A gift for you. I've been instructed that for her first Midsummer festival, a bride is always presented with a flower wreath by her husband. Hopefully I've made it well enough that it will last for the whole day."

The musicians began to play a lively dance tune, and an open space before the stage cleared for dancers to come forward into the set.

"Would you dance with me, my lady?" Conoc asked, offering her a hand.

"I would," she replied.

. . .

JENEVRA ENJOYED DANCING, and she was handed around from partner to partner with barely time to catch her breath. Her parents would never have hosted such a gathering, or not participated if they had, but she enjoyed it.

After Conoc had danced the first one with her, he handed her off to Lorent for a reel. Then the village blacksmith - a big, tall man, with a beard almost as red as his face - had claimed her and whirled her so fast down the line that her feet hardly touched the ground. After him, Finn took her up and down the line in another set. From there, she had changed partners so often, she barely knew who had her hand.

Finally, laughing, she had dropped onto a bench. Lorent offered her a cup, and she toasted him with it before drinking.

"No one watching you would believe you were not born here," he said. At her questioning look, he clarified, "They're very ordinary, the folk here. More than a trace of Northerner blood among them, unused to your ways. No one has lived in the castle for a couple of decades, due to the border wars. You could change that, insist on more formality. And you do some, within the keep. But here, instead, you stand on no ceremony. They are not your equals, perhaps, but you do not hold it against them."

Jenevra laughed. "You are speaking nonsense, Sir Lorent. I treat them no differently than I treat anyone."

"My point, my lady. You treat everyone that way."

She might have argued, for she did not understand his point, though she suspected he'd had a little too much of the very powerful drink the men were passing around and therefore did not articulate his argument as well as he might have, but he offered her a hand and pulled her into the circle dance beginning.

She swung from partner to partner around the circle, coming chest to chest with Conoc at one point, who gave her such a look that she almost missed her next steps. As if he didn't know her.

After that dance, the musicians begged off, and the men went to show off their prowess at feats of strength and skill. They started with rocks, to see who could throw them farthest, which, unsurprisingly, proved to be the blacksmith. After they moved on to archery, where the guardsmen all took good marks, but Sir Lorent proved the best.

Jenevra, her eyes often turned to her lord, noted that while he was always present to compliment a good shot or commiserate with a poor one, he did not compete himself. He did nothing to draw the eye to him and away from those who did compete, except once when he stopped to help a boy, no more than ten, draw a bow to hit the target. He cared for his people, but he was not one of them.

Which she thought odd. Father Andreu had once suggested Conoc considered himself too much one of his men, and Father Bardin, to whom he had been speaking, had denounced Conoc's manners and lack of breeding. The conversation remained with her because she had seen how much Conoc trusted his men and how much they thought of him.

Conoc had not been prepared for the changes in Jenevra. Though he saw her daily, he hadn't been aware. Now, seeing her in a new gown of a soft spring green that molded to a figure become increasingly womanly, with her head reaching his shoulder, he saw that his wife had grown into a woman. At least that she had begun that transition.

He didn't know what to make of it, and as he watched her dancing and laughing with different people, he wondered if he knew this woman at all.

He watched the others compete at archery. Though he knew Lorent could outshoot him, he wished he could join in. It went against the grain, to not put forth his best and strive to outdo others. He did not want to win, but to show what he could do.

Jenevra presented prizes to each winner, including a kiss for each. The blacksmith blushed too red for a man his age, but she had that effect on people. For all that she could laugh and join in with them, she had been bred to something finer, and they all responded to that without any words.

Lorent received his kiss and offered some jest that made Jenevra laugh. Conoc's heart and stomach clenched.

After that, he claimed her hand to lead her back towards the musicians. Some of the women were setting out bowls and platters of food, and the castle's cook had set to work carving the pig and the bull. But the musicians had begun to play again, somewhat slower than the tunes earlier.

"Will you dance with me, Jenevra?" he asked.

She looked up at him, surprise in her blue eyes, and he noticed the distance between their faces had shrunk from the first day they'd met. "I will, Conoc."

He led her out and pulled her close to him before guiding her in the steps of the dance. This was no formal court dance, with patterns and polite formalities. Nor was this like the energetic dances of the afternoon, where everyone took part. This dance was for them.

The sun had finally begun to set, and the fire cast shadows everywhere, but in-between them, Conoc danced with Jenevra. She moved with him as though they had done this many times, as though they knew each other so thoroughly in heart and body that nothing separated them. Only he could feel her trembling under his hand or see her pulse in her throat, beating too fast. Around them, other couples danced, but Conoc had no eyes for them, all his attention on his bride.

He did not look away from her face, but he was aware of every bit of her: the lock of hair escaped from her hairnet to lay temptingly against her neck, the delicate hand that rested on his arm, the skirt swirling around her ankles.

The music stopped, and Jenevra, held in his arms, stared up at him, panic in her eyes. She trembled still, and she might have fled given the chance. He didn't release her, didn't look away, and her eyes stayed locked on his.

"A kiss! A kiss!" People, villagers took up the cry, and Conoc didn't look to know that other couples had given the crowd what they asked for.

Before he could think better of it, and before Jenevra could pull away, he bent his head to hers. One hand cradled her face, his thumb brushing her petal-soft skin, then he kissed her lips. Her eyes closed, and the trembling in her body stopped, but her heart pounded where her chest touched his. For those seconds, she was completely his.

When he released her, those blue eyes fluttered open, and as cheers rose around them again, her cheeks flushed a bright pink. She stepped away from him and curtseyed to the crowd, waving and smiling at them, putting on the face they expected to see from the lady of the castle. He alone had seen the shadow of fear in her eyes for that one brief moment.

His own breath came ragged; though he could tell himself it was merely exertion, he could not make himself believe it. Something had shifted between them, and he didn't know if it was a good thing.

"You look as though you enjoyed that," a feminine voice said beside him.

Conoc dragged his attention away from his wife to the women who stood beside him. "Eseld," he said softly.

Kenan's sister stood beside him. He had not seen her arrive at the festival, though he'd known that she ought to be there. Her husband Jorin Norster, though no lord, held one of the largest portions of land underneath him. That they would come had been only right.

Yet somehow he hadn't imagined her there.

Black hair, held back from her face but otherwise loose to her waist in the northern fashion. Dark blue eyes, so dark as to be almost black as well, bright and lively. Roses in her cheeks as always. Though she was only two years younger than him, she looked still a young woman.

Eseld had wanted to be his wife, before he'd ever been knighted. Their mothers had spoken of the idea fondly when they were all children, but the idea had never come to fruition, and though Kenan had raised the idea again after he'd been granted Ravensmere, he hadn't been able to accept. Politics had been part of it; he'd needed what Jenevra brought to their marriage. But beyond that, he hadn't loved her enough. He'd introduced her to Jorin, and they had seemed well-situated together.

All that paled seeing her here.

She was everything Jenevra wasn't. Bold and hearty and earthy, a woman grown and aware of her own effect on men. Beside her, Jenevra seemed the more delicate, the more dainty, pale and passive. Yet Conoc, with Jenevra's kiss still on his lips, found he preferred Jenevra's innocence to Eseld's confidence.

"So this is Ravensmere's new lady," she went on. "She is younger than I expected. You were so firm about what you wanted in a wife."

He winced. Eseld would bring that up to jab at him, and he'd allow her that one. She had been part of a conversation he'd had with Lorent and Kenan about finding a wife. They had teased him into describing what he wanted, and a child-bride had not been on the list. But he'd seen the look in her eyes when she realized that she could never be what he wanted and known that she was hurt.

"Yes," he replied. "That is my lady Jenevra. Shall I introduce you?"

Eseld colored slightly, realizing he'd put her lower than Jenevra. "No, not now. But mayhap you will dance with me."

"I am promised to Jenevra for the evening."

"Oh, she is well enough. She is accepting someone else already."

Conoc looked; Jenevra had placed her hand into a lad's, barely older than herself. She ought to have had those moments, he thought, with shy lads trying to curry her favor. He felt a pang in his heart, but pushed it away to offer Eseld his hand. "Then as you please."

Jenevra finally left the fest, the sun long since set. Many of the other women had left or were leaving, especially those with children, all piled into one large wagon to carry them down to the village. The men, both of the village and the castle, continued to celebrate, but that seemed both predictable and fitting. Predictable in that the men always continued after the women retired, and fitting in that the god returned to dominance at midnight, and men should be the ones to honor him.

Though she was weary, she did not go to her room, where Sess would be waiting for her. Instead she went to Mellyn's room.

Her husband's mother had grown too weak to walk on her own, and even assisted could not stand long. Jenevra hated to see her thus and did her best to cheer her, always bringing fresh flowers and herbs from her garden to brighten the room and stories from the keep to entertain her.

Tonight she set the wreath from her hair onto the table beside Mellyn's bed. The flowers had wilted a little, but the lavender woven through still smelled fresh.

Mellyn smiled at her and gestured for her to sit. "Did you enjoy yourself?"

"I did." Jenevra smiled back. "You were missed though."

"I had one of the lads carry me to the solar so I could watch for a time." She reached for a drink, and Jenevra carefully handed the cup to her and steadied it while she drank. "Did you ever sit down?"

"Only for a few moments, and that while everyone ate. I think I must have danced with every man present." Her smile faded as she thought how her mother would not have approved. Such a celebration could never have happened at Allandale, but Ravensmere felt different.

Mellyn patted her hand, but didn't say anything. She seemed to know when Jenevra's thoughts went to her childhood home and her parents, but she never said a word. Jenevra loved her the more for knowing that silence would be the greatest comfort at those times.

"There was a woman at the festival," she began hesitantly. "I did not know her, but Conoc did. She was beautiful, all dark hair and flashing eyes. He danced with her. Who was she?" Mellyn would know, Jenevra was certain, because Conoc had so obviously known her.

"I saw. That is Eseld Halacre, Kenan's sister. They were children together." She coughed, then drew in a deep breath. "She always loved him."

"Is she married?"

"Oh, yes. She married Jorin Norster, who is a freeholder under Conoc, the largest one." Mellyn rested her head back against the pillow. "That was a good match for her, for she brought little but a close connection with Conoc to the marriage. She and her husband seem well content with each other."

"Did he love her?" Her heart twisted a little. She did not love Conoc, not as a wife ought, but she cared for him, and it hurt that he might hold another woman closer to his heart than her, though she had no right to think of it.

"Others pushed their match. I don't think he ever loved her

as anything but a sister." Mellyn gave her a shrewd look. "He also danced with you."

Jenevra's cheeks turned pink again, and she had to swallow back the memory of that dance. His hands had been so warm, and he had held her so firmly. She had never felt such intensity, she had barely been able to breathe for the look in his eyes, and she had trembled as much from excitement as fear. Then he had kissed her, and for one long moment, everything else in the world ceased to exist. "Yes," she managed. "It was just a dance, like any other."

Mellyn looked at her speculatively. "The fire illuminated the two of you quite well."

Alone in her room later, Jenevra sat and waited for Conoc to return to his room. She had resolved to be no different than usual, but found her resolution tested each time her mind reviewed their dance and his kiss. Each time she thought of it, her heart began to race and she held her breath. She could still feel his hand on her face, the faint touch of his breath and the pressure of his mouth on hers. She felt again the urge to melt against him.

Something had changed between them, something she could not grasp or define. Only that she knew it had. She had seen it in his eyes as he stared down at her.

She waited and waited. When she cracked her shutter, the outside lay dark and silent, even the owls quiet. No men could be heard except those on night watch along the walls. The last celebrating had ended long since.

Conoc had not returned to his room. She would have heard him. So she, mindful of her resolution, banked the fire and unlaced her kirtle to leave it on her linen chest. She blew out her candle and climbed into bed. He had never entered her room but the one time, assuring her of her privacy. He would not come tonight.

For a long time, she lay awake, still listening for his footsteps, thinking now and then she heard them. But if they were his, he never knocked or opened her door to check on her. She thought again, as she lay there, of his eyes as he danced with her and his touch as he kissed her. For the first time, he had looked at her as if she were a woman, not a girl, and butterflies fluttered in her stomach at the thought.

Finally Jenevra fell asleep, after crying a few exhausted tears into her pillow and wondering whether she had hoped he wouldn't come... or that he would.

CHAPTER ELEVEN

Conoc slept fitfully. Even in his sleep, he had thought of Jenevra and he awoke several times, reaching for her in his bed and finding it as empty as it had been when he had gone to sleep.

He had taken extra care that she should not hear him when he returned to his rooms. He did not want her to come in, young and innocent, to unknowingly tempt him into something he ought not want. He could see candlelight under the door, and for a long time, long after her room had gone dark, he stood with his hand on the door between them, wrestling with himself whether he should enter or not. Even something as simple as a kiss goodnight seemed fraught, and he would not injure her. But equally, he valued their few moments of nighttime peace. Could that truly be so wrong?

By dawn he had given up on sleep, even though he had been in bed for only a few hours. The covers of his bed looked as though he had not slept, twisted and rumpled. With care not to awaken Jenevra, he dressed in his mail and surcoat and left the room.

The keep had a stillness to it that he rarely noticed. Comparatively few lived in the keep itself, as his guardsmen lived in the barracks in the two main towers of the castle. After yesterday's fest going so late into the night, mostly everyone here would still be asleep. Even the kitchen seemed unusually quiet, especially given the cook Symme's tendency to swear when cooking did not go his way.

His feet led him, as they often did when his mind was unsettled, to the chapel, and to Father Andreu. He tried to remember how many years it had been that the priest had been his teacher and confidant, but he could not remember a time without him.

More he seemed to know Conoc's moods as well as he himself did, for he sat waiting, engaged in prayer, just inside the chapel.

"I thought I would see you this morning," Andreu said. "You might try finding the chapel more regularly and perhaps you would be less troubled when you do come."

"Then you would not be able to scold me instead of counseling as you do so often," Conoc replied. He did not take a seat but paced back and forth as he attempted to work out his thoughts. "Eseld was there last night."

Andreu's eyebrows went up. "I saw. She looks remarkably unchanged."

"You thought so? I found her very different. Or perhaps she only seemed different to me. No one else said anything."

"And what would they say? The few that knew her before are not likely to say much because the subject is so fraught. Or did you think it was common knowledge that Kenan wanted her for your wife rather than Jenevra?"

Conoc sat down abruptly. "No, I did not expect everyone... but Kenan said nothing, nor Lorent."

"Kenan is her brother, and Lorent is almost a brother to her. They see her through that window."

"I think of her as a sister," Conoc protested. Or tried to; his tone seemed too weak to sustain the argument.

Andreu gave him a look, the look he'd always used when Conoc had been an erring and stupid student. "She never thought of you as a brother, and I don't believe you thought of her as a sister."

No, Andreu was right, much though Conoc did deny it to anyone else. As a young man, when Eseld had begun to change from girl to woman, he had admired her, perhaps come close to loving his dear friend's sister. He had even kissed her once, her first kiss. But though he had not seen her as a sister, he had equally not seen her as a lover and wife, especially not after he followed his father into the king's service. Eseld, like Kenan, embraced her Northern heritage. They had fought more than once about it, for she, like Kenan, could not understand why he did not.

That had not been the only issue that had separated them, but it had been a larger one.

"She is - if not the woman I thought I'd marry - at least the sort of woman I would choose," Conoc admitted. "She and Jenevra are so different."

Andreu said nothing, and Conoc stopped in his pacing to look at the priest setting down his polishing. "It was to talk about your lady that I expected you. I watched you dance last night."

"Aye, all of Ravensmere and most of the surrounding area watched us last night. But most of them only saw what they expected to see: the lord and his young bride, looking happy together. They didn't see her trembling and panic-stricken."

"She was not ready." Andreu's voice contained no judgment, and Conoc loved him more for it. He had flogged himself in his thoughts all night.

He knelt in front of the priest in a position of penance. "Tell me what to do, Father. She is not a child any more. She is a woman, and she is still too young."

"Conoc, she cannot be the first woman you have wanted and

could not have. If she is, I will be disappointed in you." He waited for Conoc's grimace of acknowledgment. "You have always been inflexible once you have set your mind to something, and you have always been a man of honor. This is no different."

Andreu set his hands on Conoc's head in benediction and murmured a blessing in the ancient language of the church. Conoc understood only a few words, but he felt better for it anyway. "Carry the blessing of god and goddess with you. I believe that you will find your way."

JENEVRA PULLED her cover over her head when Sess opened the windows. Sunshine poured down on her, warming the room, and a fresh breeze swept in. She could hear the curlews twittering on the lakeshore, but today the sound brought her no joy and no desire to rise.

"Go away, Sess," she ordered from under the pillows. "I wish to be left alone."

Cecilie did not reply, but went about ordering Jenevra's linens and setting out the items necessary for her morning toilette. That done, she dragged a stool to a place beside the bed and on it set a tray of breakfast. The smell of warm pastries brought Jenevra's head out from the pillow, because those smelled like her favorite sweet rolls, with cream and sugared fruit, alongside fried ham and eggs.

She looked at Sess, who looked back at her. "I will not make you rise," Sess said. "Half the castle, including the guards not on morning watch, are still asleep. But you will feel better if you eat and wash your face."

Sess's practical streak had come to the forefront again, and Jenevra knew when it would do her little good to argue, so she sat up. "Have you nothing better to do with your time than wait on me? A maid could have brought breakfast."

"But then you would not eat it," Sess replied. "Jenevra, you are as close to me as a sister, and I love you. That doesn't make me less your companion or less like to care for you. Now, eat."

She did, albeit reluctantly. She did not feel very hungry, and if Sess had not brought foods that were among her favorites, she might not have tried. Sweet rolls, especially with preserves, were a treat not to be wasted. An especially rare treat, because the cook did not like her very much and seldom made recipes that she brought from her home.

"Everyone is still asleep?" she asked hesitantly, her attention on her plate.

"Not everyone. The kitchen is mostly up," Sess indicated the tray in front of Jenevra as evidence. "The watch is obviously awake. And others are waking. Father Bardin is awake and has asked for some of your time this morning when you can spare it."

Jenevra heard Sess's eyeroll in her voice, as she did not like Father Bardin any more than Jenevra did. But while she could dismiss him from her household and even send him away, he had done nothing to merit such, other than being someone she did not like. She would not abuse her authority that way.

"And Lord Conoc is long up," Sess went on. "I heard his voice in the chapel as I passed."

That was the answer Jenevra had wanted without wanting to ask. Even the thought of facing him brought flutters to her stomach, flutters that became great wings of terror if she tried to imagine speaking. He had kissed her, before everyone, and she had not known what to do.

Through the night, when she woke and could not sleep, she had played it over and over again in her mind, still not knowing what he had wanted of her. No answer had appeared.

Perhaps it would do her good to talk to Father Bardin. She found Father Andreu far easier to confide in, but if Conoc were already doing so, she could not imagine discussing the subject with him. She could barely imagine discussing it with anyone beyond Sess.

"Did you dance last night?" she asked, hoping Sess's story would give her time to settle her mind. Sess began to blush as she took the tray away, and Jenevra clapped once. "I thought I'd seen you. Who was it?"

"Some of the guards, yes," Sess replied, still blushing.

"Finn?"

"Enough! Finn was one of them. As was Sir Lorent, among others. Now, will you get out of that bed or shall I drag you out?"

SOME TIME LATER, Jenevra entered the solar where Father Bardin sat at the table, apparently translating a text before him. His hair, now slightly longer than the guardsmen, looked disheveled, as though he had run his fingers through it. She cleared her throat a little, and he rose quickly to his feet.

"My lady," he murmured.

"Father." She sat down at the window seat and picked up the sewing she had abandoned there a few days before. "Cecilie said that you wished to speak to me."

"I did, my lady. I have been reviewing St. Larione's *Profession* in light of yesterday's celebration." His lips twisted into a sneer on the last word. "I believe it is immoral, and you are the only one who can stop it before next year."

"I, Father?" Her surprise was not feigned. Though she could not claim to be the scholar that the priest was, and she had never read Larione's *Profession* in either original or translation, she had not thought the fest particularly scandalous. Low class, perhaps, but hardly immoral.

"Yes. Clearly the people here see nothing wrong with it, and if Lord Conoc were inclined to say anything, he would have before this year. Besides, he's hardly educated, is he, being half-

Northerner. You, though, have the chance to change it as you grow into your power."

He was very harsh of Conoc, who admittedly had not the education she had, but she forbore to argue in order to get the priest to come to the point. "I'm afraid I have not read the *Profession*, so I am not sure to what you are referring. What in yesterday's celebration was immoral? What would you have changed?"

"St. Larione is very clear. Here he says '*Holy days should be kept unto the god and goddess, never marred by the pagan or dissolute. Nor must they induce man into sin nor expose him to temptation.*'" He banged the book on the table, and Jenevra winced. Her eyes kept moving from the stitching in her hands to the priest, normally so calm, now so animate. "The celebration yesterday involved pagan rites, leading people away from the god and goddess to something else."

He continued on in that vein for several minutes, pacing back and forth, his face red, during which time Jenevra continued to sew. She still had no clear idea what he believed to be the problem, but clearly he needed to rant about it thoroughly before any sense would be talked. Only when he began to slow and his denunciations became mere criticisms did she dare to interject.

"I still do not understand, Father. Can you give me the exact rite that troubles you? I noticed nothing pagan. There was dancing, feasting, probably more drink than strictly appropriate but hardly a great issue. You will have to be specific for me."

He stopped mid-stride and turned to face her. "No, you wouldn't know, would you? You have never been exposed to such things. It was the dance, the dance that ended in kissing. A pared-down version of a pagan fertility rite, not a ritual honoring the god and goddess. Indeed the entire festival is pagan in origin."

Perhaps Father Bardin had been studying too hard. "I think

you have misunderstood, Father. It was a kiss. Between husbands and wives, no less. That surely cannot violate any tenet of our faith."

His face began to grow red again, and she shrank back against the window frame. "It is not the kissing, though such displays of passion are immoderate in public. It is the why of it I object to. Pagan rituals ought not be performed in a household dedicated to the god and goddess."

Jenevra drew a deep breath to steady herself. Her heart pounded nearly as much as it had the night before and far less pleasantly. "I will take counsel on the subject, Father, and speak to my husband and Father Andreu. Then we will decide an appropriate course of action."

He looked as if he might start ranting again, so she looked down as her stitching, as if she assumed the conversation done with her comment. Staring down at her fingers did not stop their trembling, but at least she could focus on that until she heard him take his seat at the table.

She did not think it coincidence that he read from the *Profession* all morning.

CHAPTER TWELVE

Jenevra sat at the window seat in the solar, staring out the window at the rain. For a week it had rained unceasingly. She had been confined to the keep, forbidden her garden, forbidden even some room to walk without half the keep in her way. Even the window in her room, which she left open as often as possible, had been closed more than her wont; the rain fell most of the time in exactly that direction and she did not wish to burden her maids more than necessary cleaning up rainwater.

She was not the only one being driven mad by the unrelenting sound of raindrops. Conoc had moved drills indoors, into the great hall. The men took down all the trestle tables in the morning and restored them for the evening meal that they had room enough to train, at least at close fighting. Even the great hall had no room for archery.

The fingers of her right hand curled. If the weather were finer, she would make some time to practice a little archery herself. The bow was too big for her; she could not draw it cleanly. But she practiced despite that, whenever time and other duties permitted. Which they often did, as Lady Mellyn ran the keep, at least in the eyes of the more senior members of the household, such as it was.

Today she longed to be home in Allandale. To have the comfort of people who enjoyed her company and the pleasure of finding something in her father's book room. To know that she could sneak to the kitchen for a treat or have someone bring it to her. To know that someone wanted and cared for her.

She rose, her book falling unheeded to the floor. Another religious treatise that Father Bardin believed she ought to know letter perfect and in which she had no interest. She had tasks enough to fill all her waking hours, but the priest would insist that she devote hours to this. She did not mind learning, nor practicing another language, for inevitably, the works he chose were in ancient religious languages. But he chose such dull ones!

Jenevra set the book on the table, there to remain until she had both leisure and desire to pick it up again. She could apply her time more usefully. Lady Mellyn would be resting at this time of day, but when she rose, they would work together on household duties. Jenevra knew more on how to run a castle, but Mellyn knew *these* people and *this* castle.

A knock on the door, and Sess slipped in. "You have a visitor. Mistress Eseld Halacre, Sir Kenan's sister, is here."

She said nothing, simply nodding to approve. She had no idea why Eseld would visit *her*. They had never actually been introduced, and until Midsummer, she had not even known Eseld existed. That is, she had known Sir Kenan had a sister, somewhere, but had known nothing else about her.

Eseld swept in, cloak dripping, hair damp, but her face flushed in a way that immediately made Jenevra feel colorless and bland. She had the same coloring as Conoc and Sir Kenan, hair black as a raven's wing, and dark blue eyes several shades darker than Jenevra's. But where the two men were ruggedly handsome, Eseld stunned with her beauty.

She curtseyed carelessly, then removed her wet cloak and handed it to Sess. Jenevra did not know what to make of her, but she felt those dark eyes sizing her up and not missing a thing.

"Welcome," she said finally. She took a seat in one of the chairs at the table, unconsciously keeping the table between them, and giving Eseld tacit permission to do likewise. "I am sorry, I am ill-prepared for visitors. I did not expect anyone."

"My husband had business with Con - Lord Conoc, and I convinced him to let me accompany him. By rights I should have visited sooner." Eseld's voice, a rich alto, carried the odd vowels that Jenevra had come to identify as a sign of Northern heritage. "Among my people, a bride is accorded the first visits."

Jenevra noticed no apology in the words and felt the insult Eseld had slipped in carefully. "You yourself are a new bride, I understand, so perhaps it is I who should have visited you. But Lord Conoc prefers that I not leave the safety of the castle unless he - or Sir Lorent or Sir Kenan - can accompany me."

Eseld's lips pursed, but before she could speak, Sess set goblets of warmed wine before each of them. Whatever she had meant to say, she evidently changed her mind, because she smiled. "He would not want anything to happen to you, of course. Everyone is all a-twitter with talk of Lord Conoc's fascination with his new wife."

Eseld's words were all that was correct; Jenevra could not find fault with any of them. Yet she felt the implied insult in every word Eseld spoke.

So she took refuge in her wine to give herself that moment to think. "I am certain that everyone has more interesting uses of their time than discussing Lord Conoc and myself."

"I disagree. You are fascinating to the people here, who have never seen such a lady. Lord Conoc is much loved, and of course, everyone hopes soon to see a young lord as his heir."

Jenevra felt the color rise in her cheeks and could not think of a single thing to say that would not be immodest or untrue. Eseld laughed. "I am too blunt; I have no courtly manners. But I speak the truth in this. Everyone hopes that Lord Conoc's obvious fascination with his wife will lead to the getting of an heir sooner rather than later and secure the castle."

She remained silent. Though it was not indelicate to say such a thing, it would be considered impolite to speak so openly with someone not otherwise a confidante. Too, it felt forced; Eseld had no reason to discuss it. She could not find the meaning hidden in Eseld's conversation.

Eseld seemed to realize the line of conversation was unwelcome when Jenevra failed to respond. Instead she spoke on the foibles and quirks of the residents of Ravensmere's territory, and Jenevra was content to let it go, telling herself she had imagined any ill intent in Eseld's words.

CHAPTER THIRTEEN

"Jenevra," Mellyn said so softly that Jenevra, sitting beside the bed, had to lean far over to hear her.

Only a few weeks after midsummer, Lady Mellyn declined so precipitously that everyone knew she would not last long. Jenevra sat with her as often as she could, though the room made her ill herself. The window could not be opened any longer, and the only person who treated Mellyn, a herbwoman from the village, set bowls of burning herbs all around the room until the smoke grew cloying and coated the back of Jenevra's throat until she felt she couldn't swallow. The smoke collected and became so thick at times that room seemed hazy, and her eyes watered.

Jenevra could barely stand to be in the room this way. Perhaps the herbs or the smoke from them eased Mellyn's passing, for she did not get any better in that time. But she could not take pleasure in it, and every night she bathed and washed her hair because she could not sleep with the smell around her.

Very few sounds penetrated into the room, so Jenevra sat often in silence. She was not used to filling the space with endless chatter, and Mellyn lacked the energy to speak much.

Though, with the room so quiet, when Mellyn did gather her energy to speak, she did not have to work to be heard over noise.

Conoc did not spend much time in his mother's sickroom. She did not ask, and he did not offer, his reasons, but she trusted that he knew his own mind in this. She would remain there, because she loved Mellyn, and she could show it differently than Conoc.

Father Andreu came in daily, to pray and to speak of times that he and Mellyn both remembered. Jenevra left easily at those moments, knowing that the priest would take as good of care as she herself. Some of the maids could not be trusted the same way.

"I'm here," she replied, taking Mellyn's hand in her own and placing her other hand on Mellyn's forehead. Satisfied that Mellyn's fever had not worsened, she used that hand to smooth the covers back.

"You're a good girl," the older woman said. She muttered words in her own native Altyran, words Jenevra did not know or could not understand, but finally came back to Merembrian. "Leaving everything to you now. You'll manage. Smart girl."

Jenevra leaned over, nodded. "I'll manage, of course," she assured around a lump in her throat. "I have good help."

Mellyn smiled a little and squeezed Jenevra's hand. Then she closed her eyes as if to sleep. Jenevra held her hand until the grip loosened, and the wrinkles in Mellyn's face relaxed, the lines of pain disappearing at last.

The lump in her throat grew bigger, and tears burned her eyes. Alone in the room now, she let her head fall forward onto the covers, tears falling out unheeded. A million tasks needed to be done, but she could not bring herself to lift her head, let alone rise.

Mellyn had been a friend, closer even, in their months together. The one person, outside of Sess, who had supported her without question and without being asked. Who had understood how hard it was to come to a new place where she knew almost no one and where the customs were so different from her own.

She had loved her.

Jenevra did not even know she had been weeping until Sess came in to check on her and found her so. She found herself gathered up in Sess's arm, crying helplessly against her friend's shoulder, for herself, for Mellyn, and for Conoc.

SHE INSISTED on telling Conoc herself as soon as she could rise and speak without stumbling over her words. He needed to hear this from her.

He would be out in the bailey training with his men at this time of day, she knew, and so she let herself, Sess behind her, out the door of the keep and into the yard.

The yard was nothing but packed dirt in the area set aside for training. The stables with the horses were set off to one side, and some of the other outbuildings lay around and behind them.

About two dozen men trained in close combat there, armed with staffs, knives or swords. A few more worked on horseback at pells set up, while others practiced archery even further over. Conoc she didn't see at all. Everywhere around her was noise, metal clanging against other metal or wood, horses with their harnesses jingling, men's breath heavy as they fought and took blows from each other, but she barely noticed these, so intent was she on her task.

One man saw her approach, which she never did, and stepped back from fighting, nudging the man beside him, who in turn stepped back. One by one as they saw her approach or as others drew their attention to her, the men stopped what they did and fell back away from her so that an aisle formed in front of her, leading her to Conoc. No one spoke, and each bowed as she passed, so that the noise of the practice field dropped gradually into silence.

That silence brought Conoc out from the tower. He looked prepared to yell at everyone to get back to their duties when he saw her there. With quick footsteps, he closed the distance between them and touched her face with one hand, wiping away a stray tear. "What is it?" he asked.

She didn't have the words, and the lump in her throat rose up again. Jenevra swallowed it back and forced herself to remain calm. "Lady Mellyn has passed, my lord."

His eyes searched hers for a second that seemed interminable to her. Then he closed his eyes and nodded. "I... Thank you for telling me, my lady."

She wanted to smooth away the lines of strain that had abruptly become so apparent, but he set his jaw and strode away from her, back to the keep, calling for Lorent to take over. She stood still and let him go, her heart hurting for him.

HOURS LATER, Conoc remembered his lady.

He had spent the intervening time at his mother's bedside, keeping vigil as Father Andreu began the rites for the dead. The ceremony was not long or convoluted, though Conoc could not have said what it consisted of, as he didn't hear a word of it. He only came out of his stupor when Andreu touched his shoulder once in silent benediction.

The smell of the incense mingled with the smoke still hanging in the room from the burning herbs, and the combination sickened him. But he didn't rise, just sat in silent thought, sometimes praying, sometimes not.

He had never been a good son to his mother. Not as good as she'd deserved, at any rate. He'd more admired his father, who had been everything brave and heroic to him as a boy. His mother had always just been there, and he had never appreciated that being there involved a great deal of work and a great deal of love.

And when his father had died and he had been given Ravensmere, she had simply left her old life to come and care for him. Without even a second thought, he had dumped his wife on her and her on his wife. They had bonded, sharing time and confidences that he'd had no part of by his own doing. Thinking back to Jenevra's pale, tearstained face and red eyes, he considered that she grieved almost as much as he did.

When two of the women came in to dress her - the body - he finally rose. He barely saw them, but he couldn't stay to see his mother so. Instead he fumbled his way up a flight of stairs and down a long corridor to his own room.

Intending to throw himself on his bed and sleep away all thoughts, he was startled to see the fire blazing away, where normally it was kept banked all day. On his linen chest sat a tray with a plate of food covered by a linen cloth, and a jug, water beading on the sides. The plate, when he uncovered it, had slices of fresh bread and cheese, nothing too heavy to upset his stomach, but enough that he wouldn't go hungry. And the jug contained chilled wine, just enough to blunt the edges of his grief. In this he saw his wife's delicate hand, supporting him even in her own grief.

He replaced the cover over the food - he would eat it later - and turned to look at the pale girl standing in the doorway between their rooms. She hadn't been there when he came in, nor had he heard her enter. But he'd known she would come.

She seemed taller than even at Midsummer, though he couldn't imagine she had grown so much in a few weeks. She said nothing, and neither did he. He didn't know what to say, could hardly think in one cohesive line.

From behind her came the sounds of water splashing as someone prepared her bath, and she turned away in response to a low-voiced comment he could not hear. Her movement jolted him out of the near-trance he'd been in, and when she looked back at him, he could almost smile at her.

"Go, my lady. Let someone care for you for a time." Her eyes remained doubtful, but he could not think of a way to reassure her. "I am well enough, thanks to your care."

She nodded and stepped back into her room, closing the door between them and leaving him to his own grief.

JENEVRA HAD NOT WANTED to leave Conoc alone, did not think it had been a wise idea, but equally could not think of a retort to his courteous dismissal. She had brought the food so that he would relax a little, as she doubted he'd eaten at all during his vigil.

Nor had the rest of the keep eaten particularly well. Dinner had been far more somber than usual, and she had felt it the more with his seat empty beside hers. Lady Mellyn had been well-liked, loved even by those who had known her longest. Symme, the cook, had been so distraught that he'd overcooked the game pies and burned the roast, but she doubted that anyone had really even noticed; few had done more than pick at it. She did not think Conoc would have enjoyed it.

Sess poured a pitcher of warm water over her head to rinse out the last of the soap and with it the last of the burning herbs smell. They needed someone with more knowledge of healing and medicine than an herbwoman in the village. Father Andreu knew a bit of battlefield care, but was unskilled in matters of sickness.

Jenevra wrapped herself in her robe and settled down before the fire to let her hair dry as Sess combed it. She hummed softly to herself, the melody wandering through fragments of songs as her thoughts took their own turns, though most were sad.

"Father Andreu will hold the final rites for Lady Mellyn

tomorrow," Sess said, beginning to braid Jenevra's waist length hair. "Being the summer, he cannot wait any longer."

She blanched at that simple truth. The summer months were too hot to wait, but the speed did not lend itself to an easier mourning period.

"There is a cemetery by the village; the ground near the castle is too rocky and that is consecrated ground." Jenevra heard the catch in Sess's voice, knew it would not be different for the rest of them.

She covered Sess's hand with her own. "You need not pretend with me," she said softly.

Sess knelt by her side. "I would not burden you with more. You have your own grief, and must be support for everyone. Besides, your loss is greater than mine."

Jenevra leaned over so that their foreheads touched. "That does not make us less dear friends. Support does not go one way."

WHEN SESS FINALLY LEFT, Jenevra went to the open window and leaned out, taking comfort in the evening sounds. She had lived a dozen days since the morning, and she needed to re-find her equilibrium.

The final glimmers of sunset, orange and pink, reflected off the lake, washing to entire area in warm light before twilight turned completely. The lake itself seemed made of molten gold from where she stood.

She breathed deep of the fresh air and the scents carried up from her garden. Rose came the most strongly, followed by rosemary's sharper scent. Subtler and sweeter, heather and lavender finished the combination. When there was time again, she would gather the flowers and try and catch that scent in perfume, to hold this bit of summer through the long winter months.

She could heard the sounds of the end of the day, the men changing to the night watch, the stamp of feet up and down the stone steps, the animals being moved into stables and pens. The ravens had mostly settled on their perches by now, but the occasional squabbling echoed over the lake.

The last low calls of the curlews floated up to her. No full moon meant the little birds went to sleep not long after the sun.

She tried, again, to whistle back at them and failed, but the guard on the wall heard her and looked up and saluted her. She nodded back before he continued his walk, and when she could no longer hear his footsteps, she closed her eyes and breathed deeply, holding these sounds and sights and smells close to her heart for strength the next day.

It felt different in the morning. Jenevra walked beside Conoc down the path to the churchyard, with others of the household behind them.

The day had dawned appropriately gray, with a thick cloud cover that left the air heavy. She whispered prayers all morning that the threatened rain would hold off until after the ceremony. The building pressure was not much of an improvement.

The procession followed the four men carrying the casket with Lady Mellyn's remains. Conoc had wanted to be among them, but Father Andreu had laid a hand on his arm and said something softly, so he'd taken his place as chief mourner. Instead, Sir Lorent, Sir Kenan, and two other men of the household had done it.

They, like Conoc, wore black surcoats, all hastily altered from other things. Most of the other men and women in the household wore black armbands; Jenevra wore dark gray, made over from one of Mellyn's dresses.

The church and the cemetery stood outside the village, between the village and the castle. Though the road turned a little with the curves of the hill, the distance from the castle gate to the cemetery gate could not have been more than a mile and a half, They moved so slowly that the walk seemed far longer than the distance could account for.

The bubble of silence they walked in kept all sounds out. Though birds must have called near the road, and cows and sheep lowed in the fields around the church, the sounds did not penetrate to anyone at the front of the procession.

The villagers waited just outside the churchyard, their faces as somber as the castlefolk, and fell in at the end of the procession. Lady Mellyn had not been known well outside the castle, but they didn't come just to show respect to the dead. Their respect went as much to Lord Conoc.

Jenevra saw it all, but she could not process it. Her attention stayed always on Conoc, whose impassive face hid his deeper emotions. She worried for the moment his control would break, and he would need more support from her than simply standing by his side.

But he lasted through the little ceremony at her grave, and when the men laid her coffin in the grave, though she could feel him shaking so slightly beside her.

Father Andreu finished the prayers and stepped back from the graveside, and over to Conoc. He didn't say anything but laid a hand over Conoc's in blessing. Then he turned to her long enough to squeeze her hand, but not long enough that she could read his expression. The priest's shoulders slumped a little, as if he carried a too heavy weight there.

After Andreu, every person there came by, one by one, to offer condolences. Sir Lorent and Sir Kenan, closest of everyone to Conoc, each offered a one-armed hug and some words she could not catch. Lorent kissed her hand before moving on; Kenan, ever more formal with her, bowed correctly and almost said something, but closed his mouth at the last minute.

Dear Sess curtseyed to Conoc, then kissed her cheek. After her came the other members of the household, most of whom said nothing but bowed or curtseyed as necessary, or bowed or curtseyed with a murmured 'I'm sorry.' Father Bardin said something to Conoc that she did not hear, but knew from the way Conoc's jaw clenched that he'd pushed too far. She glared at the young priest, but she doubted her expression did much to quell him.

After the castlefolk, the villagers came by, offering less in words, but more in actions, for many of them carried flowers that were tossed in the grave. Conoc's jaw clenched again, and he swallowed several times before he could regain enough composure to nod at each person in turn. Only Eseld dared try anything more; she leaned up to kiss Conoc's cheek lightly.

Finally it was done. She and Conoc were the only two left at the gravesite, though Sess and Lorent and Kenan waited by the gate of the churchyard. The rest of the castlefolk had already begun the walk back, and the villagers returned to their homes.

The threatened rain had begun to fall, large drops that did nothing to dispel the heavy pressure in the air but promised worse to come. Conoc offered her his arm. "Come, my lady, we'd best head back."

ANOTHER LONG MISERABLE EVENING ENDED, Jenevra sat in her room and drew her brush through her hair. Sess had been exhausted after the emotions of the day before, as well as staying up half the night to ready mourning attire for the immediate household, so Jenevra had sent her to bed, saying she was perfectly capable of taking care of herself for one night, especially when all she needed to do was comb her hair and take off the mourning gown.

She enjoyed taking care of herself at times. To be alone, for even a few minutes, had become precious and would become more so. Despite Mellyn's illness and her own marriage to

Conoc, plenty of people had seen Mellyn as the authority. From here out, she would have no one to shelter her or to stand behind her with their authority. She would be visible at all times and have even less chance for solitude than before.

The window stood open again, but tonight she had not energy to lean out and enjoy the night breeze, with all of its scents and sounds. She was too worn, emotionally as well as physically, and all she wished tonight was to crawl into her bed and sleep.

A heavy footstep, slower than usual, in the room beside hers changed her mind. Instead of waiting as usual, in case he needed time to himself, she set down her brush immediately and opened the door between their rooms.

He didn't look surprised to see her, though he'd had his back to the door and she'd made no sound. She didn't know quite what to say, other than what they had said - more than once - since yesterday.

"Are you well?" she asked.

He looked back at her standing there, but his eyes seemed to be seeing some other time or place. "That color doesn't suit you," he said finally. "Don't wear it again."

She looked down at the dress, then back at him. "My lord, mourning..."

"No." His voice firmed. "We will not observe some formal mourning period, as though my mother were the queen. She would not have wanted it, and it is impractical. Besides, I do not think I could bear to see it."

Jenevra had no useful answer to that. Formal mourning would not be done by many, but Mellyn had been his mother and her husband's mother, and that relationship deserved their respect. Though he was not wrong that Mellyn would not have wanted it done. "As my lord wishes, then."

He laid a hand on her face, to guide her to looking up at him, though the gap between them had narrowed a bit of late. "Your hair is down. I've missed seeing it so."

She tilted her head and raised an eyebrow slightly, so he clarified. "You used to wear your hair down during the day, and plaited at night. Now during the day, you wear it in a plait or in a net." He drew a few strands away from her face.

She hadn't known he'd even noticed. "Oh. I was a maid."

"You are still a maid."

"No, my lord, I am not. At least, not that any others should know." She let out a breath. "Perhaps 'maid' is not the right word." Except that it very much was. "But I am a married woman, and only girls may wear their hair loose."

He didn't speak, but gently tucked the hair he still held behind her ear. "I will take your word for it, my lady. But I'll ask you to wear it loose when I am the only one to see it." Then he leaned down and kissed her forehead.

She leaned against him and felt his weight on her as well. He shuddered once, as if he had swallowed down some emotion; a few drops fell on her shoulder, and she thought she heard her name hoarsely whispered. But when he picked up his head, although his eyes were red, they were clear of the pain he'd carried for a day and a half now.

"To bed, my lady," he said. "Tomorrow we begin again."

CHAPTER FOURTEEN

Jenevra sat at the window of the solar, wrapped in a blanket against the cold, for, despite the careful sealing that had been done at the end of summer, the large window in the solar let in drafts. She still preferred this seat to any other during the daylight hours, which were becoming fewer already.

Winter came early that year, shutting the castle in almost as soon as the last harvests had been gathered. The first storm had come whistling down from the north, dropping snow wherever it passed. For two days, no one had been able to set foot out of doors, for the wind had blown so fierce that nothing could be seen beyond the tip of one's nose. But that first storm had worn out the weather's fury, and after that, though it snowed regularly and often, the storms behaved as normal ones ought.

Her work lay behind her on the table, a ledger of the household accounts. She did not enjoy working at it exactly, but she found satisfaction in knowing how the numbers came out and what that meant for the household. The numbers added up well enough for the moment, though she worried for what the winter would bring.

The harvest had been inconsistent. Of vegetables and fruits they had more than sufficient, for the weather had suited those crops, and the fruit-bearing trees had produced so much that even Jenevra and Conoc had joined in the harvesting in an attempt to get it all done. The grain crops had done less well, and bread would be scarcer through the winter.

Sess hummed softly beside her as she continued her own work. Today they were alone, a rare thing these days, for Father Bardin preferred the solar when he studied. But today he had begged her indulgence to miss their instructional time as he'd claimed he had work in private to do.

She suspected he wrote again to his preceptor, with whom he exchanged letters whenever a courier could be found or spared. Secretly, she encouraged this, for if he wrote to his preceptor, he did not complain to her. His complaints had long since tired her, for he complained of her husband, his people, the insufficiency of their religious practices, Father Andreu, her failure to produce an heir...

Jenevra looked out at the snow-covered bailey again. This year, though colder than last, the snow had been more manageable. The men kept the snow in the bailey stomped down so they could practice outside more.

The road to the village was kept open this year as well, for the villagers too had had a hard year and Conoc felt they would need him too often to let the snow hold him in. The men of the castle cleared down from the castle, and the villagers cleared up from the village to meet somewhere in the middle. Neither side much enjoyed the work, but both sides appreciated it done when they needed something in the other place.

She saw the rider as he entered through the gates, the king's banner snapping in the cold breeze, and sat up to better look. It had been at the time of year that a messenger had come before from the king. But from the window she could see nothing distinguishing about him, only that he rode alone and was not Sir Wyeth.

She hurried from the window and down to the great hall, though she did not run as she had a year ago. By now, the women of the castle knew what was expected of them in waiting on visitors.

Conoc waved once as she entered the great hall, to beckon her over. She waited until she had found the messenger with her eyes, being served by one of the women near one fireplace. He seemed well-enough, despite the cold, and so she answered Conoc's summons.

The cold of the stone floor seeped up through the rushes and through her shoes, so she did not dawdle but sat down and tucked her feet on the crosspiece of the chair. "My lord wishes to see me?"

"I did not wish you to disturb the messenger," Conoc replied. "You would only embarrass him." She tilted her head in question, and he added, "I've already done so. He is not accustomed to lords who greet him personally."

Jenevra smiled, careful not to laugh, though the faint twinkle in Conoc's eyes almost undid her. "Then I shall sit here and not shock him further." She did pick up the pitcher of warmed wine that sat before Conoc and pour out a goblet for him and one for herself. "What does the king wish of us?"

He refolded the letter but did not offer it to her, his movements betraying a hint of tension, and the laughter in his eyes dying. "He is remarrying at Midwinter."

"Remarrying? But who...?" She wracked her brain, but could think of no sign that the king had favored any women when her parents had taken her to court. Nor had her mother's occasional letters mentioned anything.

"Gailana of Balyun." He tapped the letter on the table.

Jenevra stilled, but a knot formed in her stomach. "In Hunslind?"

Now Conoc looked at her, concern in his eyes. "Yes. Her father rules one of the principalities there. What is wrong?" When she didn't answer, he touched her face to look at her. "Jenevra?"

She forced a smile in case anyone watched them. "I don't know. Maybe nothing." He stared hard at her, but she didn't say anything else. She barely understood what had caused that skitter of fear down her spine, she could not tell him. The great hall was too exposed; bits of conversation had a way of echoing around the room.

Finally, he nodded once. "He and his new bride will go on progress in the spring, and he intends to visit Ravensmere."

Her spine went cold, and she tried - and failed - not to shiver.

"Jenevra, tell me. What has you so distressed?"

"Later," she whispered. "Not here." Before he could ask her anything else, she rose and fled from the room.

Conoc paced his room that night. Jenevra's distress, the fear in her blue eyes, gnawed at him. She maintained her calm, even in moments when she could by rights lose it. This should not have provoked such a reaction, but it had.

He built up the fire to warm the room. In just his shirt and hose, the room felt cold, and he did not want Jenevra to be cold either when she arrived.

She would come. He'd hoped to speak to her sooner, but between their conversation and dinner, he had been unable to find her. At dinner, she had kept the conversation away from anything of significance, wearing as she did her mask of calm. Only he had been close enough to see her real emotions under the surface.

He picked up his room without thinking as he paced. Unlike Jenevra, who had Sess and a maid to take care of her, he took care of himself and his things. He tended to not take care as well as he ought, though, and he suspected she had started to do it for him. He'd found dried herbs in his linen chest, and his clothes were always neatly folded, regardless of what state he left them in. Only his mail and weapons were never touched, but those he took good care of.

The work allowed him to push his thoughts aside for the moment, to focus on the mundane rather than the more pressing worry in his mind.

When she opened the door between their rooms, before she could say a word, he grabbed her hand, pulled her into his room and shut the door behind her. "Will you tell me now, lady?"

Though she looked startled - he had never shut the door on the rare occasions she'd been in his room and she was now effectively trapped - she showed no fear of him, which loosened a tension he hadn't realized he carried. He never wanted her to fear him.

Her kirtle, the same shade of blue as her eyes, made her skin look paler than usual. Or perhaps her emotions caused that. He did not know and would not ask.

"I hardly know," she said. "But I know of Gailana of Balyun." He let her go when she began to twist her fingers together nervously. "She is very learned, but the Hunslind principalities do not share our faith, and I have heard that she is fanatical. If I know this, the king must."

He covered her hands with his, preventing her from her nervous gestures, which looked painful to him. "She will be queen consort, not regnant. Her faith will not matter to us."

"Fanatics will not allow for differences, Conoc. Will you tell me truthfully that she will have no influence with the king her husband? I do not believe that. And though she may never be queen regnant, she could become queen regent."

"That is not likely. The king is not so close to death as that, and the prince -"

"Does not stand to inherit, or not if the king can sway enough magnates to stand with him. She could bear the next heir, and she is barely five years older than me." She pulled her hands away from him. "And why would he bring her here? We should be summoned to her, not her come to a border castle that still faces attacks."

Conoc drew her back to him, tucking her head against his chest, and he measured the strength of her agitation by the fact that she let him. "You are worrying about what might happen, but it hasn't happened yet. You do not need to upset yourself so. Are there no scenarios where they visit, and you and she become friends? You have the rank and lineage to stand as one of her companions."

She gave him such a scornful look that he would have laughed had she been less serious. "That request would have surprised me not at all, but the king's letter did not say that, did it?"

He sighed. "It did not. I am not sorry for that, save that it gives you more space to fret, for I have no desire to spend time at court."

"Answer me this, Conoc. Why? Why does the king do this? It cannot be for love, as he has never met her. He gains something from this, but I do not know what and that is what worries me."

He stroked her hair lightly and murmured soothing words that made no sense. He had not married a stupid woman, and she had learned at the feet of other intelligent women. Her fears, as little as they made sense to him, were grounded in her knowledge and experience. His lay on a battlefield, and he would not believe himself in danger from the king. "What would you have me do, Jenevra?"

"I don't know that either," she whispered. "I simply do not know."

With some coaxing, he convinced her to sit on the bed and relax. Though he would have preferred to sit beside her, where he could hold her, he dragged a chair to sit in front of her, with the fire to his side. A cup of wine in her hands seemed to settle her enough that she no longer seemed likely to panic.

The color had come back to her skin, so that her blue dress seemed no worse for her than any other color. She did not speak now, lost in her own thoughts as she stared at the fire. He could admire her to his heart's content.

She was rapidly becoming a woman, and he had the uncomfortable thought that Andreu had been right once to counsel him not to wait long to begin courting her. He did not worry about her fidelity if he failed to win her, but he wanted her to one day look at him with something other than her serene expression, to see him for himself.

For the first time, she had said his name that night. Not a title before it, no formal surname, just... his name. And she had trusted him with her fears, not because he could solve them, but to let him help her bear it. After more than a year, they began, however lightly, to pull together as partners.

He had time; she had a few weeks more before her fifteenth birthday. She was still a girl, not a woman grown. Almost against his will, his eyes traced her silhouette, her long eyelashes, slightly curled at the ends, the delicate upturned nose, the slightly pursed lips... Not a woman, but not a child.

Her mind had not wandered as his had. "The magnates will not deny the king the marriage; that is a battle they will not win," she said thoughtfully. "Neither my father nor Courcy of Gilshire have the strength to force that issue, not unless they unite against the king, which is unlikely. Most of the other magnates will follow their lead, except for a few of the king's own men, Lefric of Oakhalgh or Waldef of Netherwhit."

"You are worrying over something you cannot change," Conoc said. "We do not even know the truth of your information, so all we know is that the king is marrying again."

She tilted her head in what he took as acquiescence, her

expression unresolved. He would accept that for now.

ALONE IN HER ROOM LATER, Jenevra curled up in her bed to think. Heavy comforters covered her, so that she hardly felt the chill that seeped in through the shutters despite the coverings. The stone walls absorbed little heat, so in the winter, her room felt perpetually cool. But with enough covers, she would sleep warm enough.

The only light in the room came from the fire. Sess had added wood before she'd left, to make sure that it would burn through the night. By morning, it would be mostly dead, with just enough embers to stir up. For now, she had light enough to not be in complete darkness and that was enough.

She had not told Conoc everything she knew, and that might constitute a lie. Her mother's friend, her own godmother, Lady Berdina Reize had come from Balyun to serve the old queen. It was from her that Jenevra knew of their customs and beliefs. Lady Berdina had remained in contact with her family there, so Jenevra's knowledge of Gailana was not mere rumor.

Gailana was a fanatic, who argued for no mercy to heretics. She was unusually educated for a woman in Balyun, where women were expected to obey their fathers in everything until they married. But despite being kept closely guarded and veiled in public to prevent anyone from seeing her, Gailana wielded a great deal of influence with her father.

Jenevra shivered and pulled her blankets tighter. A loose piece of hair kept falling in her face, as she'd hastily plaited her own hair before climbing into bed. After Conoc had expressed that he wished to see her hair loose, she had left it so every night, but then she had to take care of it herself and she could not do it as well as Sess.

As the people of Balyun understood their faith, the goddess

came subordinate to the god. They found the Merembrian idea of god and goddess sharing the rule of the year heretical, as they preferred teachings of Gilon and Sibico over Marke and St. Crepin. That would be all well and good - those were, after all, valid teachings - if they didn't insist on executing those who disagreed with them.

She could not shake the feeling that something else lay behind this. If the king meant to push the magnates his way, he went about it wrongly, for her father, at least, would trim his sails to match the king's wishes. He did not desire the crown for himself, though he would not object if it were offered him, but he wished to have power, to rule if not to reign. He had tried once to betroth her to the prince, the king's only child, but the king had refused. Only then had the king proposed that she marry Conoc. And the prince had been banished some months later, though no one knew the truth of that.

This marriage would not be popular. The magnates might not oppose the king openly, but they would have tried and would still try to change his mind. The Council, when they acted in concert, wielded a great deal of power. The king had yielded to them before, though never with good grace. The prince's banishment still lay sorely between king and Council.

Going on progress with the new queen seemed an ill idea as well. That would force the magnates to acknowledge her, welcome her, before they'd had time to reconcile to it. Too many insults lay that way, with no room for grace or polite excuses. And nothing made sense about bringing her to Ravensmere.

Conoc was right in that she ought not worry about something she couldn't change. But somehow, it kept nagging at her. She was missing something, something important.

Eventually the fatigue from all her worries, combined with the warm bed, overcame the anxiety, and she fell asleep, still trying to make the pieces work together.

CHAPTER FIFTEEN

Morning brought her no clarity, nor did any of the days that followed. Before long, Jenevra gave over worrying at it. She did not wish to, but before much longer, increasing snow trapped them, so that farther than the village was simply impassible. Whatever would happen would happen without them.

She had matters closer to her to deal with. Her fifteenth birthday had come and gone, and she had become, sometime or another, fully the lady of the castle. Her wish was law, and with that came her responsibility to everyone.

In theory, at any rate. It did not work as well in practice, for even more than a year after she had come to the castle, too many regarded her as an interloper. She received no credit for the work she had done, as they gave all credit to Lady Mellyn. That she had become popular with the guardsmen did not help, for some of the castlefolk thought she distracted the guardsmen from their duties, especially when she'd had the bad judgment to be caught out in an attack and require half the castle to search for her.

Especially in the kitchen. Symme, the cook, still could barely tolerate her, and their fights had become a source of amusement for those in the kitchen. He won, for he simply would not do what she asked of him, no matter how she asked it. Unless Conoc gave an order, Symme regarded everything as a suggestion, to be ignored at his discretion.

That day, a few days after Midwinter, she went down to the kitchen to discuss meal plans. The king's and new queen's progress would begin in a few very short months, and before then, the castle had to be prepared. She wanted Symme and the rest of the kitchen to begin making the kinds of dishes the court would expect.

At Allandale, she had loved the kitchens, and she'd never been unwelcome there. The old cook there had always had time to make treats, and as she grew older, he taught her about the kitchen and how it worked. She could not claim to cook, but she knew what to ask for and what would be a burden on the kitchen staff. She'd seen how her mother and the cook worked together in a partnership to keep everyone in the castle well-fed.

This kitchen was not so welcoming as Allandale's. The floor direly needed scrubbing, as a layer of grease and food scraps lay everywhere. Though a few people worked at peeling and chopping vegetables or preparing meats and one kneaded loaves of bread, others loafed around pretending to work.

The fires, from where she stood, put too much heat into the kitchen, as though they weren't venting properly, and something smelled distinctly of burning, food burning, not wood or coal.

A faint hum of chatter stopped as soon as everyone realized she was there and dropped whatever they were doing, productive or not, to watch.

Symme stood near the entrance of the kitchen, his arms crossed over his chest. He towered over her, even now that she'd grown, and he scowled whenever he saw her. He'd lost a leg during some battle and now had a peg, which did not slow him down for even a moment in the kitchen and never prevented him from stomping around in a temper. Like many others, he had been one of Conoc's men who could no longer soldier and so worked in the castle. She could not criticize the quality of his food, for he cooked very well, but he did not run a kitchen as well as he cooked.

"Lady," Symme said, giving her a quarter of a bow. "What do ye want?"

The rudeness rankled. She was never rude to him, no matter what he said or did. "I brought some recipes for dishes that the court -"

"No." He did not even let her finish her sentence. "I'll not be lookin' at them. Those fine and fancy dishes," his voice mocked her, and she flushed, "might be alright for nobles, but this castle is full o' fighting men, and I'm not interested in making them sick so ye can play at being a lady."

She pressed her lips together to stop the immediate rush of words. "Master Symme, I am not asking. The court will be here, and this is what they will expect."

"Lady, I won't cook this. Those spices are unhealthy." He didn't move a muscle, just continued to stare down at her. "And expensive to boot."

"I brought the spices with me. It will not stretch our resources. And they are not unhealthy; every noble household in the realm uses them." Across the kitchen, the young man who'd been kneading bread slid it into the too-hot oven, and Jenevra drew a breath to tell Symme but he cut her off.

"Not this one. I won't do it, and ye can't make me."

"You would have done this for Lady Mellyn," she snapped back.

"Aye, I would. Because she wouldn't of asked. She knew what ordinary folks needed." His jaw tightened, proof of his irritation.

"That is your final word?" she asked.

"It is."

Jenevra turned away, angry and hurt that she would not be listened to. She tried not to use her authority as a bludgeon; her mother had never done so. But she began to not know what else to do. "I will have a different cook for the royal visit then."

She stomped away from the kitchen, her only consolation that she could hear Symme banging a pot around, indicating he was as irritated as she. She did not have time for this. She could not order everything done as she wished, due to the season and the snow, though she had a long list of orders to be sent as soon as the snow melted and the roads opened.

Before she'd gone much farther, she smelled something burning and heard the faint cursing that indicated Symme had smelled it too. Shaking her head, she continued up the steps. She hoped that some day Symme would learn to listen to her; she did not want to displace him, she wanted to work with him.

At the top of the stairs, she turned the corner into the hall and almost ran straight into Father Bardin, who dropped the two books in his hands as he caught her arms to steady her. Then he let go of her as if he'd been scalded. "My lady, I beg your pardon," he stammered out.

"Not at all, Father," she replied, bending down to retrieve his books. "You obviously had matters of great importance on your mind, and I am not hurt."

"No, but I ought not have touched you so familiarly." He bowed. "You are a virtuous lady, in all sense of the word."

As priests took vows of celibacy, she didn't expect him to be touching any woman with any familiarity, nor did she find her arms a particularly familiar place. But he seemed embarrassed enough without bringing that up, so she smiled a little and nodded to accept the apology. She handed over his books, noting the titles as she did so. Hano's *Letters* and Thieme's first essays, both written by Balyese religious apologists. She hadn't even known he'd possessed those books.

"Reading heresies, Father?" she asked lightly, to distract him from concerns of her virtue.

He looked away for a moment, which she found fascinating. She had never seen him so uncertain. "I wished to understand their perspective. The new queen…"

"Yes, the new queen." She sighed once. "In that case, I shall leave you to it, and trust that you will acquit yourself well, should it come to a debate when she visits." She smiled again, and he stood aside to let her pass, and she continued down the hall, never noticing that he stood still, looking after her far longer than necessary.

Conoc found the time to pass slowly. Knowing that the king would be coming, and that his defenses would be called upon to protect the royal persons, he drilled his men more fervently and exactingly than even his usual wont. But the days stretched too long, no matter how he worked.

Jenevra's uncertainties wore on him, though she had not mentioned them since their initial conversation. But he wavered in his own mind whether he gave the right credence to her fears and if she had the right of it all. His own mind said no, that they would be in no danger from his king. He had pledged his life and loyalty to the king's service; to believe the king capable of endangering his vassals, from highest magnate to lowest peasant, betrayed that oath.

So he occupied his body with drilling and his mind with worries, and the days wore on while he wrestled with these problems.

He left Jenevra to deal with her own problems inside the castle, though under other circumstances he would have supported her as much as she needed. But she did not ask, and he, his mind on other things, did not notice that she struggled at times.

He did, however, notice that at dinner that night, as they shared a trencher since there were no guests, that she did not eat well and picked at the food. Jenevra was a slim girl, and compared to the men in the castle, she ate very little. But he'd always observed her appetite to be healthy. "Is something wrong, my lady?"

On Jenevra's other side, Cecilie had turned to look at him and was shaking her head, clearly warning him not to pursue this. But he'd already committed himself to the question, and if something was wrong, he would try and fix it.

"I am simply tired," she replied, a sharp edge in her voice. She smiled faintly, but he could see that it didn't reach her eyes.

"Tired, lady?" He touched her cheek gently and ducked his head to meet her squarely.

"Yes, tired. I am tired of not being listened to within this castle, of being sneered at for having been born to a noble family, of being held responsible when I have not even been given the chance to show what I can do, and of having to take it all in silence!"

"What are you talking about?" he asked. "I have seen no one treat you thus."

Cecilie's head shaking had grown more frantic.

"Perhaps you might ask Symme then, or anyone else down in the kitchens. Because I can assure you, it happens!" She pushed away from the table and rose, but not before he'd seen the hurt in her eyes. "I am not hungry tonight." And without waiting for him to say anything, she stomped off in a swirl of skirts.

He beckoned Cecilie over. "What happened?"

She sighed, looked over at where Jenevra had gone, then back at him, her divided loyalties obvious on her face. "I should not say... But she and Symme had another... disagreement."

"Another one. I had not known they had a first one." Conoc

did not know what to think. Jenevra had kept something from him, when he thought they were beginning to trust one another. Something that had hurt her, for her temper had come from hurt, he'd recognized that clearly.

"Once a week or so," Cecilie admitted. "She didn't want you to know."

"Why not?" His own voice sharpened, and Sess flinched.

"Because..." She sighed, then shrugged. "Because she wants you to believe her capable, that she can solve her own problems without running to you. No one will ever treat her appropriately if she has to hide behind you."

Now he sighed. He understood that only too well. Since taking over Ravensmere, he'd suffered from doubts about his abilities that he could not show, lest it change how people saw him. He'd had to separate himself from his men, to no longer be one among them. She had never been one of them.

Cecilie watched him, and a flicker of guilt hit him. He'd pushed her to break a confidence, from someone she loved dearly. He'd have to prove worthy of it.

As soon as dinner was over, he went down to the kitchens himself. He hadn't been down there since Jenevra had come and taken over helping his mother. He'd never given the matter another thought, beyond an occasional bout of guilt that he was relieved of such an onerous task.

He didn't remember it being so dirty. His mother would never have allowed such a thing, and, having seen how clean Jenevra kept the rest of the castle, he doubted she approved either.

He didn't even want to know what the smell was.

Symme hurried over to meet him, wooden leg pounding on the floor in his haste. "M'lord, I didn't expect ye to come down here. How can I help you?"

Symme had served with him for a long time. He was older than Conoc, at least a decade, and Conoc had grown used to his ways. Or maybe he'd just overlooked them, since Symme had lost his leg protecting Conoc, in a battle where they'd been separated from the rest of their forces.

"I... What did Lady Jenevra want this afternoon?" He'd meant to ask more subtly, but the hurt in her eyes came back to him and the words escaped without thought.

"She wanted me to make some fancy dishes, with some outlandish spices from foreign parts. I told her no." Symme didn't appear ashamed of it at all, and Conoc wondered how he'd missed this more than once. Symme lowered his voice, but didn't conceal his laughter. "She said she'd get a new cook for the king's visit. As though the king wouldn't like me own cooking."

Conoc nodded slowly. "I see."

"Did she sulk or pout at ye?" A knowing smirk, that the little girl would run off and tattle.

"No. She said very little, and I had to get the details from others. Had she told me, my reaction would have been the same." Conoc sighed. "Symme, this cannot happen. Whatever you may think - and I don't know where you got the idea you were her equal - she is my wife and the lady of this castle. When she gives an order, I expect that you'll follow it."

"She's no' one of us," Symme said urgently, his accent thickening. "She's a lady," he spat that word out, "with no idea what she's doing."

"She is attempting to keep us all from being embarrassed when the king arrives. But even if that were not so, she is acting as she ought. You are to follow her instructions."

"Or what? Will ye throw me out, m'lord?" Symme gestured to his leg. "Will ye really?"

"I wouldn't want to, no. We've come a long way together. But I will not tolerate disrespect for my wife." Conoc shrugged.

"And I would leave it to her. She has full control of those under her."

Symme glared at him. "So I'm to obey Lady fine and fancy, even when she's making ye all sick? Or I'll be gone?"

"I expect her to be given the respect she is owed. And that means using her correct title."

Symme had nothing else to say, though Conoc could see the words choking him. Andreu had been right, as he so often was, that staffing Ravensmere with his men, men he had been one of, would prove troublesome. They saw him as one of them, the minor improvement in his birth meaningless in light of his upbringing. Always before, he had encouraged that camaraderie. Now he had been elevated above them, and his wife was above that. He could never be one of them again.

Shaking his head, Conoc turned to go, but a slight hand on his arm stopped him. One of the kitchen women had a tray that she offered him. A plate of rolls, filled with fruit, sat there.

"Lady Jenevra didn't eat much at dinner," she said. "These are her favorites."

"Thank you," Conoc replied courteously.

HE TAPPED at the door between their rooms. Though Jenevra never locked it from her side, he respected that her room was, for the time, still hers and hers alone. Besides, she'd been angry enough at dinner that he could believe her capable of locking the door, and he did not want to discover this by trying.

The tray he had set down on his table, which had not been changed from the disarray he'd left it in this morning. Jenevra had been too busy of late to come in a tidy up after him, but he hadn't noticed that either. She did so much within the castle, and not with the full support of the people within it.

As of today, that would come to an end. He would ensure that all gave her the respect to which she was entitled, and any who chose otherwise could leave his lands. He didn't think that would be necessary. From what he had seen, the only people who still objected to her were those, like Symme, who had been with him long and had been used to doing as they saw fit.

Most of his guardsmen, whether his own or the levies from Jenevra's land, respected her and some of the younger lads fair worshiped the ground she walked on. Their wives, the bulk of the castle staff, trusted her for her knowledge and respected her rank.

He sighed once. He understood Symme's dislike to an extent. Some of them had fought in wars for nobles and lost their lives and limbs to a battle that should never have been fought. They had thought, by following him and coming here, that they would be safe from that.

Jenevra's existence brought that world, the one they thought they'd escaped from, a little close. And she could not help it; she was a lady in every sense of the word. She carried it in her words, her gestures, her carriage. She had been born and raised to wealth and privilege.

They would not see what he saw, what so many of the guardsmen saw, that she treated everyone else as if they were as valuable as any noble. Not the same, she saw the distinctions in rank clearly, but valuable. No one was merely a commoner to her.

She opened the door. "Yes, my lord?" She stood stiffly, her back perfectly straight, her chin up. Her cheeks had the remnants of tear tracks, and it took a great deal of control not to gently brush them away. But he suspected, at this moment, she would not appreciate the gesture.

"I have brought you something to eat, since you did not eat supper." He gestured to the table and had the pleasure of seeing her carriage soften and her eyes brighten a little.

"I am surprised the kitchen was so obliging," she said.

"You have friends there. But I am surprised I had not heard how disobliging the kitchen has been to you."

She grimaced. "Sess told you."

"She did. But you ought to have. You are my wife; did you think I would allow anyone to treat you otherwise?"

"I - no..." Her face crumpled, and she lost her battle to keep tears from falling. This time, he did not hesitate to draw her close to him and brush the tears off her face.

"Tell me," he said softly. "Let me help you. You have shouldered part of my burdens since you arrived, and I have let you. Let me return that favor."

When he received a tremulous smile, though a few stray tears still slid down her cheeks, he guided her to his chair and set the tray in her lap. "I'm told these are your favorites." Then he took a seat at her feet.

She gave a teary half-chuckle. "They are." Then, between bites, she told him of her experiences with Symme, how he would follow Mellyn's instructions, but if she brought them, he would send for confirmation; how since Mellyn's death, he had refused to work with her on anything; how she had pleaded with him to take steps to prepare for the king's visit; and finally how she had gotten so angry today and declared she would find a new cook.

Conoc sat and listened, not interrupting her, letting her tell the tale as she would. He suspected that she still downplayed the situation, that she did not tell him everything that had gone on. But he also knew that he could not force her confidence.

When she finished, he took her hand in both of his. "I wish that you had told me sooner, but I will say no more on that if you will promise to bring me your problems in the future."

She nodded. "I will. I wanted to, but you have been so worried over the king's visit that I have not wanted to add to your burden."

"Burdens are lighter when split, lady. Though I grant that I have not been particularly welcoming of late." He smiled up at her. "As to this problem particularly... I have instructed Symme that you are the lady here and you will be treated with all the respect owed to you. Your word is final, and if he chooses to disobey you, you have the right to dismiss him from your service."

"Conoc, I - "

"No, Jenevra. This is my decision. You have the right to dismiss anyone who does not meet your standard, and their past relationship to me should not have bearing on your decision." He waited for her nod of acquiescence. "I do not say that Symme will ever love you, but he will obey you. And in time, I expect that he will come to respect you for your own sake as he knows you better.

"Now," he added briskly. "If you are quite done," she nodded and he removed the tray from her lap and moved it to the desk. "I have a favor to ask of you."

She nodded. "Anything within my power, of course."

He handed her a wooden case, finely carved. "I - Open it first."

Inside the box, on a bed of soft silk, lay two knives, delicately fashioned for a woman's hand. Her eyes widened, then flew to him. "My lord..."

"My lady. I have wanted you to have this for some time, but they had to be made, for your hands are very small." Holding the box, her hands appeared even smaller than usual. "I cannot be with you always. Nor can Lorent or Kenan. I would have you able to act in your own defense at least until I can get to you."

She started to protest, again, but he stopped her. "My lady, I know you can handle a bow. Did you think I had not noticed your practices?" She blushed, and he smiled.

Almost from her first weeks in the castle, she had coaxed a few guardsmen into guarding her while she practiced with a bow far too strong for her. She demonstrated more skill than most of his guardsmen, though her shots lacked in distance. He had taken months to discover who the archer was, and even once he knew, he had allowed her to keep her secret.

"I have known that for some time, and if it were not inappropriate, I would add you to the castle's defense. For that matter, should it come to a prolonged battle, I may still add you. But that will not help you if someone should be close to you."

After a long pause, during which her expression remained unreadable, she nodded.

"I will train you, or Kenan will. Lorent had made a goal of finding a bow properly sized that will remain yours."

"My lord," Jenevra said finally. "Why?"

"Because spring is coming, and I fear what will come with it."

CHAPTER SIXTEEN

With the first breath of spring, Jenevra sought the outdoors and the comfort of her garden. Winter had blown in hard and early, and spring blew in equally early. At least to places like her garden. The mountain passes were slower to melt, as they always were.

The smell of the fresh earth as she turned it over and planted the carefully saved seeds from the previous summer relaxed her. She did not lead a hard life by any estimation, but in the garden she could let go the restrictions of her life for a few moments.

Outside the wall, her newly returned curlews had begun to chirp and call, and she closed her eyes to just listen to them. She missed their sounds so much during the winter, and this winter had been full of tension and anxieties. They would have been a comfort then and were a comfort now, settling a part of her soul.

She planted the last seeds of the chervil, covering them gently against the faint chill, and moved on to the next row of dill. Her elbow bumped the still unfamiliar hilt of the knife she wore at her belt. Conoc and Kenan had spent more time training her over the winter than she felt strictly necessary, but she had at last achieved a grudging commendation from Kenan. Conoc, both harder to please and quicker to compliment, had insisted that she wear it always, especially once she reached a level of proficiency. She didn't like it, didn't feel it necessary, but he was lord and he sometimes planted his feet and did not budge.

Another row of seeds, for mint, and even the seeds carried the faint sweetness of the flower. These had produced an abundance last summer, and the rest waited in a jar in the stillroom, finally cleaned and ready for her in the moments she had time. Time came at a high price of late, around the preparations for the royal progress as well as the more ordinary preparations for the spring. Only yesterday Conoc had ridden down to the village to meet with the farmers about crop plantings and what lands would be open for hunting.

An anxious cry from one of the curlews, followed by a rush of wings, made her look up to see what bothered them. An unusual number of ravens had gathered on the walls, beaks clacking, and she made to shoo them away, though she'd never known them to bother the curlews before.

"My lady!" someone shouted, and she turned towards the voice, the birds forgotten. Finn, still her constant guard inside the castle walls, had a hand on his weapon already.

A boy ran up, one of the young levies, and began gasping out his message before he'd even caught his breath. "My lady, Lord Conoc sent me to tell you. An attack at the main gate. You're to get inside and - "

Jenevra drew her breath and nodded. "I know." A plan, discussed often, in case of a more serious attack. Conoc had planned it carefully and laid it out for her, so that she could see why he would mandate certain actions. Now they would test the practice of them.

She picked up the skirt of her kirtle with one hand and picked up her basket with the other. "Go, both of you. Lord

Conoc has more need of you than I now." Finn opened his mouth to protest, and she shook her head. "I'll be inside and following Lord Conoc's instructions. Go!"

She let herself in the kitchen door and shut it behind her. The wooden beam that would bar it was too strong for her to manage on her own, and one of the kitchen hands came to help her lift it and slide it into place.

Symme looked at her. They'd had an uneasy truce since Conoc had intervened in the kitchen, and she didn't doubt that he would disobey her if she didn't have the weight of Conoc's authority behind her. "My lady?" he asked, tone turning it to a veiled insult.

"An attack at the main gate. All the outer doors are to be barred and remain that way until Lord Conoc says otherwise." She heard the hush that fell over the kitchen as she said that, and Symme nodded once as though that did not surprise him.

"I'll check the other doors myself, then," he replied. "We'll be ready in case of intruders as well. Any other instructions?"

"No. I trust you to have it well in hand." Another nod. She believed that, too, that he would be prepared. He'd been a soldier before he'd been a cook. The kitchen would be safe.

Quickly she took the look hallway and the short flight of steps that led from the kitchen to the chapel. Father Andreu would be the next person she alerted. Her pattons clunked on the floor and she paused long enough to untie the laces so she could walk more easily and quickly in her slippers.

He didn't seem surprised to see her, but then, nothing ever surprised Father Andreu. Even though he'd his back to her, seemingly lost in prayer, he spoke, "You are welcome, my lady. Come in."

"Father Andreu, I - "

He stood up and came over to her. His face, weathered brown from the years and with wrinkles enough for two, inspired trust; he smiled always and never lost the serene calm he exuded.

"Take a moment, my lady," he said, taking her basket and the pattons from her and setting them aside. "Breathe. You do not have to rush; the situation is not so urgent as that."

She drew the breath as instructed, but let it out in a huff. "Father, I - "

"Have come to tell me that there is an attack, and Conoc has instructions for me." When she stared at him, astonished that he knew what she was going to say, he smiled. "Conoc sent one of the lads with that much. He said you would be along with those instructions. So again I say, breathe."

When she had taken another breath, and the nerves she hadn't noticed had settled some, she began for the third time. "Father Andreu. Conoc's plan requires that the true noncombatants - the children and those women who cannot act in support - wait here in the chapel as much as possible. He believes the Northerners will not attack a holy place and that it is more defensible that many other places. He said you would understand."

"Aye, and I do, my lady. I think he's right, for they share our faith. They would not despoil the chapel. I'll borrow young Father Bardin to gather everyone. It will be good for him."

Jenevra hid a smile of her own. Father Bardin disliked the 'unwashed masses', as she'd once heard him refer to them. He preferred his scholarly life, away from those who didn't understand him. "I believe he would see it otherwise, Father."

"That is the benefit of being old, my lady. We may instruct the young without being taken to task for it." His eyes twinkled a little at her. "Will you keep us company here?"

"I think I would crawl out of my skin," she replied. "To be trapped, never knowing what happened... I have a safe place to watch from."

His eyebrows went up. "I do not think Conoc would

approve. He wishes you safe above all others here, and you know that, my lady. Besides, the people in this castle need to see you among them for their comfort."

"And they will. I will come back, and certainly if..." Her voice faltered; she would not give voice to the idea that the defenses could fail. "I will be here if there is trouble. But I cannot stay waiting the entire time."

Andreu shook his head. "I would tell you otherwise if I thought you would listen, but I suspect you are as headstrong as Conoc when you wish to be. I wonder if he knows that." A pause, then a grudging nod. "As you will, my lady. But if you do not return in a timely manner, I will send someone after you, and I will ensure Conoc knows."

ON THE WALL, Conoc stood with Kenan and Lorent. The spring sun beat down on them, and their armor, always too hot, now left them dripping with sweat. His padded gambeson soaked up the sweat until he felt damp and sticky.

He kept watch on the attackers, but he lacked focus. This attack barely constituted such. He had forty men on the walls; the Northerners had a hundred. They couldn't take the castle that way. A siege under these conditions made no sense.

A projectile hit the top of the wall, sending shards of metal and stone flying into the defenders. Conoc ducked, but caught a piece of stone on his cheek, where his helmet left his face slightly exposed. Lorent had fared better, but Kenan had taken a chunk of stone to his forehead, cutting him and leaving blood dripping down his face.

"This cannot go on," Kenan said as he wiped the blood away, leaving it smeared on his hand and face. "They'll destroy the castle stone by stone that way."

Lorent examined scraps of metal. "It's almost like the shot from a cannon, but they haven't got one."

They watched the Northerners regroup out of reach of the archers. Something about their tactics bothered him. He had fought Northerners for years, and one reason they lost so often, despite their fierce passion, was that they fought as individuals or very small groups. "They're thinking as a group," he said aloud.

Conoc shook his head. The Northerners were too aggressive in this. They'd repelled ladders as well, men trying to climb the wall to engage hand-to-hand. This was not their way. They preferred the open battles; Ravensmere existed to prevent them from marching south for a grand battle. They did not use siege tactics.

Lorent shaded his eyes. "No. It's an accident. They don't trust each other enough to work as a group."

Men shifted on the walls, tightening defenses, redistributing arrows to archers. Kenan took his turn to look out. "It's no accident. There's a plan there, something they all understand. Someone taught them this."

Conoc stared out. He agreed with Kenan that someone had taught them this. He'd caught the markings for half-a-dozen different families here. Too many for a single clan, for a single group working together. This was organization, and that had never been part of Northern fighting.

He kept his eyes out there, watching the way the men interacted. Something about it... "See! They're reforming, but it's as you said! They've learned these methods. I'll wager that the one who taught them isn't there, and they can't improvise a group strategy."

He waved to the archers, gesturing for them to concentrate on the formation. "Break it up, make them break apart from each other! Then we'll see what they've truly learned."

The archers began firing arrow after arrow. Most of them hit no specific target, and at that range, a killing shot would have been difficult. But the arrows accomplished what Conoc had sought. They forced the Northerners to stop making a formation and turn to defense, and the formation broke apart into individuals as they protected themselves and not the men on either side of them.

A few began charging towards the castle wall, but the archers had an easier time picking them off as they drew closer. Others, including one man shouting from the back, retreated farther into the woods.

Kenan nodded on Conoc's right. "That's finished that then," he said, though with no satisfaction. Conoc felt the hurt in Kenan's voice down in his bones; they came from two worlds, and they were charged with defending one against the other. Kenan took no satisfaction in it.

"The one in the back," Lorent said. "You think he was the one orchestrating this?"

"No. If he had, they'd have listened to him better. That one was in charge today, but he isn't the one behind it all." Conoc gave orders for manning the walls so that everyone could have some relief. Those who would have night watch were sent off for food and bed without delay, and Lorent went with them.

Kenan stayed with him, and Conoc shook his head at his old friend. "Something has changed. You saw it too."

"Someone. Someone has changed them." Kenan's eyes looked away towards something that wasn't there. "The great families among them, they don't give their loyalty to many. Someone earned it and is uniting the clans. I'd give a great deal to know why."

Jenevra, perched at a narrow window intended for archers, saw the moment the stand-down order was given. Half the men left the walls immediately, and the other half shifted in their postures. Alert still, but a more general alert, less immediate.

She stood up. The ledge of the stone window had just

enough space that she could perch there like a bird, her feet dangling beneath her. The window itself was no true window but an arrow slit, narrow at the outside of the wall and widening inside so that a man could shoot without being vulnerable.

The small alcove, round as it was in one of the corner towers, had three such windows so that one man could defend multiple directions alone. Because of that, and because the alcove was tucked back from the hallway, Jenevra could see what went on without herself being exposed.

She watched as Conoc and Kenan walked down the stairs from the wall together, still speaking. Then, a quick forearm clasp between them, and Kenan went back up the wall to supervise the watch. Conoc glanced up at the castle, and, though Jenevra knew he could not see her there, she felt the pressure of his look.

She ran down the stairs, her hiding place abandoned, hoping that she would reach the chapel before him. Though Father Andreu would not keep her secret, not if Conoc asked, so it made little difference. He would know she had not been in the chapel as he'd instructed.

Her skirt gathered in one hand and her feet moving as fast as she dared lest she slip on the stone floor, she set her hand on the door handle of the chapel only to have a male hand settle over hers.

"You weren't in the chapel, my lady," Conoc said mildly. She looked over her shoulder at him. Sweat matted his hair down and had left tracks in the dirt and blood on his face. His hand on hers was grimy, and his knuckles had blood on them. His armor showed no new marks at least. But his eyes, intent on her, belied the tone in his voice; they were filled with a hot anger.

"I was not." She nodded once. "I was well-hidden elsewhere, but I needed to know, to see what went on."

"That is not good enough!" His hand over hears tightened

slightly, then pulled her fingers off the door handle and turned her around to face him. "We made a plan, Jenevra, and that included actions for your safety! You cannot simply decide another place is safe. Did anyone even know where you were?"

"No," she said, looking away and down.

"I am not surprised that Andreu let you go, you have a way about you. By god or man, what if something had happened? We might not even know you were hurt if we didn't know where to look!" With his free, he forced her chin up so she could see his face. "I'm lord of this castle and your husband, and you'll obey me in this."

She pulled her head away and retreated as far as she could with him still holding her hand. "I did not do it to disobey you. But to sit and hide, without knowing what happens... I shall go mad! You are lord here, and I do not dispute that or your right to give me orders, but how am I to reassure the people in this keep when I cannot even tell them what goes on!"

The chapel door opened, forcing Conoc to release her hand lest he be knocked over, and Father Andreu leaned out.

"Children," he said mildly, no censure in his tone or expression. "If you do not want everyone in the castle to know that you are not in accord, perhaps you should argue somewhere less public - or at least with lower voices."

Jenevra drew herself up straight. "My lord?"

Conoc shook his head. "I have nothing further to say, my lady."

LATER IN HER ROOM, Jenevra sat at her window seat and wept angry tears until she gave herself a headache. She had not intended to fight him, had not intended to do anything but state her argument calmly. But he had pushed and she had responded defensively, more than she would have otherwise.

He had never been so angry with her, nor she with him. She

had once or twice been frustrated, and once taken her anger out on him, but never actual anger at him.

She pushed her window open to allow the night air in. The birds were finally quiet; they had taken unusually long to settle tonight. Even the owls were silent tonight, so the only sounds she could hear were the footsteps of the guards on watch, and the faint lapping sounds of waves brushing against the lakeshore.

Only a faint moon lit the night, a tiny waxing crescent. Though she found it beautiful, the darkness seemed more encroaching as a result. She felt isolated and alone without even nature to comfort her.

Even Sess had deserted her. She had, perhaps rightly, scolded Jenevra for disobeying Conoc, endangering herself, and fighting where others could see or hear. Sess's desertion hurt, for if Sess did not agree with her, than no one would. She might be wrong, though she did not think so, but no one would be convinced.

She heard footsteps in the Conoc's room and knew them for his. The pace was wrong; he moved more slowly than was his wont. The first twinge of guilt struck her. To hurt him had never been her intent, and she had.

Jenevra walked to the door and laid her hand upon it. She did not want to apologize, did not want to own any of her behavior was in the wrong. But Conoc cared for her, and she ought not to abuse that.

Giving herself no time to think or talk herself into another position, she yanked the door open. Only to find herself face to face with Conoc, his own hand upraised and flat, as though he too had been resting it on the door.

He stared at her, and she stared back. Though he had washed the grime from his face, there was a weariness still in his eyes that no washing could wipe away. His clothing was wrinkled, and blood had soaked in, though none of it seemed to be his.

New lines creased his face, and Jenevra reached up to smooth one away.

He caught her hand lightly in his own and turned it so he could place a kiss on her palm. "I have come to beg your pardon, lady, for the way I spoke to you earlier."

She shivered; the touch of his lips on her hand set her nerves to tingling, from her hand to her spine, and she curled her fingers into her palm. "I intended to ask forgiveness for disobeying you."

"I will take the greater share of the blame," he replied. "That I am lord here and your husband is true, but you are not an object to be put in its place. You are my wife and my lady; I owe your more courtesy than I showed today."

"No, Conoc, that cannot stand. If I have qualms about what I was asked to do, I should have spoken to you in private. To do otherwise, especially to argue with you where others could hear and believe it gave them leave to disrespect you, is unfair and wrong of me. Especially when you had come from a battle."

Conoc stared down at her for a moment, then smiled and drew her close to him. "My lady, what am I to do with you? You argue as fiercely against yourself now as you did in your defense earlier." He dropped a kiss onto her hair, and Jenevra relaxed against his strength. "Father Andreu and Kenan, both, took your side, you may be glad to hear."

"Oh, Sess scolded me roundly as well. My arguments did not move her, no matter what I said. So you and I are even there." That Kenan would take her side surprised her; he did not even like her, so she would have thought he would argue against her simply for that reason. Father Andreu had disagreed with her from the first, but he rarely took sides in anything, so she supposed Conoc had been intemperate in his language.

"So tell me, lady, what did you learn from watching out your well-hidden location?" Conoc let go of her and went to sit in his chair. Though she knew he would welcome her in his room, she remained at the open door.

"Nothing of much merit," she admitted. "I could not see much, other than the backs of the men on the wall. Of the attackers, nothing at all. What happened?"

"They found a way to throw something much like cannon shot up to us. It can hurt a man, but it did more damage when it hit the wall and shattered into flying metal and stone." He touched the cut on his cheek. "They brought ladders as well, though those are easier to defend against."

"Those are not the tactics they employed last year, are they?" She drew closer and touched his cheek below the cut. "You said those were testing our defenses. This is more serious."

He held her hand. "Yes. These attacks indicate a far deeper plan, and by someone who knows our strategies and can anticipate our reactions." For a moment, he remained silent. "I will not lie to you, my lady. An this escalates, we will not be in a good position."

Jenevra brushed the hair away from his face and pressed a light kiss on his forehead. As if in response, his arm snaked around her and pulled her closer to him. "You will manage, I know. Ravensmere is not in the condition you would have chosen, but don't the stories tell us that Carbevan was defended by only ten men? You'll find a way."

She grew silent in her turn, for a thought had occurred to her, and she did not think Conoc would like it, not if she knew her lord at all. "You have another option," she said, drawing the words out slowly. "My father is your kin now. More than that, he has made alliance with you. Should you call on him, he is obliged on his honor to come to your aid."

"Is that what you would have me do?" Conoc's voice rose from his chest, and she could feel that rumble against her side.

"No! Not if it can be avoided. My father is..." She paused, but her loyalty to her father held her far less than her loyalty to

Conoc. "He did not gain the power he has in the Council by helping others unless he saw something for himself. If you call on him, he will answer, but he will turn it to his own ends."

"So I should not ask him for help then?"

"I do not know! I only wished that you should know it is an option. Why do you ask me?"

"Because, my clever lady, you know more far more of what goes on among the magnates and the Council than myself or anyone else here." He looked up at her, and she tilted her head down to him, drawn by the warm light in his eyes. Conoc never lacked sincerity, which made his compliments the more to be treasured.

"I thank you for the compliment." She shook her head. "You have had a long day, my lord. I should not keep you sitting. Let me call for a bath and some food before you sleep."

"I do not want a bath now," he said, leaning up to kiss her lips. His mouth was strong and unyielding. She could taste the sweat on his lips, feel the heat of his skin near hers. "Come to bed, my lady." His breath caressed her skin, his words only slightly louder than the sound of his breathing.

Jenevra froze, though her heart, already twice as fast as normal, began to race beyond her reckoning. She ought to say something, but she could not make her mouth move, let alone any other part of her. She could not forget the way his kiss to her hand had sizzled along her nerves, but she could also not forget the panicked feeling of last summer when they danced together and he had kissed her mouth.

A shadow fell across his face, and Conoc released her. Without waiting for a dismissal from him, she fled to her room and slammed the door behind her. Her breath came fast as she leaned back against the door, listening for his footsteps, though she doubted she would hear them above the pounding of her blood in her ears.

He had never indicated, by word or deed, that he desired

her, save for that one moment last summer. At all other times, he behaved with all courtesies, and she might have been a sister for all that treatment resembled a wife's.

She ought to have said yes, to have gone with him as he wanted. She had not been prepared for it, though they had been married more than a year. She had not known what to do in that moment.

Uncaring of anything, she threw herself down on her bed to weep again, not stopping until she fell asleep fully clothed.

THE MOMENT HER BODY TENSED, Conoc knew he had said the wrong thing. He had not even meant to say it, but she had been warm beside him and she caught him with the light in her eyes as she'd looked down at him. His girl-child wife had become a woman. Not almost a woman, but one grown. She had not hesitated in being close to him, nor hesitated to touch his face. She hadn't shrunk at his touches.

Until he violated the one boundary between them. God above but he was a fool!

He rose and went to the door silently, his footsteps careful to make no sound on the floor. He could hear nothing from her side but a harsh, ragged breathing. His wife, terrified of him.

He turned away, not willing to even try the door and make the situation worse. Though he knew he need apologize, to do so now would help neither of them. Instead he took to pacing as he tried to work off the manifold irritants of the day as well as his irritation at himself. He knew better. He knew she was not ready, and he would have to proceed with caution, but when the moment came, he had failed so completely.

A light knock on the door, and Kenan leaned his head in. He looked better - blood no longer marked his face as someone had tended the wound on his forehead - but more, he looked clean. "Good. You are alone."

"What of it? And who would I be with?" Conoc shoved the chair against the wall in a flash of temper.

Kenan looked baffled. "Your lady, perhaps. It is late, and her room is beside yours. Also, she ordered water enough for everyone to have a hot bath tonight, and I expected to find you having one."

Jenevra never stopped thinking about others. Water might always be available for bathing, but it usually remained cold. To ensure everyone had warm water, she must have issued the order while still angry with him. Conoc felt small, which irritated him further. He knew, better than any, that she thought first of the folk of the castle.

"No, I have not had one." He stopped his teeth from grinding against each other.

"So I see," Kenan said, his expression decidedly and utterly neutral. "Those on night watch had theirs as soon as they'd eaten, before they slept. The rest of us have taken our turns. You are the last. Do you want it in here?"

"No, I'll come down." He knew there would be a tub nearby, for Jenevra bathed in her room, but there were baths in other places in the castle, and it would be less work for everyone if he used one of those places. Besides, the longer he stayed in his room, the more he'd convince himself that he should open her door and check on her, and she did not need him crossing that boundary as well.

Kenan walked silently down the hall beside him, and Conoc didn't know if he preferred the silence or the questions that were sure to follow once they had privacy to speak.

Once he was in the tub with its curtain drawn mostly around and no one else in the room, Kenan obviously felt the time had come.

"What happened?" he asked with no preamble.

"What do you mean?" Conoc asked, then ducked his head under the water before Kenan could answer. The hot water soothed muscles he knew ached as well as those he hadn't, and he felt himself relaxing overall.

Kenan was undeterred. "You were not in such a temper before you went to your room. Though you were angry with her, I expected that you and Lady Jenevra would find your marital harmony again." His voice carried an edge of mockery. "Instead, I find you fierce as a bear."

"I upset her because I was thoughtless. I apologized for earlier, as did she and all was well. Then I... I made it all worse." Conoc scrubbed at his arms, washing away the layers of sweat and dirt, the scent of steel from his mail. He would have been no fit partner for his lady, covered in grime and smelling of a battlefield.

"She will forgive you, especially if you apologize." Kenan dumped a pitcher of water over Conoc's head, grinning at his friend's sputtering.

In return, Conoc flipped a handful of water at Kenan. His heart wasn't in it; his concerns about Jenevra niggled away at him. "Sometimes I think you were right. She is too young, too different from us."

Kenan shook his head. "I wasn't. Perhaps about her being young, but I do not know what you could have done there. The Merembrian marry young, younger than Northerners. But her differences are better than I thought, much though it pains me to admit it. She softens you." He sat back. "Besides, if her maids are to be believed, she meets you sometimes at night. That is not the action of a girl too young."

"Her maids? Sess?" He did not think anyone knew of their time together, though they had nothing to be ashamed of and it was no true secret.

"Not Mistress Cecilie." A quick dismissive shake of his head. "She is even more close-mouthed about Lady Jenevra than you. No, the maids who tend the fire and the room. They gossip at times."

He didn't know that. Truthfully, he could not even put a face or a name on any of them, though he did not doubt that Jenevra would know. She had a way about it. But she would not appreciate being gossiped about, and he would have to tell her so she could handle it.

Conoc scrubbed at his hair, the action doing more than cleaning the outside of his head. Somehow, the bath washed away the little tensions and stresses, so much a part of him as he'd anticipated this attack. Even fighting with Jenevra had been about his tensions more than her transgression. He'd wanted to end this stress and had gone about it in the stupidest manner possible.

Another pitcher of water poured over his head - Kenan, to rinse out the soap - ad he looked over at his oldest friend. "Why are you doing this?"

"Because you needed someone. Lorent and I talked about it; if I'd had night watch, he'd have been here instead. It should be for your wife to do, but apparently you messed that up yourself."

"You need a wife of your own," Conoc said as he reached for a towel. But Kenan didn't answer, and Conoc was surprised to see him staring off, seeing somewhere else. "Kenan?"

"Someday," he said. "Someday when I meet someone who can take me as I am, and when I've more to offer her than what I have now."

Conoc raised his eyebrows. Kenan had never expressed such thoughts before, and he wondered if he'd found such a woman already but had not the words for it. He could only wish him well if that were so.

CHAPTER SEVENTEEN

Jenevra let herself out of the chapel quietly and ran up the stairs to her alcove in the tower. The noise of the attack outside did not penetrate to the chapel, on the wrong side of the keep and towards the back, and she desperately needed to know what went on.

The attack had come in the predawn half-light, before the mist had burnt off the lake. She had been rousted out of bed by Conoc's single heavy thump to her door and his command to get moving. She'd run down to the chapel in her kirtle only, a gown held over one arm, and her hair loose and disheveled.

Sess had spent some of the time while they sat and waited fixing her hair and lacing up the sides of her gown so that she looked less the lost waif and more the lady of the castle. She had to look the part; the women and children who lived there all gathered in the chapel. She doubted whether any of them had heard the sunrise service Father Andreu had said.

But the strain of being the lady for everyone, comforting women whose husbands fought on the castle wall, soothing irritations from too many minutes with nothing to do, had taken a toll on her. She needed a moment to hear her own thoughts, to breathe without being watched and to find out what she could so that her words would not be empty.

The alcove was empty, as she'd expected. If the guards were forced to retreat into the keep, archers would take this position, but none could be spared now.

She leaned up to one window, her fingers holding on to the rough stone. Her ears could pick up the sounds of fighting before she could see anything, the distinct sounds that together made up a battle: the metal striking metal of swords on shields, the twang-hiss of arrows, the heavy thuds of rock and metal flung up to strike the walls, and, above all, the shouts of men fighting... and the groans of those who were not.

Her fingers clenched tighter on the ledge, so tightly the stone cut into her fingers. From here, she could see the number of men who had fallen back from the wall, though wounded or dead she could not tell. Conoc still held the center of the wall, Lorent and Kenan near by. No attackers stood on the wall now though.

A shower of rocks and that metal shot from a catapult caused everyone the wall to duck and throw up shields. When the metal hit the stone of the wall, it shattered and fragments went in all directions, and no shield could stop all of it.

Jenevra saw the moment the gate gave. The Northerners had been pounding on it - she'd been able to see the heavy blows causing the gates to bend despite the metal bands supporting them. The portcullis should have been closed to prevent that, but the pounding continued 'til the gates gave way and attackers rushed in.

Men ran down the stairs to stem the tide, but the sanctity of the bailey was breached already. Conoc leapt halfway off the stairs to get down faster, and he was at the forefront of the men.

The fighting beneath her had become a complete melee, and no more could she separate the different sights and sounds. She kept her eyes always on Conoc, even though some part of her knew she ought to retreat to the chapel, to safety, for if the castle wall had been breached, the keep could be as well.

The fighting continued, Conoc always in the center of it. Kenan and Lorent were never far from him, and the three were easy to pick out for they moved differently than the other men, more skillfully. But gradually she began to notice that the number of people in the bailey had decreased, and not because they had become too wounded to fight. The fighting had moved into the keep itself.

Now she could hear the distant sounds of fighting coming from behind her, within the keep, and her heart rose in her throat. She left the window, only now noticing that her hands had cuts and scrapes from the window ledge, and tucked herself behind the wall that sheltered the alcove. She could not risk leaving here now to try and reach the chapel and could only hope Conoc's men found her before the Northerners did.

The sounds of metal on metal came nearer and nearer. Shouts - both in Merembrian and Altyran - but often not intelligible from distance and the echoes around the keep. Soon she could pick out other sounds: swords hitting the stone walls because men had no room to swing freely; heavy footsteps; individual voices.

She breathed a prayer to the goddess to hold everyone in the chapel safe and another to the god to keep her in the shadows so she would not be found.

"Lady?" The familiar voice whispered incredulously, and she looked to see Finn staring at her. "God's hand, Lady Jenevra, you ought to be in the chapel." He moved behind the wall with her and looked her over. "Are you hurt?"

She shook her head no. Finn looked no worse than expected and certainly far better than the time in the woods. Some blood, but no signs of serious wounds. "I was afraid to move from here."

He leaned out to look out into the hallway. "I can't take you to the chapel. It's clear now, but no certainty how long that would last. There's fighting up and down the halls. We'll have to stay here. It's defensible at least."

He gestured for her to flatten herself back even further. "Gather your skirt back so it doesn't move. Lady, they can't see you."

Jenevra did as told, not asking for more details. She'd heard enough stories, even back in Allandale, about what happened to women captured in an attack like this. Conoc would come for her, he would always come for her, but better to not be kidnapped away at all.

Time stretched oddly while they stood there. Finn kept nearer the opening of the alcove that she, his sword in his hand nearer the wall, so no stray light could catch it and reveal their hiding place. He did not move, barely seemed to breathe, and Jenevra found herself imitating those faint breaths.

The sounds of fighting rose and fell, but their hallway remained clear for long enough that Jenevra began to wonder if it might not be safe to try and made the chapel. She opened her mouth to say that to Finn, but a shout echoed in the hallway and she shrank back a little more.

By their speech, Northerners, though she could only pick out a little from Mellyn's teachings.

... sure this way? one asked, voice deep.

... said she... this hallway, another answered.

Her whole body grew cold. They were looking for her. They knew she would be here. Someone had told them where she was. She pressed her hand to her mouth to stifle the shriek forcing its way out.

Finn might not have understood the words, but his fingers tightened on the hilt of his sword, and his arm tensed. When a Northerner finally stepped into the alcove, Finn's sword nearly caught him in the gut before he had a chance to get his own up in defense.

His shout and the sound of sword on sword brought the others, but the shape of the wall meant that only one person could attack at once, and when Finn brought the first attacker down, he stepped forward, further blocking the entrance.

But they outnumbered him, and they kept coming. Jenevra watched, still stifling her cries with her hand, as he fought off one, then another. He had improved since last summer, but the best swordsman couldn't fight everyone. The third attacker managed to get inside Fin's guard and stab him in the side before Finn finished him off. He pressed his hand to his side, though the blood oozed out between his fingers.

By the fifth attacker, he could hardly stand, and that man didn't even fight him, just shoved him to the ground. Finn's skin had grown pale, and she wasn't sure he was still breathing. But his lips shaped an apology meant for her.

The Northerner saw her now and grabbed her wrist. Her skirt smeared Finn's blood as he dragged her out, to the point she thought she might be sick.

Once out of the alcove, while the Northerner gloated about catching her, she looked around. The group of Northerners was smaller than she'd thought, only a half-dozen men including the one holding her. If she could get free, if she could get past them, the hallway was clear.

With a quick motion, she drew the dagger Conoc had given her and stabbed it directly into her captor's hand. He swore and jerked his hand back, and the moment her arm was free, she ran past the rest, who hadn't even realized what happened.

She was fast, even encumbered by a dress that tangled her legs. She only had to make the end of the hallway, where a door guarded a back stair that would take her down to the rest of the keep.

Something hit her, and she went down, her hands going out too late to break her fall. Her chin hit the floor, her teeth bit deeply into her lip, and flashes of light danced in front of her eyes. She shook her head to clear the daze and tried to get to her feet, but too slowly.

Hands grabbed her and hauled her up by her upper arm, and the pain of that grip forced her to focus. The man who held her stared at her, his eyes hard. His face was weather-beaten, more so than the others had been, and he carried himself with a sense of authority. He shook her once, hard enough to rattle her teeth. "No more of that," he said. In his own language, he called back over his shoulder, *"She's the pretty one but -"*

Whatever else he might have said did not get finished as a sword went through him and stuck out his front. Jenevra shrieked and jumped back from the now lifeless body, her eyes tracking its fall, and then looked up to see her husband there staring at her. Behind him, other men, including Lorent, had taken down the remaining Northerners, and all of them looked over at her.

"My lady," he said, his tone the mild one that spoke of more deep anger than simple fury could, though he softened almost immediately when he saw the blood on her face. His skin looked too pale under his tan, and she felt guilty that she had worried him more. "You're hurt."

"Not very. But, Conoc, Finn -"

"I know. He's already being taken down to Andreu." He indicated where two men were picking up Finn under Lorent's direction. "Andreu will take care of him. But you... god above, when no one could find you and Northerners inside the keep... Jenevra." He rested his forehead against hers. His skin felt clammy, and she looked up in time to see his eyes roll back into his head.

"Lorent!" she called out as Conoc's weight came down on her, and she sank to the floor with him in her lap. Her hand was bloody where she'd caught him, and she pawed frantically at his mail, trying to find where the blood came from.

When she shifted his arm, she saw the wound in his left arm

just below his shoulder, just where the shoulder piece would leave a gap when he raised his arm. He'd been bleeding and in pain while he searched for her, and had probably made it worse. Her head dropped, and a single tear ran down her face.

Lorent knelt down beside her. "Lady?"

Jenevra took the moment to draw in a deep breath. If she asked, Lorent would take the burden of command, would give the orders that needed giving. For Conoc's sake and for hers, he would. But she had a responsibility as well, as lady of the keep, and she could not shirk it. She straightened her spine and lifted her head. "You and you," she said, voice firm and clear, picking two soldiers with her eyes, "take Lord Conoc to his room, get him out of the armor and get the fire built up. I'll be there soon. Sir Lorent, for the moment, command of the castle is yours."

She didn't see that everyone snapped to follow her orders or that they stepped back to allow her to pass. All she could see was Conoc's pale face.

BY THE TIME she reached Conoc's room, after running down to check with Father Andreu briefly on the disposition of the wounded and leave it all in his hands and to gather what she needed from the stillroom, Conoc lay in the bed, his armor removed and discarded in a pile. No one had removed his padded gambeson and she could see both the hole and the blood that had soaked it.

The fire did blaze, but metal tools lay on the hearth, half in the fire. Symme sat near the fireplace, sharpening a large knife that looked like one she'd seen in the kitchen. Kenan, near the bed, watched him, one hand resting on Conoc's uninjured shoulder, keeping him from tossing around.

With two big men occupying the space, as well as the fire blazing, the room seemed smaller than usual. Sess, holding the bag of supplies, stood in the doorway to Jenevra's room, out of the way for the moment.

Ignoring Symme for the moment, she went to the bed, Kenan giving way to her, and laid her hand on Conoc's forehead. His skin felt damp, but no longer cold or clammy; fever had set in.

"Sess," she called. "I need scissors, then some rags. And water heating on the fire." She didn't need to look to know that Sess had gone as silently as she'd come. Sess would find all of that faster than anyone else, without wasting time.

"You need?" Symme said, his voice rising in disbelief. "Ye need to get out of the way." He'd finished sharpening the knife, a heavy one for separating joints of meat, and stuck it in the fire.

"I'm caring for my husband, and I won't get out of your way. I didn't send for you." She never looked away from Conoc. Instead, she checked the padding over the wound and winced at the sluggishly seeping blood.

Kenan touched her arm gently. "Lady Jenevra, this is no place for you, and Conoc would not have you here. Symme knows what he's doing."

She focused her attention on Kenan, whose presence she had barely registered to that point. "What is he doing, sharpening knives more fit for a butchery than a -" The color drained out of her face. "No. No, Kenan, I won't have it."

He spoke softly, turning her away from Symme. "Jenevra. It's the only way. His arm is probably already infected. Removing it now means the infection doesn't spread. Symme is the best in the castle at this."

Her eyes searched his and found only sincerity. Kenan loved Conoc and would only do what was in his best interest. "I won't allow it." She turned back to Conoc, lying still in the bed, and breathed a prayer.

"Get out of the way," Symme said. He'd pulled the knife out of the fire and now approached the bed. She could feel the heat radiating off the metal, and flinched inside at the thought of that applied to any person, but especially Conoc. Conoc, who already lay wracked with fever and loss of blood.

"No." She pinched her lips together and lifted her head. She could not yield. "I have already said no. If you have no other help to offer, then you must leave."

"Have ye lost what little wits ye have?" Symme demanded. "He'll die."

Jenevra drew in breath, intending to try and reason with him again, but worry and temper spiked when Conoc moaned. "I am Lady here! This is my keep and my lord, and no one will gainsay me when it comes to his care. Now, be helpful or leave!"

Symme looked down at her, and she stared back up at him, towering over her. For once, she did not feel afraid of him. Then he looked at Kenan, and fury mounted in her that he would look to someone else before obeying her. "Get out!" Kenan nodded, subtly backing her, and it was well he did, or else she'd have thrown him out as well.

"When he dies, it'll be your doing!" Symme slammed the door on his way out, and Jenevra immediately put him out of her mind. She had no time to worry about him.

"Sess, the scissors, now." She held out her hand, and when Sess had handed them over, began cutting away the gambeson. The fabric had stuck to the wound, helping to slow the bleeding, and as she pulled it off, the bleeding began again.

She reached for a clean cloth and dipped it in the water Sess had brought, then began cleaning the blood away. It did not bleed as quickly as earlier, but she worried that Conoc had lost too much.

With gentle fingers, she examined the wound more closely. Though it bled profusely, whatever had stabbed him had not severed the muscle. The bleeding had washed away any dirt that had entered.

"My bag," she said, holding out her hand for it. Sess handed it to her, and she dug through it until she found the slim needle and fine silken thread she'd put in there. Her fingers shook so much that she could not thread the needle, and Sess took it back long enough to do so.

She drew in several deep breaths, her focus on steadying her hands long enough to do this. Carefully, she made one small stitch, as small as she could make it, through the muscle, to keep it from tearing any further. Her fingers shook again as she dabbed away the blood that continued to seep out. Then, jaw clenched, she began to stitch the outside closed, forcing her hands steady.

First one stitch in the center. Then one to the left and one to the right, each halfway between the center stitch and the edge of the wound. She did not look at Conoc, could not listen to the sounds of pain he made. If she did, she would never finish. Again and again she placed the delicate stitches, the silken thread once yellow and now stained red with his blood, always halving the distance between the stitches, until a line closed the wound.

She sat back and, for a moment, allowed herself to hope.

But only for a moment, because she could not claim the victory yet. Instead, she reached into her bag and pulled out herbs - fresh yarrow leaves, dried rose and oak barks that crumbled under her fingers, thyme - that she ground up. Sess brought warmed water, and Kenan ran off, without questioning, to fetch honey from the kitchen. When all had been mixed into a paste that smelled refreshing and clean, though it looked more like mud from a bog, she used it between layers of the bandage that she wrapped around Conoc's arm.

She wiped her arm across her face, the sweat and oils soaking into her sleeve. She hadn't noticed how hot she'd become.

Sess pushed a mug of warmed wine at her, the spices she'd added tickling Jenevra's nose. Her fingers shook, more than when she'd been working on Conoc, and Kenan steadied the mug for her.

"First battle nerves," he said. He waited until she looked at him, then nodded his head. "You've done well."

"We hope." She managed a sip of the wine and savored the clove on her tongue, giving herself that minute to marshal her strength. "Sir Kenan, does Lorent have command of the castle?"

"For the moment, yes, my lady." He nodded once. "I'll relieve him later, after I've rested, then he'll rest. We'll split the night watch tonight."

Jenevra let her breath out. The castle secured, she could focus on the inhabitants. "Then rest while you can. Sess, you'll stay here with Conoc. He should have steeped willowbark when he wakes." Sess nodded, and Jenevra was again grateful for the practicality and absolute faith that meant she didn't have to argue with her oldest friend.

"You will rest too?" Kenan asked.

"Later." She drew another deep breath and ignored the sick feeling in her stomach. Unconsciously, she pulled her shoulders back and straightened her spine. "For now, there are injured men to tend to, and Father Andreu will need my help."

FATHER ANDREU DID NEED her help. Easily two-thirds of the guard had been wounded and now filled the great hall. The unwounded, or those whose wounds had been superficial, stood watch under Lorent.

The less-injured sat or sprawled along the walls while the castle's women brought warmed wine and food to them. Though water had been prepared, none had time or energy for bathing, so dirt and blood coated many of them. The more grievously injured lay on the floor, sometimes on hastily rigged pallets, but just as many on cloaks or piled rushes or nothing at all.

A steady hum of sound filled her ears. Men's voices, women's voices, the sounds of pain from those most wounded

Father Andreu worked steadily, she noted, helping one man as best he could before moving on to the next. His steady and unflinching countenance seemed to reassure the men before he even began to treat their wounds. Father Bardin, on the other hand, looked as though he had been given an impossible and disgusting task. He tended only the less injured, and he did not hide his feelings, though whether he objected more to the blood or to the common man, she could not say.

She skirted the mass of wounded to reach Andreu. "Father," she said.

He nodded once. "How is Conoc?"

"Sleeping for the moment, and hopefully on the way to mending."

"And does he still have his arm?" She nodded, and Father Andreu closed his eyes and let out a deep breath. "God and goddess be praised."

"Where can I be of use?"

Andreu looked at her, his face drawn. "Shall I tell you that Conoc would not approve of you being here, that this is not the place for a lady?"

She looked at him, then around the room at all the men, then back at him, lips pressed together. "Conoc is not here, and I am. And no lady of a keep worth the name would be elsewhere."

He smiled ruefully. "Very well then, lady. Do you take that side, and I will continue from this. With divine grace, when we meet, we will have saved all who can be saved."

JENEVRA DID NOT KNOW how long she worked, but Andreu's words had proved prophetic.

Sometimes when she knelt beside a man, he could be treated. Many had wounds from arrows or spears or swords, and those, if they were not too deep or too badly placed, could be packed with poultices and bandaged or stitched with one or two small stitches. Those men often spoke while she tended them, telling her highly embellished versions of the battle, for each claimed he'd been pivotal in the Northerners' defeat.

"Got their leader, right in the stomach," one man boasted as she wrapped a bandage around his middle.

The next man grinned at her, then sucked in his breath as she poked too hard at a stab wound. "It were an accident," he said, referring to his companion's tale. "He missed the one he was aiming at."

She laughed, as much because they needed it as because their banter amused. Their spirits rose if she kept hers up, and tomorrow they would boast about having the lady tend their wounds.

The second man needed stitches, just two, and flinched away when she slid the needle in. "What're you doing?"

"Do not be a child," she replied, finishing the first stitch. But she gave him a cup of wine to occupy his hands and mind while she placed the second stitch. His friend smacked him in the shoulder, causing him to slosh wine out of the cup. He swore at his friend, but the distraction meant she placed the second stitch before he had time to complain. He would recover in no time.

Others did not fare so well. The next after the bantering pair, a boy her own age, lay on a pallet of rushes. His skin looked white under his dark hair, and his eyes had a farseeing and lost look. She did not need to look under the blanket that covered him to know that she could do nothing for him, but she did look. The gaping hole in his abdomen made her wonder how he had hung on this long, even with a hurried bandage, now soaked in blood, on it. Nothing could have been done for him even if she had been at his side when he'd been wounded.

She took his hand in hers, and his eyes focused on hers for a moment. "Lady," he whispered.

"I'm here," she said.

"Do you remember dancing with me? At Midsummer?" His eyes darted around, seeing something other than the walls and ceiling of the great hall, and his breathing grew shallower and faster.

She did remember him, though he'd grown since. A shy lad, hesitant to ask for that dance, and far too innocent to be a guardsman already. "I remember." She did not loose his hand, but with her free hand she poured a few drops of poppy oil in a cup of wine. She could do nothing for him but ease his passage. "Drink this."

He did, and his whole body relaxed as the poppy took effect. "You w're too perfect for me, but I'll remember that forev'r."

"I hope we will have the chance again this year. I shall insist upon it, in fact." Her voice shook, and she fought for control of herself, forced herself to smile at him as though neither of them had a care other than dancing. "Do not tell Lord Conoc, but I shall dance with you first of everyone."

"Than' you." A childlike smile, innocent and sweet. "Lady?"

"I'm here," she said, squeezing his hand and leaning closer that he could hear her clearly.

"Don' tell - don' tell the others - I wasn't brave enough. Shoulda had him before he got me but I... afraid. Rather be thought... bad at fighting."

"No one shall hear it from me," Jenevra said. "Though I think you very brave indeed for telling me so."

His eyes closed, and his breaths evened out and slowed. She remained, holding his hand, unwilling to leave him alone in his last few moments, though others needed her, until finally his chest stopped rising and the hand in hers released its grip.

She pressed her lips together tightly, her eyes closed against anyone seeing the look in them. Her shoulders slumped down. She did not even know his name.

A hand came to rest on her shoulder, and she looked up to see Lorent there. He had cleaned up and rested, for he did not look as weary or battleworn as the others in the room, though his eyes held the same sick look as all the others.

"Did he have any family?" she asked.

"No, my lady. He was an orphan until he joined us." Lorent began to speak, but she did not give him the chance.

"See that he's buried in my household colors." She laid the boy's hand, still held in hers, on his chest in a formal pose, then drew the blanket over his head, pausing only to brush the hair out of his eyes.

Then she turned to the next man waiting.

SHE DID NOT KNOW how many hours passed while she cared for the men. Some, for by the time Andreu forced her to leave, the stars were out as she could see through the window of her room. The clear sky seemed insulting to her, given the griefs of the day. The boy - she had not even known his name, though later she had learned it was Cole - had not been the only death she had witnessed. She had sat beside two others, helpless to do anything for either except to ease their pain as she had Cole's. With the second, she had given him more poppy oil than necessary, just to see the pain leave his face.

She had not cried.

Not for lack of caring. She cared for each of them, for duty's sake if nothing else. But each of them had been a someone, a person with a life, a family.

Tears were a luxury she could not have afforded. Too many depended on her strength. If she had surrendered to the tears, they too would have fallen to their own fears.

Besides, she did not deserve to cry.

She had been sheltered, growing up. War had touched her very little, for her father's land had no boundaries that needed defending. War had been something that happened on borderlands here in the north, or away in Gallrech. Even there, more posturing was done than fighting. Never had she lost someone she cared about, even a little.

Peter Wright and Bartly Miner had families, wives who even now mourned them. Cole had no one, but burying him in the colors of her household, deep blue for Ravensmere and wheat yellow for Allandale with silver threaded between, tied him to her that he would not be forgotten.

An owl hooted once, drawing her out of her heartsick brooding. She had missed her curlews tonight, when their mournful cries would have given voice to the feelings within her.

She entered Conoc's room. Sess had left watching over him when she had come up, correctly deciding she would be in the way. She would sleep in Jenevra's room tonight, to be nearby if she were needed.

Jenevra laid her hand on his forehead. His fever remained strong, but that alone did not worry her. He was strong, and he would fight. No signs of blood poisoning spread out from the wound in his arm. She adjusted the covers over him, that he would not grow cold.

Not even bothering to change, she threw herself down on the pallet between Conoc's bed and the fire. Sess had made it up for her at Father Andreu's insistence, though she had every intention of sitting up with Conoc. She did not think she would be able to sleep, that she would see their faces over and again, but exhaustion won out. Within minutes, she was so asleep she did not even hear Father Andreu come to take up the post watching over her and Conoc.

. . .

CONOC WOKE to a dark room lit only by a dying fire. For moment, he did not know where he was, and, even after he recognized his own room, he did not know how he had come there. His fingers searched for but did not find his sword, always close to his hand.

He tried to sit up, but his left shoulder burned like fire when he tried to move, and he hissed in pain.

A gentle hand settled on his forehead. "Lie still," Father Andreu said.

Against his inclination, Conoc did just that. "How did I get here? What happened?"

"Shh," Andreu said. "Do not make too much noise. I will tell you everything I can, but I do not want your lady woken."

Conoc turned his head slightly to see better. Just beyond Andreu, on a pile of blankets on the floor, her hair shining in the firelight, lay Jenevra. Pain and irritation blended to a sharpness he rarely felt, let alone showed.

"Why is she sleeping on the floor? She ought to be in her own bed."

"She would not leave you. Cecilie and I could barely convince her to lie down, so certain was she that you would need her during the night. But you can see yourself that she was beyond weary."

He did not understand, and that must have shown for Andreu waved him to silence. "What do you remember?"

"I remember finding her in the upper corridor, where she should not have been. I... dispatched... the man holding her, and we took the others prisoner." Conoc shivered a little, for he clearly remembered the fear on Jenevra's face as she struggled. He also remembered the tone her captor had used, a tone that boded nothing good, which had made him more deadly than he might have been otherwise.

Andreu sighed and began to fix a mug with herbs and hot water. "Let me begin at the beginning, and you may ask what you need after. You collapsed just after you found and rescued her. She had you brought here and came to tend you herself. She is responsible for the fact that you still have an arm, for Symme would have taken it off. She mended your arm and bandaged it, then while you lay unconscious, she went down to the great hall and began to do the same for your men. Only when they were all cared for would she return to your room. She would not agree to sleep in her own room; this was as far from you as she would consent to be."

"How did she convince Symme? They barely tolerate each other." Jenevra had not even managed to stand up to him over something as small as the food she wanted served.

"As Kenan told the story, she did not convince him. She threw him out." Andreu shook his head. "If she was a girl-child, she is no longer. She has steel in her."

Conoc knew that, though she had never shown it so openly before. Always hesitant, his lady, afraid to put herself forward. Afraid that others would judge her, and they had. "And she tended the wounded?"

"Aye. Bandaging wounds, applying poultices, stirring medicines... Listening to all those who lived, and sitting with those who died. She was grand, and she would not be gainsaid. Where she knows herself to be right, she will hold fast to her decisions." He helped Conoc up enough to sip the drink that had now steeped. "She said this would help you relax enough to sleep again."

"I don't want to sleep. I am not tired." Conoc could hear the petulance and the fatigue in his own voice, which only made him the more determined to stay awake.

"Lady Jenevra did not ask that. Her instructions were to give you this if you woke. But you fought off an attack today, were wounded and lost more blood than was good for you, and you need the rest if you are to recover. It is a serious wound, Conoc, and the full healing will be long."

"How bad is it, truly, Father?"

"You are lucky to have your arm. The healing would be simpler and faster had it been removed. But, if all goes well, Lady Jenevra expects that you will regain the full use of it."

Against his will, Conoc relaxed. Though he'd objected, Jenevra's potion did work to reduce the pain, and he knew that as soon as he let go, he would fall back to sleep. He looked over again at her, sleeping so deeply that she had not stirred during the conversation. He could not believe that she had done so much since the fighting ended, but Andreu had never lied to him.

He wished she could sleep beside him, that way he would know she got the rest she had earned. But he did not want her moved and risk waking her, as he suspected she would then not go back to sleep easily.

All he could do now was follow her example and let himself drift back off to sleep. Tomorrow he would take care of her.

THAT DID NOT PROVE as easy as Conoc had anticipated.

By midmorning, when he woke, Jenevra had already awaken and the blankets she had slept on been removed. If he had not himself been awake in the middle of the night, he would have no idea that she had been there at all. Somehow he suspected that had been her intent.

The sunlight streaming in through the unshuttered window - proof that Jenevra had been there - illuminated every corner of the room. He'd never been here during the daytime hours, he'd no idea how much light could come in. The fresh breeze that blew in, smelling of Jenevra's garden, scattered dust motes to dance in the light.

Not much had been cleaned since yesterday. He could see no sign of any medicines or treatments, but his armor lay in a heap not far from the bed, discarded in a hurry. Blood still coated it, and he would spend too much time cleaning that off when he finally was well. His sword lay on the table, far away from him, also uncleaned.

Faintly, he heard voices, feminine ones. Though the door between his room and Jenevra's was shut fully, he could just make out the sounds of water splashing. If she were bathing, she could not have been up for long. Perhaps, if he took his time, he could rise and dress himself before she finished. Then he could check on her.

He pushed himself to a sitting position. At least, he attempted to do so. But the pain in his shoulder, thus far reduced to a dull ache, came screaming back, and he gasped as ache turned to agony. Beads of sweat dotted his forehead, and he couldn't decide which would be more painful: to push up the rest of the way or to go back to lying flat.

A faint knock on the door, and Kenan leaned his head in. "Good. You are awake."

He tried to think of something clever to retort with, but nothing came to mind, so preoccupied was he with the fiery pain in his arm.

Without a word, Kenan came over and supported his back, taking the weight off his injured arm, and helped him to sit up. "I do not think you should attempt this on your own for today," was his only comment.

Conoc still failed to think of an appropriate response. Without his weight on his arm, the pain had gone down to merely intense, rather than agony. His lieutenant didn't seem to mind the lack of their normal banter, instead stirring up the fire a little and setting a kettle to boil. Though he appeared clean and neat, his shoulders slumped with fatigue, and Conoc wondered how much sleep he'd actually had.

"She will be pleased to see you sitting up," Kenan said, now offering a cup of something that smelled less than appealing.

"She who?" he asked, sniffing at the cup. It smelled worse up close.

"Your lady wife." Kenan's tone suggested that should have been obvious. "Drink it. It will help."

That everyone was determined to bully him annoyed Conoc. "I don't want to drink another potion, and it smells dreadful."

Kenan's jaw clenched, preventing whatever words he wanted to say from slipping out. He put his hand on the cup, the other on Conoc's good shoulder, and held it to Conoc's mouth. "You can drink it on your own, or I will help you." His fingers tightened, confirming this was no bluff.

The anger surprised Conoc, being unlike Kenan's normal temperament, and he drank the potion, which did not taste quite as bad as it smelled. "Why are you so angry?"

"Because you nearly died and you're complaining about something to help you heal! You just kept bleeding yesterday; I was here and I saw it! And I saw Lady Jenevra's face while she dealt with Symme, and I watched her bending over you, putting tiny stitches in your arm to try and hold you together. She kept her face calm, made it seem simple, but her eyes gave her away." Kenan's fury poured out with the words. "You sit there, white as the moon, and have the nerve to complain about the smell!"

He slammed out of the room, imparting so much force to the door that the metal catch barely held, and leaving Conoc alone with his thoughts.

He had not thought to make Kenan so angry, and he was surprised that he had managed it. For all his passionate nature, Kenan remained cool-headed at all times. Under normal circumstances, he might have threatened to pour a potion down Conoc's throat, but the tone would have been jesting, not furious.

It had been thoughtless to complain. Even if he hadn't known how severe his injuries were, Andreu's words overnight had made clear the seriousness of the situation. He had ignored his friend's response to relieve his own irritation. Now, his irritation still lingered and he had no friend who might have helped him over it.

Kenan's words about Jenevra remained. He had argued more than anyone against her coming and had advocated that she be sent away even after her arrival. She believed he did not like her, so apparent was his dislike. Yet he had spoken of her even more than Andreu had. He did not know what to think, between his own knowledge of her and the fact that she had impressed two such different men with her actions.

He wanted to see her. He wanted her here, beside him, so that he could see her face and know that she was well. He wanted her to assure him that he would be well.

He simply... wanted her.

Jenevra had awaken not long before Conoc, but after quickly checking on him, she had sent Lorent, who had drawn the last shift to watch over him, away to bed. Conoc's fever had finally given way, though he could bring it back easily enough and would, given half the chance.

But he no longer needed someone to sit beside him and watch him sleep. She felt confident that Lorent's time would be better spent sleeping, as neither he nor Kenan had slept more than a few hours each. She hadn't even known they would be watching over Conoc; only Father Andreu had spoken to her, and he hadn't listened when she'd insisted it was not necessary.

She'd retreated then to her room and to the bath that Sess had ordered the maid Mally to prepare.

In her own room, she stripped off the gown from the day before. Blood stained it in more than one place, Conoc's, Finn's, Cole's and others. A sleeve had ripped when she'd struggled with her attacker, and the skirt had strips torn off near the bottom when she'd needed to bind a man's arm and nothing else had been available.

Her kirtle had fared little better. Though it had no tears, the blood had soaked through in multiple places. Judged solely on her clothing, she must have looked like the injured person.

She left it all piled on the floor; Sess would see if it could be cleaned enough to be usable again.

The peace and quiet of the room after yesterday's chaos and the disorder in Conoc's room smoothed out the rough edges in her mood. She hadn't been angry, but the constant anxiety wore on her, leaving her drained and weary. Now she began to find her balance again.

She could not see any damage from the window. She faced away from the front gate and the road, so the open window showed her the edge of the wall and the lake, and the lake remained as peaceful as ever. Lakes did not trouble themselves with the petty problems of men.

The curlews chirped and called as much as ever, and that sound soothed Jenevra's troubled heart as much as reassured her that no attacks were likely today. 'Her' birds flew away or hid if danger approached the castle.

In the bath, she scrubbed hard enough to make her skin sting. But no amount of scrubbing could take the feelings off her skin: another man's hands on her, a boy dying beside her, her guard fighting almost to his death for her. All of it indelibly marked on her skin. Nothing could take that away; something had changed within her forever.

Sess and Mally came back into the room, Sess with a tray of food and Mally with another bucket of water for the bath. Without being asked, Sess set the tray down on he bed, then knelt down beside the tub to scrub Jenevra's hair.

"You should be prepared," she said, pitching her voice not to carry farther than Jenevra's ears. "The castle is abuzz with the events of yesterday, and you have become a heroine in more than one pair of eyes."

"I?" Jenevra stared at Sess. "Why?"

"Because you saved Lord Conoc. Because you tended to men who are far below you in station." Sess paused long enough to pour some water over her hair and rinse the soap away. "That is not what they expect of well-born ladies. Even Lady Mellyn would not have knelt down on the floor to bandage wounds."

Jenevra's skin felt warm with blushing. "I did not do anything so special."

"Sir Kenan and Father Andreu have said otherwise. The people of this castle would have you know they value you, so you may expect demonstrations of such." She held out a sheet, scented with rose. "You cannot soak today, the bath water is filthy. Come wrap up, then you may lie down and eat, for I doubt you had much yesterday."

Jenevra let Sess bully her. The peace she had gathered about herself had fractured at the idea of everyone praising her for what she had done, and Sess's bullying was so normal that it balanced the rest.

Though she did not lie down right away. Sess combed and plaited her hair into two plaits that fell to the middle of her back, then twisted them up with ribbon to keep them out of her way. "Now eat, then sleep again if you can. It is early yet, you can be spared a few hours."

JENEVRA SLEPT, and woke again near midday. The sun had shifted far enough that the light no longer shone on her, but instead illuminated her mirror and table against the wall. Despite the warm sun and the late spring air, she felt chilled, proof enough that she'd been worn. Though if she felt so, she could only imagine how the soldiers felt. She had not had a battle to fight first.

Sess had left clean clothing laid out at the foot of the bed: fresh linens, a kirtle the same yellow as the poppies growing on the slopes beyond the lake, and a gown of deeper golden tones. She did not wear yellow often, as it made her look sallow, but Sess had an eye for color and a sense for the appropriate.

When she had finished dressing herself, she tapped very lightly on the door to Conoc's room, then cracked the door.

The light shone bright in his room too, but the angle of the window meant that he himself lay in shadow. He lay asleep on his back, his body stiff even in sleep.

The room had not been picked up, and Jenevra began to do so as she made her way to the bed. His armor she could do nothing about, but she picked up the remains of the bloodied clothing and put them outside the door. Too the tray containing the remains of breakfast, a sight that unknotted a bit of tension in her shoulders.

That done, she drew near the bed to examine him with her eyes. His skin still looked pale, and faint lines of pain marked his face, but not so deeply as yesterday or this morning. Though dozens of tasks more urgent waited for her, she sat down on the edge of the bed and drew her hand across his forehead to check his fever. And started when he took it in his good one.

"My lady," he said, his lips turning up in a slight smile. His eyes, dark as ever, carried no pain. "I did wonder when you would come see me."

"You ought to be asleep," Jenevra said, her heart beating too fast. She hadn't expected him to be awake, had not planned on what to say to him. She felt uneasy, off-balance with him. Since he had kissed her a month before, they had not fully regained their ease with each other, and seeing him unclothed while she tended him had compounded her discomfort. "You need rest to heal."

"So I have been told, more than once," Conoc said. "But I wished to see you. You are not hurt?"

"No, my lord. Not even a scratch." Their eyes met, and she felt he saw too much of her thoughts, despite her smile.

His words proved that, as he reached up to brush a finger along her lip where she had bitten it the day before. "Not all hurts are physical, my lady. I think you know that. So I will ask you again, are you hurt?" He looked at her sharply, missing nothing.

"Nothing that will not heal, given time." Her lips trembled against her will, and she pressed them together to hide it. Her heart ached, and she could not forget all that she had witnessed the last day. But he did not need that burden on top of everything he already carried.

"Then I will say no more today." He shifted his body over, as best he could, to leave more space for her. "What is your assessment of me, lady? Shall I admit to surprise that you are a healer too?"

"Only a very little." Jenevra felt his forehead, noting his skin no longer felt clammy, though a hint of fever remained. She loosened the bandaging on his arm enough to assure herself that the bleeding had stopped and no signs of infection spread out. "My mother considered it a useful skill. I think you are doing very well, and perhaps tomorrow you may rise."

He took her hand back and pressed a kiss on her palm, a kiss that sent tingles all along her nerves. Her face blushed rosy pink, but she could not extricate herself even if she would.

"Thank you, my lady," he said.

"You should rest now." Her throat felt thick, her voice coming from a distance away. She wanted to lie down beside him, curled up in the space he made for her. But she did not dare trespass so.

"I will, if you will promise to come back later."

"I promise." She smiled and brushed her lips across his forehead. His eyes closed, and though he did not sleep immediately, she saw the lines in his face smooth as he relaxed. "Sleep well, my lord."

Conoc did have a visitor later, though not Jenevra. Lorent came in the midafternoon to bring him an update and, Conoc was certain, to check on him.

He felt much improved. Hours more of sleep, combined with whatever potion Jenevra had prepared for him, had left him feeling more himself and more energetic, though he knew that to be temporary. His arm still hurt whenever he moved it, but he no longer felt the constant pain that left him drained. He even managed to sit up on his own.

With this improvement in his physical condition came an increased alertness. He could not rise, but he could begin to deal, through others, with the state of the castle and the people.

The sun had moved far enough over that it no longer shone directly in the still open window, but he could, if he leaned over farther than he ought, see it just above the wall. He'd seen it this way from atop the wall and knew it would be turning the lake to shades of liquid gold. He could hear the guard on the wall, mail faintly clinking as he walked. In an hour or two, the guard would change and someone else would take up the post. He didn't know who either guard was, immured as he was in this room.

A faint breeze blew in, shifted from the morning. Now it came from the west and brought the scent of the lake and the heather on the hills with it. He began to understand why Jenevra kept her windows open as often as she could and only wished she were there to share it with him.

Lorent changed that.

He knocked, but did not wait for a response before he entered. He looked lankier than usual, as though he had lost weight in the last day, and his farm boy thatch of hair even more disheveled. And, though Jenevra frowned on the wearing of mail in the keep, he wore his mail shirt and his sword. He carried one of the small vials that Conoc had already come to recognize as his lady's work.

A maid, vaguely familiar to him though he could not say where he had seen her before and he was certain he would recognize the flirtatious look she directed at him, carried a tray covered with a linen cloth. At Lorent's urging, she set the tray down on the table and left, though not without a sway of her hips that drew both men's eyes for a moment.

As soon as she was gone and the door shut, Lorent looked him over. "You look better," he said. "I have a potion for you, courtesy of your lady wife. I imagine it tastes disgusting, as every other potion she has prepared today has. But she has said you may have it in a cup of wine."

Conoc smiled, almost against his will, as Lorent had known he would. "Have you had many of her potions today?"

"No. But I have heard from almost every man who *has*. To the man, all have said they are horrible." Lorent poured each of them a cup of wine from the pitcher on the tray and added the contents of the vial to Conoc's cup. He handed it to Conoc, then toasted him with his own cup.

He drank it quickly, wanting to be done with it. And though he would not call it either horrible or disgusting, he couldn't deny the odd bitter aftertaste that the wine couldn't hide. He grimaced, but at least it was finished.

Lorent set the tray in Conoc's lap. The linen cloth, now covering his blankets against dropped food, revealed a bowl of stew, with a healthy serving of roast sitting in the broth, surrounded by early spring vegetables, and half a trencher beside it. A smaller dish, not even the size of his palm, contained honeyed fruit.

Conoc ate quickly, more hungry than he'd realized, and

Lorent sat beside the bed, sipping on his wine. "You've eaten?" he asked.

"I will. It is early still, but you need to eat before you sleep again."

"I've slept too much; I won't be able to sleep all night." At this moment, Conoc felt very awake and equally determined not to sleep again until Jenevra returned.

"I doubt that. You don't know how much recovery you will need to do."

"I do," Conoc admitted. Men died often from wounds such as his, and he did not doubt that without Jenevra's intercession, he would be either dead or armless and still fighting to recover.

"Then you will know that you will sleep easily enough if you don't fight it."

They had been friends too long. In the alternately playful and scolding tones of his friend, Conoc saw that Lorent had something he did not want to share. "What is it?" When Lorent tried to demur, Conoc shook his head. "You're trying to hard to not let me see. What is the bad news?"

"The winch on the portcullis is broken." Lorent shook his head. "I don't know how long it will take to fix it."

"How badly?"

"Badly enough. Someone hit it with an ax. Kenan and I believe we will have to replace it." He shrugged. "It is up at the moment. We can lower it, but then you will not be able to raise it again until everything is repaired."

Conoc shook his head. Without the portcullis, only the wooden gates bound in iron guarded the front gate. "Meaning we'd have to use the postern gate." Which was much less defensible. Nor did he want to draw attention to it, for when they did have to use it. "Leave it up for now."

Lorent nodded his head. Then, without waiting to be asked, he began to list off the other damage to the castle: the main gate bore cracks due to the battering it had taken, the entrance to the keep required a new bar to the door, and other, more minor issues. The damage to the castle, though, compared little to the damage to the people.

"We lost ten outright on the walls," he said. "Mostly the Caermor levies who didn't fall back when ordered. Though," he grimaced, "they kept their portion of the wall clear. We lost a few more to wounds before they could be treated, a few are poised between life and death still, and four more lost a limb. In short, half our force was lost."

"God and goddess above," Conoc muttered. "And how did they get in? Their force shouldn't have been able to break into the castle so quickly. Forty men should have held for weeks, even with the poor shape of the castle."

Lorent ran his fingers through his hair and in that gesture, Conoc read his friend's lack of composure, as well as the source of the tousled hair he'd noticed earlier. "I don't know. Either they had help or they know something we don't."

"Help? You're suggesting one of our own provided them access." The thought cut Conoc to the core; so many of the people in the castle had been with him for years, had been his men when they had nothing. Their wives staffed the keep. They were almost a clan, bound by something more than blood. Bound by their time together, their shared experiences. He trusted these men, had trusted them more than once, with his life. Could someone betray them so?

Lorent shrugged. "They came in behind us. They could not have gotten the gate open otherwise. Kenan agrees; the wall would have remained clear, and the gate was battered, but would have held, especially with the portcullis." He paused, and Conoc saw again the hesitation. "That small group inside the keep... They were there a-purpose to find Lady Jenevra, and they knew to look for her in that hall. Someone told them something, my lord. Several somethings."

Conoc's heart sped up in a way that would not help his

recovery. "You have suggested before that she could have been a target."

"I have. Those times could have been coincidence. Once she wasn't in any danger. This was different. She heard them, Conoc. She heard them looking for her."

He swore, words that Jenevra would definitely not approve of. "Who else knows?"

"Kenan. No one else. They were speaking Altyran, and the guard with her didn't understand it. Everyone else considers it ill luck that she was found."

He swore more. "I need to be up. I need to be doing..." Something went on here that he didn't understand, and until he did, Jenevra would be at risk. His child bride had wound herself into his heart, and he could not allow her to be in danger.

"You need to be resting." Lorent put his hand on Conoc's shoulder, and though he did not apply any pressure, Conoc could not muster enough strength to push him off. "Another day and you'll be able to rise."

"And in the meantime, who protects my castle and my lady?"

A hurt look flashed across Lorent's face, gone almost as quickly as it had come, and a hint of guilt hit Conoc in the gut. "Kenan and I will always guard what's yours as if it were our own. And, of late, your lady does a fair job of caring for herself."

CHAPTER EIGHTEEN

Conoc rose the next day, though he felt weak enough that he needed help wherever he walked. Jenevra, tall though she was, had not the strength to hold him, so Kenan or Lorent walked with him. His arm lay bound in a sling, contrived carefully so that his neck and middle carried the weight, rather than his healing shoulder. He'd argued it unnecessary, but Jenevra had been unmoved, and Lorent and Kenan had backed her.

Although it tired him, he went first to the great hall. The dead had been removed, and the wounded taken to rooms where they could heal in more peace than a common area provided. But the remnants of the battle fought here had not been fully cleaned away.

Pallets soaked in sweat, dirt and blood still lay on the floor, with remnants of clothing laying nearby after being cut off. Puddles of blood had dried into sticky stains, the rushes too soaked to accomplish anything. The tables had been stacked along the walls to free as much space as possible and hadn't been replaced. Only a few tables remained in use, and men and women clustered in those spaces.

He stood in the entrance, Kenan supporting him, and

surveyed this battlefield. This battle, that Jenevra and Andreu had fought to save men's lives. He could see too easily in his mind the bodies lying there, and the two working 'til they wore themselves out to save each one. Andreu in sober gray would have blended in amidst the mail-clad soldiers. Jenevra, wearing a green dress, would have stood out.

She should not have been here, but from the stories he'd heard in the last day, he didn't think anyone could have stopped her. The spine and spirit wrapped up in her slim form amazed him, and he knew her better than most. Everyone else could only marvel.

He turned his head, and the object of his thoughts caught his eye. She supervised a group of the kitchen women in removing the blood-soaked fabrics and scrubbing the stone floors. Soon they would lay fresh rushes, and men would return the tables to their proper places, and no traces would be left of what had gone on here.

She stood out among the others. Yesterday she had worn yellow and gold and looked like a sunbeam among them. Today it was deep blue, the shade he thought of as Ravensmere blue, with bits of silvery trim, an evening sky with hints of stars.

Kenan helped him to a seat at the head table, which stood in its accustomed place, either never moved or already returned. He suspected it hadn't moved, for it was far larger and heavier than any other table, and no one would have had the energy to move it after fighting.

No one else stood or worked nearby, and pride threaded through with a touch of embarrassment washed over him. From his seat here - and his seat and Jenevra's were carved and distinct - he felt every inch the lord his rank made him. Surveying his people at work, above but not part of them. He had seen the king sit thus over the court.

And yet, that breath of shame. He was not so much above them save by an accident of birth and a little luck. Another man might have led the armies that broke the Northern attack and been rewarded by the king. He had no true right to sit above them.

He watched Jenevra move among the guards and the serving women. Always a smile for someone, a moment to stop and listen. With one hand, she directed the women in something, then laughed at a jest from a guardsman with his arm in a bandage. Yet she truly was not one of them, and they all felt it, despite the laughter. She carried herself differently, spine straighter and head raised to meet the world. But she had no false pride either; she worked every day for the people of the castle.

His heart nearly burst at the pride he felt in her.

Kenan murmured something about a meal, something that Conoc nodded an assent to, and left him there at the high table. He took one of the smaller doorways that led to the working areas of the keep, passing a woman with a basket of rushes under her arm. Conoc couldn't see her face, but he could see the moment when Kenan's hand went up slightly to meet hers and their fingers brushed lightly as a kiss.

His eyebrows went up, and he looked to see if her face came visible. But she turned behind a group of guardsmen, and he lost sight of her. Nothing about her dress or her hair had been distinct from any of the other women.

He wondered, and he regretted that Kenan had little choice of partners here at Ravensmere. Kenan and Lorent and Jenevra's cousin Cecilie, along with Father Andreu and Father Bardin formed a class of their own, and he could not see Lorent and Kenan fighting over Sess.

Jenevra walked around the table to stand beside him. She seemed pleased and relaxed. "The work goes well. By tonight's meal, I think we will be able to use the hall again."

"Indeed," he replied. "Sit." He drew her by her hand to sit in her chair beside his. The heavily carved chair dwarfed her, despite her height, and emphasized her delicate features and her youth. He forgot, sometimes, that she was barely fifteen, that though she had the all skills necessary for a wife and a lady, she lacked in simple life experience.

She smiled, though he noticed a hesitation. "For a moment, my lord. I - There is much to do."

"I know. And I am about to put another burden on you." Her eyebrows went up, and her lips pursed slightly. He would have kissed those lips, had they not been in public and he not known that she would not welcome it. "Kenan has taken an interest in one of the women in the keep. I did not see her face, but I saw the way he touched her fingers. I wish to know who she is."

Then her smile softened and she laughed. "You wish me to find Sir Kenan's ladylove, based on only a brief touch? I shall question everyone most thoroughly, but it is not much to go on."

"I have every faith in you, my lady." Conoc drew her hand to his lips and placed a kiss on the back of her hand.

She nodded once, accepting the compliment. Then she looked out over the hall, her hand still resting in his. The last of the blood had been scrubbed away, and several women laid fresh rushes everywhere. A few of the guardsmen helped to move the trestle tables back to their proper positions.

"We should have more people," she said absently.

"My lady?"

She started, as if she hadn't realized she'd spoken. "We are a small keep, I realize, but this is becoming a noble's household. We should have a household. A musician or two, skilled craftsmen like a blacksmith, a mason, a carpenter. A steward. Sir Kenan and Sir Lorent share the duties of marshal and huntsman between them, but a clerk or two to assist them would not be amiss. You should have a chamberlain. And pages and squires."

Conoc smiled. "You have thought about this, my lady. And how do you propose we support all these people?"

"I do not suggest we immediately bring in everyone at once. But we will need some of these people for long-term stability. They would become part of our castle. As well, when we need travel to court, we would need someone - several someones - to take care of Ravensmere. And to take care of us at court." She licked her lips, and he read nerves in the gesture. "We would have to pay some for some people, but having experienced help would allow Ravensmere and Caermor to profit more."

He considered the matter as they continued to watch the goings on. Her thoughts tracked his earlier ones, though her concerns had been practical, rather than romantic. But she knew what went into the running of a castle. He had married her for just that reason. If she recommended this, she had given the matter a great deal of thought and believed it necessary. She rarely spoke out otherwise.

"And you believe we can begin that process?" he asked.

She nodded. "I have kept the accounts, and I believe a steward to begin. There are things I simply do not know, for the castles I've lived in have always had one. Also, the blacksmith and the mason are necessary. When we go to court, you will have to have a chamberlain, but that can wait. And Father Andreu can take on more and will if you ask him."

He squeezed her hand gently, and she started again. In her fervor, he suspected she'd forgotten he held it. "How long have you thought this?" For these were not the plans of a week or a month. She had been thinking this for some time.

"A year or so." Now the hesitation crept into her voice and her eyes.

"My lady, you must not be afraid to bring these things to me. You are lady here; I would listen for no other reason than that. But I know you to be learned in such matters, so much that you must teach me. And," his voice dropped. "I would have you trust me, to feel safe bringing anything to my attention. I should stand as your shield in all things, great and small."

The shadows lifted from her eyes, now clear and blue as the summer sky. "Thank you, my lord."

"I DO NOT KNOW, CONOC," Andreu said. "I must give the matter thought."

Conoc nodded once. An hour spent with Father Andreu had restored him as the nap he had taken earlier in the afternoon had not. He tied Conoc's past and present together, reminding him that he had not abandoned what he had grown up as. He had shared his earlier feelings of guilt and shame and had received a verbal clout in return. Father Andreu might have made the clout visible, judging from the older man's expression, had he not been injured. As it was, Andreu had asked him if he'd received a blow to the head to be thinking such nonsense.

When Conoc had entered the chapel, assisted to the door by Lorent, he'd found the chapel as scrupulously clean as always, a rather astonishing feat given the number of people who had retreated there during the attack. No stray lacing lay discarded on floor, nor sticky fingerprint marred the wall. Andreu must have cleaned every moment he was not tending the wounded.

He'd begun to understand that Andreu did not clean because he enjoyed it. Not even because he enjoyed the finished product. He cleaned to work out his emotions, and between the attack and Conoc's injuries, the priest had certainly had a great deal to work out, and the chapel showed it.

But he was not cleaning the chapel when Conoc arrived. He actually sat in his little room attached to the chapel, sharpening a sword long disused. "I do not wish to be in a position where I am unable to defend the people I am called to care for," he said when Conoc asked.

Conoc could not recall ever seeing Andreu with a sword,

though he knew that Andreu had been a knight before he'd been a priest. But that had been long ago, before Conoc had even been born.

Still, the sword had been well cared for. He had seen no speck of rust on the blade, and the leather strapping of the hilt gleamed. The pommel stone, a clear crystal with hints of red, caught the light and shone as though a fire burned within.

They talked of many things while Andreu worked. Conoc's guilt, though first among them, did not even rate the most important. Jenevra's suggestion that Andreu take on more within the castle had provoked the longest conversation. They had discussed and circled around the topic, then gone back over it.

Andreu understood, better than Conoc, what Jenevra suggested, and it was he who explained that chaplains, the best educated people in the castle beyond lord and lady, often worked to answer the lord's correspondence and knew a great deal of the business and personal matters of the castle and lord. As to the record-keeping aspects of the position, he did those already and felt no qualms about keeping those tasks.

What he did not say, but what Conoc heard nonetheless, was that he had chosen to step away from the politics of the realm. He had chosen the priesthood, and the role of Conoc's advisor, when he could have had a much greater role - a high ranking prelacy, even the preceptor of his order - had he wished. He did not know wish to be drawn back into a role he could not easily set aside.

"I will not force you," Conoc said. "But I think I must give some credence to Lady Jenevra's thoughts. If she believes it time we behaved more as a noble household than a war camp..." He shrugged.

Andreu smiled. "I believe I suggested something of that nature to you, once upon a time."

"Aye, you did. And though I did not understand then, I begin to. And you - and she - are both correct in this." He looked down at his hands. "Before Jenevra, I did not think of myself as a noble, because I was not born so. But she can be nothing less, and she lifts us up, whether we will or no."

"I am pleased you see her as she is now, not as the useless girl with only worthless skills you once thought."

Conoc grimaced. He remembered saying that, dismissing the value of anything she knew. Now he could not even imagine the keep without her.

Conoc realized, as he sat at the evening meal that night beside Jenevra, how little he knew his wife.

Despite her better efforts, the evening meal most often remained less than formal. Rarely were full courses served, as it made no sense to waste food that way. And though she had asked, the cook had steadfastly refused to make the sort of formal dishes that were served in a noble's household.

He understood Symme's position; their upper class consisted of - at the broadest definition - seven people. Otherwise, they were a military unit. But he understood, better today, Jenevra's unspoken position that if they were to be anything besides that armed force, they must act as such.

But he could not account for the sudden shine in her eyes or the bright smile she gave when Symme himself, following a platter carried by one of the serving men, presented the dish to her and set it at the table before her. Nor did he understand the mixture of shame and regret on Symme's face as he bowed and backed away.

With his arm in the sling, he could not serve her as he would normally. With a tilt of his head, he signaled Lorent, sitting on his left, and he immediately rose to serve.

Conoc examined the portion on the trencher between himself and Jenevra, the slices of browned meat, covered in a delicate sauce that smelled of exotic spices. He did not know what it was, and though he had grown used to eating whatever he was served, it bore little resemblance to anything he knew. Symme usually roasted whatever meat or game they had.

Jenevra did not seem to share his reservations, as she had calmly begun slicing some of the meat, and her eyes closed in pleasure when she tasted it.

"What is it?" he said softly. A quick glance around showed him that Sess, like Jenevra, had begun eating, while his guardsmen had regarded it more cautiously.

"Duck," she said. "It is a favorite of mine, this recipe. It would be a good choice to serve when the king visits." She paused, a little crease in her forehead. "If he still comes. Should he, under the circumstances?"

Conoc took a bite of the duck, which tasted flavorful, though he couldn't distinguish the spices. Bus his palate had been shaped by the flavors of camp food. Based on Jenevra and Sess's reaction, nobles might find it otherwise. "I will write to him and suggest this is a poor time for a progress in the area. But he is the king, and he does what he wishes."

A shrug, and a slightly distant look was her response.

"You disagree?"

"No. The king's wish is law, and he brooks no opposition to it. But I wonder..." She paused again, that little crease appearing once more. "The queen is no stranger to having her wishes obeyed. So whose wish will triumph here, I wonder."

Jenevra prepared for bed, wearier in heart than body. Though she had worked the day away, restoring the great hall to its proper state and then turning her attention to the barracks, more tasks waited her attention the next day. The day after that, they would bury all the guardsmen who had been lost in the attack.

Her fingers brushed the ribbon that lay on her table before her. She had worn it at the midsummer festival when she had danced with Cole. Tomorrow it would be tied around his arm as a token of remembrance as he was prepared for burial.

Her throat tightened, and she laid her face in her hands. Too many lost, and she could only be grateful that Conoc was not among them. Nor Sir Kenan or Sir Lorent. Her own guard Finn would walk, though he might never lift a sword again.

She herself had lost so little, she had no right to weep. But her heart ached still, for all those losses she'd had no power over, those men whose names she'd never known and those who were little more than names. And one boy, not quite a man, who had danced with her.

The evening breeze brought the scent of flowers, and she smiled weakly. She tied off the end of her plait and sat at the window seat, leaning her head against the wall. She could smell the heart's ease planted below her in her garden and the rosemary and heather. Curlews cried lowly, and she imagined that they cried for the dead as well.

She did not call back to them as she might once have done. The guards knew this to be her room, and they guarded the nearest section of the wall more alertly than almost any other; she would not do anything to distract them.

Conoc's footsteps sounded heavy as he entered his room. If she had worked to the limits of her strength today, so had he, and he had much less to give at the moment. Even walking wearied him. She had no excuse for herself.

He should be resting. His shoulder healed as well as could be expected, but he was far from well.

She did not hesitate to open the door between their rooms and stand in the entrance. Only when she watched him did she think she ought to have knocked, lest he be in some state of undress. But that did not worry her as it once had.

He stood near the fireplace, one arm leaning on the wall

beside it, head bent, weariness etched in the slump of his shoulders. The firelight played over him, casting shadows behind him where no other light shone.

"Yes, my lady?" he asked without turning around.

"I came to see if you were well."

"No," he turned to look at her, his face hidden in the shadows, "you came to bully and nag me into resting."

But for the faint tease in his voice, she would have shut the door and retreated to her room. Instead she responded to the unvoiced request and took the hand he held out to her. He drew her close enough that he could lean his weight on her.

"Tonight, my lady, I will not even fight you. On one condition."

"You are not in a position to make demands of me, my lord." She helped him to the bed, where he sighed in relief.

"No, you are right in that. But I will ask all the same. I will take whatever potion you require, rest as much as I am able, if you will take your own advice and rest as well."

She opened her mouth to argue, but he laid a finger over her lips and she subsided, almost with a smile.

"You are tired, lady, and you have people who will need you tomorrow. I have seen, and I am not the only one, that you are determined to care for your people. But they cannot trump your own well-being; you are the only lady here."

"And for this, you will take the medicine that I have made and not argue? You will sleep until you wake?" Jenevra laid the back of her hand on his forehead to be sure he had no fever.

"I will." He stripped off his tunic, so that he sat there in shirt and hose, and she loosened the ties of his shirt to check his shoulder.

"Then I will agree." He healed well, and in a few days, she would be hard-pressed to keep him resting as he began to feel that improvement.

She did not notice that she stood between his legs until he

set his hand on her waist, the pressure slight but easily felt through her kirtle. She stiffened, every muscle in her back tightening in response, but did not pull away, though her heart pounded and her breath caught in her throat.

"I will not push you, Jenevra," Conoc said softly. With him sitting on the bed, his face was nearly level with hers. "But I would be remiss if I did not tell you that you have been brilliant these days. Everyone has relied on your strength and your sense, and though I have been a poor patient, I have valued you as well."

He leaned forward and kissed her forehead. "Go and rest, my lady, as you promised, and I will do the same."

CHAPTER NINETEEN

The days stretched slowly. Midsummer came and went without remark or celebration this year, for the castle could not be opened with the threat of Northerners attacking hanging over every head...

Too, the king and queen's progress still continued on its way to Ravensmere. Conoc had written to the king and expressed that this was not a safe time to visit and that the progress should be postponed, but the king's response, though Conoc had not permitted Jenevra to read it, had carried both a note of threat as well as finality.

The same messenger had carried letters to Jenevra, from her mother and her godmother. Both had been vague warnings, too vague to act upon but enough to worry her. Neither woman was inclined to paranoia, and both had served in the previous queen's court. To be warned against the queen - for so Jenevra interpreted their words - set her nerves on edge in a situation already fraught.

For the Northerners did not attack. The men trained and watched, and searched the castle and keep when time permitted. Though Conoc, and Sir Kenan and Sir Lorent, had never admitted to anything, every man, woman or child in the castle knew that someone had found a secret way into the castle, and that was how the Northerners had almost broken the castle defense in their last attack.

Why they did not press that advantage, when the defenders were weak, no one could say. Nor could anyone even guess where the entrance was located, or how it had been found by an outsider when no one within could find it.

Jenevra did not spend much time in searching. Not that she didn't believe Sir Kenan and Sir Lorent's conclusions, but she had no time to spend. Her own duties consumed her full days, the more so now that she had begun instructing some of the castle's women in her own limited knowledge of herbs and healing. Whenever Northerners did attack, she had determined they would not find them so unprepared. She would have no other dead on her soul.

The stillroom, already small for her alone, had no spare room as three women sorted, chopped and stirred under her supervision. The fireplace allowed only one person to reach the pot hanging there, and two women could just fit at the table built into the wall. All had to be cautious not to bump the shelves on the wall behind them, filled with jars, bottles, boxes and bags of herbs and potions.

When time could be had, Conoc had promised her that a better room would be found for the storage, if not for the actual stillroom, but thus far, neither time nor room had materialized.

In the mean, she had three students with much information to cover. She had taken for granted her own knowledge as something that many women would know, but as she taught, she had learned how wrong she was. Though she could not claim great knowledge, she knew every plant in the room, could identify them by leaf, root or berry as appropriate. She knew their scents, both good and bad.

The women she taught knew little of that, their knowledge

limited to what they had seen around their own homes and what they needed as wives.

"That is well done, Tansy," she nodded as the other woman, at least ten years her senior, turned to her for approval... The potion, one to reduce pain, was both less complicated and less dangerous than poppy syrup. "It is almost ready to be packed into bottles - where did the extra bottles go?"

The three other women looked at each other, before looking back at her, one wincing and another shrugging. "I'll get them," the third offered.

"No." Jenevra shook her head. "I will. Tansy, strain the potion so there are no bits of bark remaining. Then it will do no harm to sit before we bottle it. Janat, finish chopping those and start brewing it as soon as you're done. Sarre, finish sorting. For that mix, nothing can be damaged or bruised. We'll start brewing that next. I will not be long."

Indeed, Jenevra relished the few moments of time away. Though she appreciated that the women worked hard and had left other tasks that meant others would work equally hard, and she gave them her fullest attention and the best of her own abilities, Jenevra was a girl used to her own company. When around others, she must always be the Lady of Ravensmere, and it wearied her. A few moments to run down the stairs to the storerooms and locate an errant crate of bottles, then find a man to carry them back up for her, would give her a bit of breathing room.

Until she heard her name called behind her. "Lady Jenevra!"

She drew in a deep breath as she turned and greeted Father Bardin. "Father." She inclined her head respectfully. "How can I help you?"

"I have missed our mornings together." The lines on his face had grown more pronounced since coming to Ravensmere, giving him a sterner look than before, even when he was pleasant. "It is unlike you to forfeit your studies."

"I have been much occupied with the well-being of the castle," she said calmly. "As well as the visit of the king and queen."

"That is what I wished to speak of," he said, almost running over her words in his haste. "I am informed... That is, I have studied the queen's beliefs. Do you think it right to allow Father Andreu to preside over services while she is here?"

"Father Andreu is the priest here at Ravensmere. I have no intention of displacing him."

"She will find him heretical." His voice carried an edge she could not identify, a savageness at odds with his scholarly persona.

"I believe she may find all of us heretical, a thought that concerns me greatly." Jenevra eyed him, trying to see with impartial eyes the man before her. "And yet, Andreu remains. He is not only a fine priest and man, he is Lord Conoc's oldest friend. He is also your senior. Until his preceptor recalls him, he shall serve our castle."

For a moment, she saw a flash of irritation in his eyes, then Father Bardin bowed. "As you say, my lady. I only wished -"

She nodded once back. "I am certain you only wished for the well-being of the castle and inhabitants." But a niggling doubt, too vague to name, as so many of her concerns had been of late, remained as he bowed again and departed, taking her words for the dismissal they were. Too much made her uneasy.

The steps down to the storerooms were empty this time of day, and no one troubled her. Her thoughts returned to Father Bardin. Despite his attempts, she had never fully warmed to him, nor, though he was her confessor, had he become her confidante. Even in her inexperience, his occasional questions on Conoc and her relationship with him had been intrusive. Yet one could not doubt his knowledge or his faith. He was not evil.

The hallway down which lay the storerooms did not look different from the last time she had been here - the walls the same bare stone that made up the majority of the keep, the wooden doors shut or not shut as appropriate for their contents - but something felt different. The hair on the back of her neck rose, and she suppressed the momentary urge to run for Conoc or Kenan or Lorent. She could not run at every little unease.

She drew in a breath and closed her eyes to focus better. The air carried a faint hint of fish and mud, and she rubbed her arms against the cool dampness that seeped into her gown.

Her eyes popped open, and she began to run back down the corridor and up the stairs, almost tripping on the hem of her gown in her haste. She bundled it up in her fist to move more freely and continued to run, nearly slamming into Conoc and Lorent as they turned a corner, laughing at some joke between them.

Conoc put out his arms to catch and hold her. "My lady, you should be more careful." But the laughter on his face faded as he took in her flushed face and ragged breaths. "What is wrong?"

She could not speak at first and so waved her arm back the way she'd come. "Storerooms. Lake. Smell." She forced herself to slow down, to breathe enough to speak coherently, for Conoc's hands had tightened on her arms, and Lorent had his hand to his sword. "The hallway to the storerooms... I can smell the lake, and the air is damp."

Their expressions of courteous confusion irritated her, and she went on. "The air is moving. There's another entrance."

IN THE END, they took her with them. She hadn't given them much choice in the matter. She had argued vociferously with Conoc while Lorent had hurried off to fetch a few guardsmen.

Both had seen her point when she fully explained her observations, and she'd had the pleasure, albeit limited, of seeing both confounded that no one had been down in the storerooms long enough to notice what she had. She had the greater pleasure in being complimented on her perceptiveness.

Then they had suggested she return to her own work above stairs while they explored the situation, and she had protested.

"I do not think that Northerners lie in wait on the chance that someone should happen upon them. It would not even be sensible, for the more they are present, the more likely it is that they would be found."

Conoc stared down at her, as he often did, and though his sober expression did not change by even a hair's width, a hint of sparkle appeared in his eyes. "An I agree, you must agree to stay back behind us. If there should be any trouble, you would be both protected and best able to run for more help."

She nodded once, accepting with some grace the restriction placed on her, though she did feel it unnecessary. She did not think he would have tolerated any more argument from her, nor would she have done it with others watching.

Six storerooms lined the hall, three on each side. Jenevra felt slightly ridiculous walking down a hallway with half a dozen guards before her, checking each room. Had anyone been willing to listen to her, she would have told them that it would not be the first two storerooms, as those were foodstuffs, and people were in and out of those rooms every day.

The final room, she could see from down the hall, still had the lock on it that her father had put there for her dowry. Conoc had the only key, so they had not come in that way either. That left only three rooms, because the hallway ended in a wall.

The next to the last room proved to be the correct one. Mud from the lakeshore had dried on the floor, leaving bootprints from the back wall to the door. Jenevra hovered in the doorway, while the guards examined the walls for a hidden entrance.

A shout went up and two men jumped back when a section of wall swung open before Lorent.

"I've seen that kind of door before," he said. He held out a hand, and one of the other guards handed him a torch.

One by one, each went into the tunnel following Lorent, Jenevra last, behind Conoc. Despite her worries, the door did not shut behind them, and that faint light glimmering behind her reassured her.

Brick lined the walls and ceiling. This had been no hastily dug tunnel, but carefully planned and executed when the castle was built. Jenevra, running her fingers along the wall, felt dampness and more dampness hung in the air, and she scrubbed her hands on her gown to wipe them clean, though nothing marked them.

The tunnel stretched on, and the darkness pressed more heavily against the light from the torches half the guardsman carried. The other half kept hands to weapons, muscles tense. Conoc drew her forward, closer to him, and she let one hand rest on the hilt of the dagger at her belt. But no sounds disturbed that dreadful silent darkness except the men's harsh breathing and the occasional footstep.

A whoop ahead of them, and light brighter than torches shone before them. Each of them stepped out though a small door hidden between two of the boulders that lined the lakeshore. The door itself, disguised as driftwood stuck in the rocks, could barely be seen when they stood back a few steps.

From that door, across the lake, the castle stood silhouetted against the sun. Jenevra shuddered. The lake, wide though not deep, guarded the castle on two full sides. This tunnel negated that defense. As long as it stood open, they were vulnerable.

"What now?" she asked Conoc, whose own eyes were trained on the mountains in the other direction.

"We return to the keep," he said, turning to her as if he had forgotten she was there. "Back the way we came." She shuddered again, just once. "Too many people already know about the tunnel. We cannot risk even more discovering it. A watch will be posted on it."

"Do you think they will use it again?"

Conoc shook his head. "Not unless they intend to throw everything at us. The more it's used, the more likely we are to find it. No, I think it more likely that our traitor will use it to deliver information. And that is someone I wish to speak to."

CHAPTER TWENTY

Conoc did not rest well that night. Alone in his bed, the blankets simultaneously too hot and too cold, he tried vainly to sleep. But each time he began to nod off, his brain seized back on the answers that eluded him. Who knew of the tunnel? And more, who would use it to hurt them? He could not answer that, no matter how he tried.

Faintly he heard the change of watch on the wall. Midnight then.

He rose and stirred the fire to life, bringing more light and warmth into the otherwise dark room. Not so much light that it would disturb Jenevra in her room, though he hoped she slept peacefully enough that he would not wake her. He had not heard any noise from her room in several hours.

Then he opened one shutter. The moonlight pouring in lit the room even more, and that he knew would never disturb Jenevra, given her fondness for light and air and open windows. If Sess had not interfered, her own window would surely be open now...

The stone of the walls reflected back the light, giving everything a silvery sheen. Nothing softened that, for he had never seen a purpose to decorations, and Jenevra, though she made her own decisions elsewhere in the keep, had left his room alone.

A draft from the window brushed against him, and the bare skin of his upper body cooled. He breathed it in, trying to pick out the scents carried on the wind, but he smelled only the lake and plants, nothing that meant anything to him.

Turning away from the window, he took his sword down from the rack where it hung. His father had given him this sword when he had been knighted, and he had carried it every day since. It had been his grandfather's, who had died before Conoc had been born. Someday he would pass it on in turn to his grandson.

In the middle of the room, where he would not disturb anything, he began to drill. This oldest form of swordwork, learned long before he was allowed even a prearranged bout, settled something inside him, allowed him to focus. He was a knight, a warrior, first, and returning to that cleared his mind.

He had barely used his sword since the last Northern attack and his arm injury. Kenan and Lorent had united in their refusal to work with him until his lady wife gave him permission, and of the rest of the keep's inhabitants, only Father Andreu knew enough to hold his own. He had not even asked Andreu, knowing that the priest would be less likely to yield than his friends.

As he continued, his muscles remembered performing these motions over and over, until he no longer needed to think about them. That was how he had learned, practicing each motion individually, then combining them until they came without conscious thought. Attack after attack, first his strong side, then his weaker. Patterns of parries, followed by more attacks.

His feet moved silently on the stone floor, cold as it was. Despite moving with the drills, he stayed in that patch of moonlight, though both moon and patch moved as time went on.

In that silence, that seemingly endless moment, his thoughts coalesced, becoming sharper and clearer. Though he found no answers, his mind no longer felt torn in many directions. He began to find a plan of action.

The tunnel would not be used again by Northerners. Too many had heard of it, and news crossed the border more easily than people. They would know in days. Even the traitor would hesitate to use it soon, expecting that the watch would be heaviest in the beginning before eventually dying down.

When his arm began to ache, a clear sign that he had worked as hard as he ought for one night, he lowered his sword tip to the floor and rested his hands on the hilt, breathing and trying to hold on to the peace he had gained.

He never heard a sound, but he wasn't surprised to see her there when he turned around. Framed in the doorway, one hand resting on the wall, dressed in an off-white chemise that took on the same silvery tone as the stones, her hair unbound as he liked it best, Jenevra looked more divine than human.

Without a word, he crossed over to her and took her hand in his. She looked beautiful and tempting, without any intention to be so, but her eyes held a moment's flash of fear. So, against his own wishes, he simply pressed a kiss to her palm.

"I had not intended to disturb you, my lady," he said softly, voice rough.

"I woke and saw the moonlight," she replied just as softly. "I came to check... Your arm..."

"Is well enough. It is healing, and I did not re-injure it."

Her eyes went to the scar, and her hand left the wall to hover a fraction above the injury, though she did not touch it. "You should not press too hard. If you damage it while the muscles repair themselves, it may never regain its full motion."

"An that were so, it would still be more than anyone else would have left me. But," he added to forestall the words she started to say, "I will be careful. I will not practice with anyone until you believe it time."

Her smile suggested acquiescence, but he suspected she would verify that with Kenan and Lorent herself. "Now, my lady, what keeps you wakeful tonight?"

"Nothing. Or nothing I can explain. I find myself examining everyone, weighing their words and actions more than I would have before. But I can express nothing certain, only a vague dread." Her fingers twisted nervously together. "I sound ridiculous, even to myself. But I wake at night and worry."

He took both her hands in one of his. "You are observant and wise. I do not doubt that if you worry, you have cause, even if you can't explain it. I do not find you ridiculous." He kissed her fingers again. "When you can name your worry, I will act on it. Until then, my lady, you must trust me to share these burdens."

"But you need your rest..."

"My own worries keep me awake. Yours will not weigh me down." And if it lightened the cares on her delicate shoulders, he would be only too happy. He had not known, when he married her, that protecting her meant more than protecting her from others. It meant to protect her from herself, for she would give whatever she had in the service of her people. He had underestimated her once, he would not do it again.

"Then you must share yours with me," she said.

"And I will do so, in the daylight hours. You should sleep."

"As should you."

"I will when I have returned my room to order. Now, lady, you must to bed."

She looked steadily at him, her eyes too wise in her otherwise young face, and he saw for a moment a glimpse of the strong and beautiful woman she would become. Then, without another word, she stepped back into her room and closed the door.

CHAPTER TWENTY-ONE

Eseld came to visit the next day.

She came often, far more often than Jenevra would wish. Often, her husband would have business of some sort with Conoc, and she would join him with the stated intent of visiting her brother. But Kenan worked too hard to waste days visiting with his sister, and so she joined Jenevra and Sess in the solar. Other times, she came specifically to visit Jenevra, who she always claimed would be lonely without another woman around her.

Jenevra had tried, without success, to explain to Conoc that she was not lonely and did not need Eseld's company, but he believed that she was a good influence on Eseld and helped her to be more of a lady. And surely she must tire of only having Sess for company?

She never dared to say that she did not *like* Eseld. The one time she had hinted in that direction, Conoc had treated her to what could only be called a lecture on how Eseld was an old friend and the sister of his oldest friend and was it truly so hard for Jenevra to learn to get along with her, for his sake and for Kenan's?

She had resigned herself to the visits after that.

Invariably, Eseld brought work with her, so that Jenevra and Sess did not have to stop their work to entertain her. Though she spoke enough that Jenevra sometimes wondered how she accomplished anything.

Today she sat on Jenevra's favorite seat at the window, spinning wool on a drop spindle, humming a little between bits of conversation.

"Tell me," she said. "What of this secret tunnel? I had barely made it through the gate before I heard of it. And though no one seems to know much, they all agree that you were part of this."

Jenevra, at her embroidery frame, her back to Eseld, did not answer for a long moment. Eseld's question did not sit well with her. Though containing the secret of the tunnel would have been impossible, especially with half a dozen men there when it was found, everyone had been bidden to keep that within the castle itself and not to outsiders. She supposed that many would not consider Eseld to be an outsider, as often as she came to the castle of late, but still, it felt inappropriate to discuss it so openly.

"I do not have much to tell," she said. "'Twas Sir Lorent who found the entrance. I was merely present."

"You need not be so modest with me," Eseld replied. "Before Con - Lord Conoc and the others, you must be discreet and let them have their victories, but when it is only women, we may speak the truth. Weren't you the one who sent them to that part of the castle?"

That Eseld used Conoc's name without a title did not irritate Jenevra near as much as Eseld's clear expectation that it *would*, which was why she corrected herself after failing - again - to do it correctly. But then, most things about Eseld irritated her.

"Truly, I have no claims to either discovery or great modesty. I did little that anyone else would not have done, and the greater share of the credit does belong to Lorent." Jenevra twisted around on her stool to face Eseld. "Why will you not believe me?"

Eseld raised her eyes. "I have seen that you take very little credit for the changes you have made in the castle. I merely wished to know the truth of this occasion."

Jenevra turned back around, frustrated, and stabbed at the fabric. Whatever peace she managed to acquire for herself, Eseld inevitably destroyed while doing and saying *nothing* of any consequence.

Behind her, Eseld must have returned to her spinning because Jenevra heard her humming again. The melody felt familiar, but she could not place words to it. The music carried the swell of waves in it. Jenevra found herself humming in harmony.

Abruptly, Eseld stopped. "I would not have expected you to know that song. It is an Altyran song."

"I do not know it. I simply followed you." Her eyes traced the design she strove to create before her. "I liked the sound, as if waves rose against something."

The humming did not begin again, and Jenevra ignored the palpable silence behind her. If Eseld wished to be offended, as she clearly did, Jenevra would let her. She had done nothing of which anyone could complain.

Her fingers began on the next set of stitches, a carefully placed unicorn tucked in the leaves that formed the border of the piece. When finished, she would hang it in her room or here in the solar. She looked forward to seeing it finished, though she estimated that she had several months of work before then.

"How old are you?" Eseld asked suddenly.

"I will be sixteen at Midwinter." Jenevra tightened her fingers on the needle and missed her stitch.

"You are almost a woman, then. I suppose no one will think you too young any more."

No one said she was too young *now*. No one thought it, save perhaps her husband and Eseld. She had proven herself enough for all her critics. But she did not speak, just continued on with her stitching, trying to focus on that and not Eseld's voice.

"Shall it be a grand feast, the Lady's coming of age?"

The mockery made Jenevra's skin crawl. "I am a married woman; I have no need of feasts. And surely no one shall celebrate my coming of age when I have been of age for three years now."

"Surely Conoc will celebrate? He must prefer a woman to a child for his wife."

Jenevra turned around, face pale with the implications in Eseld's words. "Why, Eseld? Why do you come here? You do not like me."

Eseld stared back at her, then laughed mockingly. "So the kitten has claws after all. I did wonder if anything could move you to speak." She set down the work in her hands and gave her full attention to Jenevra. "I come because it suits me so. I wished to see what was of such value."

"And did you learn what you wished?" Jenevra shook her head. "I do not believe that was your reason at all. You come to bait me into upset, but why? What do you gain from it?

For a long moment, they stared at each other, Jenevra pale with cheeks flushed, Eseld cool and composed. Then Eseld stood. "You would never understand."

"It is too many for a progress," Jenevra said, shaking her head.

She stood beside Conoc on the keep's tower, the highest point in the castle and the one with the most commanding view. Together they surveyed the encampment at the base of their mountain.

As high as they were, she could not make out details. No matter how she squinted, she could not identify the banners to see who had joined the king. Little sound carried up on the south wind that wrapped around the castle today, only the occasional neighing of horses.

The castle too was quiet. The guards stood their watch upon the wall and did so unflinchingly. But the camaraderie that usually characterized the men failed them today, and everyone worked as though their focus would define the fate of the castle.

Conoc remained silent. He had advised the king not come on the progress, that he should not put himself and the new queen in danger. The king had decided otherwise, and now sat only an hour or two away. Even though the sun had begun to set, the fall days had a long twilight; if the king wished, he could be within the walls of Ravensmere before nightfall.

He clearly did not wish.

She had expected a large group. The king had not made a formal progress in four or five years, when the Prince had been formally invested as heir. Several members of the Council would be with him, as would a portion of the queen's household.

But she counted the tents again and the banners she couldn't identify and compared the number against the lords she had expected. She could not even fathom who some could be. Could her mother and father, her godmother, be among them?

She shivered once as the wind blew over them again. A south wind should be a pleasant thing this time of year. Instead it chilled her.

That drew Conoc's attention from wherever it had been. "You are cold," he said and brushed a lock of hair away from her face. "We should go inside."

"I am well enough." The wind chilled her less than her fears. She did not know what this meant, and she did not like it. Something felt... off, and she said as much.

"I know, my lady. I know." Conoc looked over at the encampment, then back to her. "But for now, we can do nothing. The next move is the king's, and I do not expect that we will wait long for it."

He led her down the steps from the tower, a guard waiting to take their place. A guard rarely stood watch there, for, though it stood tall above everything and had an unmatched view south, mountains and trees blocked the north. They had never before felt the need to guard their backs against their own people.

Others waited for them at the base of the tower, and Conoc handed Jenevra over to Sess while he went with Kenan and Lorent.

Sess didn't say anything, but then, she rarely did. Instead she looped her arm through Jenevra's and began walking down the hall. No urgency marked her movements, no concern her face, but Jenevra felt the tension in her friend's body.

"Symme has the evening meal ready; all he waits on is your word," Sess said finally.

"He should serve it. The king will not come tonight, and Lord Conoc," Jenevra looked over her shoulder at Conoc with his lieutenants, "is occupied for the time. There is no need to hold it."

DINNER CONTINUED THE SOMBER MOOD. Conoc, Kenan and Lorent did not attend, leaving Jenevra and Sess, along with Father Andreu and Father Bardin, to occupy the head table. But the grand chair beside her, standing empty, drew every eye, and Jenevra felt that attention, though she tried to act otherwise.

Even the dinner, a veal tart that would put the king's own chefs to shame, failed to win more than a smile, however genuine, from her. Though she ate it, and complimented Symme, she could not say what it tasted of.

Conversation stayed at a low murmur, well below the volume of most evenings. At the head table, they did not speak at all. Sess tried once or twice, but Jenevra could not speak on anything with any semblance of sense. Father Andreu and Father Bardin had a spirited, if quiet, discussion on some text that Father Bardin had been studying, but even if Jenevra could follow it, she had no interest in it tonight.

When Conoc finally entered the hall, flanked by Kenan and Lorent, what little conversation existed ceased. Everyone watched them and strained to hear any word.

Jenevra saw that Conoc saw it, and she saw his jaw tighten slightly. But no other expression gave him away, nor did his voice betray his strain when he greeted her.

"My lady," he said, taking her hand and kissing it. "I beg your pardon for my lateness."

"My lord," she replied, trying to smile and play her part for the people. "No pardon is necessary."

When he sat, she served dinner to him, and, though he wasn't fond of Symme's more formal dishes, he ate tonight without either hesitation or attention. The faint buzz of conversation began again, though almost everyone continued to look to the head table often.

"Later," he said softly, when no one watched them.

LATER TOOK TOO LONG. Jenevra was impatient and fretful long before Conoc retired to his room. She snapped one of the lacings on her favorite green gown in her hurry to remove it, and both Sess and the maid left her earlier than usual, the maid taking the offending gown to re-lace it.

She paced back and forth in the confines of her room, a room that had previously felt too large and now felt not nearly large enough for her energy. Twenty steps took her from one side to the other, twenty more back, her kirtle swirling around her ankles with her impatient steps.

She stopped before the mirror over her table and undid her hair from the long braid she had worn during the day. Unbound, her hair rippled down past her waist. The mirror had been a gift from Conoc for her last birthday, and she usually enjoyed looking in it simply for the pleasure of admiring the mirror itself. Carved birds flitted from vines carved along the frame, some wholly exposed, some just revealing a glimpse of wing or tail feather.

Pacing did not settle her, so she tried to sit and read her book, but almost immediately she put it down and rose again. She did not even touch the embroidery frame sitting nearby.

Another turn around the room, and she opened the window. Her window looked to the lake, so she did not see the encampment at the bottom of the mountain. But she could not ignore its existence, because the nighttime had a quiet that was unusual, a tense, watchful quiet.

No birds called. The curlews did not come out unless the moon was full, but she did not hear any owls, any nightjars or even the robins, who usually called incessantly. None of the wading birds were audible on the lakeshore.

She told herself that she imagined this, that a quiet night betokened nothing more than a fox out hunting. But she knew that not to be true. A fox, once spotted, would send the birds into a panic; she would hear every single one of them.

She sat at the window, the cooler night air starting to chill her, listening to the sound of the silence, until she heard the sound she listened for most: Conoc's footsteps entering his room. Jenevra flew across the room and flung open the door between them before he'd barely closed the outer door of his room.

He showed no surprise at seeing her. Instead he smiled, though it contained no joy.

"Come in, my lady. I was expecting you."

She stopped just inside the door, suddenly hesitant as he stripped off sword belt and mail shirt. Nor did she know what to say; her impatience had not waned, but to question him incessantly did not seem apropos for the moment.

When arms and armor had been arranged to his satisfaction, he turned back to her. "You need not hide by the door, my lady. Sit," he gestured to a chair before the fire, "we need to speak."

Jenevra took the chair, half-facing the fire, as he settled another opposite her for himself. "Will you tell me now what you would not say at dinner?"

"Aye." He drew a breath and let it out again. "Kenan, Lorent and I agreed with you that there are too many men for a progress. We sent out scouts; if their counts are at all accurate, the king brought nearly two hundred soldiers with him."

"Two hundred?" She stared in horror. "That is more than half the standing army."

"True, though only fifty or so wear the royal colors. The others wear the colors and badges of the lords he brought with him, and we hope that you can identify them for us."

She took a sheet from him, her fingers seeming unconnected to the rest of her, and stared at it uncomprehendingly for a moment before she focused on the words. "The white boar on red… That is Fitslan; they are the king's maternal kin. Orange and white is the Courcys. The coronet over the lion rampant… That is the king's younger brother, the Duke of Durere." Her voice dropped to a whisper, all she could manage around the lump in her throat. "This is no progress; the king is prepared for battle."

Conoc took her hands in his. "So we thought. I do not know what I have done to offend the king, but I think we will know tomorrow. For tonight, I have sent messengers to the village and to the nearby freeholders. I do not think them in particular danger, but I want them in the castle for their own safety."

Jenevra nodded, accepting his action and the implied work for her. But he caught her face in one hand so he could look at her.

"I think we will find what angers the king and make it right. I am preparing for worse than I expect. I do not wish to worry you unnecessarily."

She shuddered once, from cold or premonition. "But we need worry," she said. "We do not know what the king intends, and until we do…"

"Until we do, we prepare." Conoc kissed her forehead. "If I ask you to rest, will you? Tomorrow will bring an influx of people, and you will need to handle them. I would have you get what sleep you can before then."

"I will try." She smiled wanly. "Will you as well? I know your shoulder still pains you, and you have used it too much today."

His smile was as weak as her own, though containing a bit more humor. "A bargain, my lady. My hand on it." His hand, warm and strong, callused from his sword, took hers.

She squeezed back, then stood and, greatly daring, leaned forward to kiss him ever so lightly before she retreated to her room.

MORNING BROUGHT with it all the people Conoc had expected. The villagers had come streaming in as soon as the sun rose, to be greeted by the Lord and Lady, both clad, at Jenevra's urging, in Ravensmere blue.

Conoc, as he did when worry or upset besieged him, appeared cold and intimidating, his face stiff, lips shaped into a frown and eyebrows drawn together. Jenevra remembered the expression from their first meeting, when she had believed him angry to meet her. Now, anger truly did beset him, and he did not conceal those emotions well.

To Jenevra fell the task of welcoming people and soothing worries. Her smile never slipped, no matter who approached her. Each villager she greeted and directed off with one of the castle women she could rely on.

She did not see, until after their arrival, Kenan's sister Eseld and her husband. They arrived on horseback, and Conoc greeted them himself. She did not want to see them; her last meeting with Eseld still rankled, and she misliked having them in her home. But Jorin was the largest freeholder in Conoc's domain and deserved to be protected here as well.

Jenevra did not intend to spend any time with Eseld alone.

It did not take so long for everyone to be gathered within the castle walls. Before midmorning, the gate had closed again. The portcullis had never been repaired, and Conoc had kept it up all this time. She wondered, with a shudder, if he would lower it during this business.

Guards lined the walls. Though the garrison had been decimated by the last Northern attack, new levies, some from Caermor, some from the Ravensmere land had come. They could not shoot an arrow straight, nor use the pikes they carried, but they could guard the wall as well as any.

Jenevra stayed outside as much as she could, though the first breath of autumn chilled her in spite of her wool gown. She felt the tension in the air and knew that others did too. Every back - whether guard or villager, man or woman - stood straight, every head erect. And every eye watched the road, because they all knew something would come.

As the sun reached its highest point, it did.

A blare of trumpets broke the tense silence, and a messenger, flanked by the trumpeter and a pair of guards rode up to the gate.

"In the King's name, open for his messenger," the trumpeter called.

The gate opened, and half a dozen guards took positions around the quartet. The trumpeter and the guards wore the King's livery; the messenger did not, nor did his horse wear trappings in the King's colors. Jenevra recognized the messenger as he guided his horse to the foot of the stairs upon which she and Conoc stood. Conoc must have recognized him as well, for he went down the stairs to meet him.

"Sir Wyeth," he said, face and voice calm.

Sit Wyeth did not share that calm. His mouth twisted into a smile that more resembled a grimace, and his face was pale.

"Lord Conoc," he said clearly, for everyone to hear. "I bear a message for you from His Majesty the King. And," now his voice dropped, "I wish I did not. Were it my choosing, I would not accept such a task."

He handed over a scroll, which Conoc unrolled. Jenevra descended most of the steps, so that she remained higher than Conoc and could read it herself.

Let it be known that our sometime servant Conoc Torval, Lord of Ravensmere, is accused of harboring heretics and conspiring with the enemies of our throne, the Northerners he had pledged to stand against. If he be innocent, let him present himself before us and defend himself against these accusations.

By my hand, Renier, King of Merembria

Jenevra pressed her lips together. This was the new queen's urging, for the King had never before cared about heretics. Nor did they have any in Ravensmere. Indeed, that puzzled her; such an accusation came from nowhere. *She* was the most devout person in the castle, save Father Andreu and Father...

Horror choked her, for she had a sudden insight where this had come from. She did not want to believe it, that he would betray them, betray her so. But her heart knew with sudden clarity that it could not be other than truth.

Conoc re-rolled the scroll and handed it to Jenevra. "Have someone saddle a horse for me," he said to Kenan, who with Lorent had come up to his side. "I will answer this before the king."

Her heart racing, Jenevra reached for his hand, even as he turned towards her. "No. Do not do this."

"I must. You know that I cannot let this stand. He is my king, and I have given him my loyalty. He must see that and judge me himself." He clasped her hands inside his. "Kenan and Lorent will remain with you. Jenevra, should something happen, I leave the castle in your hands."

She nodded, her mouth too dry to speak. She did not allow herself the privilege of tears, knowing he needed to see her strong. Without another word, he pressed a kiss to her lips, too fierce to be gentle and too quick to be anything but goodbye.

Then he strode off to the horse prepared for him, mounted,

and rode off through the gates beside Sir Wyeth without a glance back.

"Sir Kenan," she said and fought to keep her voice clear. "You have the guard 'til Lord Conoc returns. Sir Lorent, take this," and she handed him the scroll, "to Father Andreu and tell him what has gone on. When Lord Conoc returns, he'll want Andreu's council. And someone find Father Bardin and send him to my solar. I want to speak to him immediately."

JENEVRA PACED the solar back and forth in the minutes while she waited for Father Bardin, rehearsing the words she wanted to use, trying to maintain a semblance of calm. The sunlight filtering through the window filled the room with light, but it failed to touch her. She had never felt such anger. Temper, yes, some, but not to such an extent. Always before it had been a quick flash that faded quickly. Now she could not see it so.

Seconds passed so slowly that she did not know whether she had waited for minutes or hours. The sun did not move so much as she felt it should have, though, so only minutes must have passed.

When he came through the door, as fiercely self-righteous as always, his eyes lit with the fire of fanaticism, a flame that lay banked most of the time, she lost the little control she had maintained while watching her husband perhaps ride to his death.

"Why did you do it?" she cried.

"I do not have the pleasure of understanding my lady," he replied. But she saw that he did know and did not repent, for he met her eyes unashamedly.

"You wrote to someone - your preceptor, perhaps? - and accused us of harboring a heretic. You accused Andreu of being one. Which of us is it that you hate so much?"

The flame flashed into full blaze. "You think you understand me, my lady? I have lived in this... den of iniquity for two years. You could have prevented this, but you failed to heed my warnings more than once. Yes, I accused him, but of nothing that was not true and full of proof."

"Proof? Truth? You do not know what those words mean."

"I know he encourages barbaric and heathen practices. They are like children and should be taught the correct way, not coddled on 'tradition' that condemns them. And you allowed it, you who know better than anyone else in the castle what is right."

"You have been studying Balyese philosophers too much. Those are their words." She stared at him, though he stood several inches above her, and did not hesitate to use words as her weapons. "You condemn him for caring about the people, for not condemning *them*. There is no truth in that.

"But I will give you this truth. Leave my castle. You are no longer welcome within its walls and its protections. You are no member of my household. Let others protect you, as you have chosen them in this." He started to speak, but she did not hear a word he spoke. "Go! If you are still within these walls when I come down, I will have you thrown out."

She held her stance as he, silenced but not ashamed, backed out without offering even the slightest courtesy. Then she dropped onto the window seat and hid her face that no one would hear her sobs.

Had she been so wrong? She had never liked Father Bardin, but equally she had never believed him other than a good, if rigid, man. Her misjudgment might cost her husband his life, and for that she would never forgive herself.

CONOC RETURNED JUST BEFORE SUNSET.

He saw her, standing on the steps, almost where he had left her. Though she had worked throughout the day, as much to run from her fear as because work needed doing, she ran out as soon as the lookout passed the word that the Lord was coming home.

She knew he saw her, saw the way his eyes lingered on her for a flicker of time. But he spoke to Kenan and Lorent. "Close and bar the gates. We will get no more visitors tonight."

Only then did he approach her, face grim, lines more pronounced than usual. "My lady," he said. He offered her an arm, but when she moved to speak, he laid a finger on her lips. "Not here. I will tell you all, but not here."

In a short time, she had arranged for a small meal to be served in the solar, the only room large enough to suit those who ultimately joined them and equally private enough that no one else would hear what was said.

Jenevra sat at the window with Sess, a trencher with chicken pasties, soft rolls and honey between them on the long seat. Conoc and Andreu sat at the table, while Kenan stood leaning against it, and Lorent paced as he ate. The table held the food and drink for the men, which they shared communally.

Only after Conoc had eaten some did he begin the conversation they had come to hear.

"I rode down to the camp as I was ordered. Sir Wyeth never left my side, though whether by order or his own will, I could not say. I was shown into the king's tent, where he sat on a throne almost as grand as that Valles Castle in the capital. The queen, or so I assumed, sat beside him, fingers stroking his hand. She was beautiful, captivating even, but she had a hardness in her eyes.

"Around them, various lords stood in their places. At his right hand, the only lord I knew by sight, stood the Duke of Durere. I knew no one else present." He glanced over at Jenevra and shook his head once; her father had not been among them, and she did not know if that meant good or ill.

"The King... is not how I remember him. He was quick to anger, quick to defensiveness. He accused me of harboring and encouraging heretics. Then he accused me of conspiring with Northerners and claimed that is why I did not want the progress to come here.

"I did my best to defend myself. No one spoke for me; I had no friends there save Sir Wyeth. The king did not seem to give me his attention; only the queen drew his full attention. She did not speak aloud, though she leaned to whisper in his ear more than once.

"Finally he dismissed me. I would hear his judgment on the morrow, he said. I do not think the time will matter; I believe he has already determined my fate, and this proceeding existed for some reason of his own." He put his head in his hands, tension and fatigue obvious in the slump of his shoulders.

In the silence, Jenevra spoke. "He would want the lords, and more, the magnates of the Council, to believe this trial. They will rise up against him if they believe he will act against them without cause. But I do not understand why he acts at all. You have been loyal without question."

"I cannot answer that question any more than I could answer his accusations." Conoc looked at her. "I will apologize to you, my lady. You expressed fears, months ago, to which I gave no credence."

She shook her head, but he went on. "No, I will say it. You were concerned about the queen's power, and I dismissed your concerns because I thought I knew the king better than you could know of the queen. I was proved wrong."

"Well, we will have no more accusations of heresy, at least," Lorent said. "I saw Father Bardin through the gate myself. I believe he headed towards the king's encampment."

"Oh no!" Jenevra groaned. "He will tell more tales, to a very willing audience. I did not think, when I sent him away, where he would go. I only wished him to leave, for I was very angry."

"If I was uncertain before, lady, I am now very clear that I do not want you angry at me ever," Lorent said. Since neither Conoc nor Andreu had heard the story, he told what he knew with great vigor. "He stomped around, a bag of books on his shoulder, and muttered often in languages I did not understand. Then he demanded a mount, which I refused to give him as he was no longer an inhabitant of this castle. So he glared at me, and if he offered this look to you, lady, he is fortunate no one was there to see it. He continued the stomping and muttering down the road, though I could not say if he still glared."

Kenan laughed, and even Sess hid a demure chuckle behind her hand. Andreu did not, though his eyes, as he looked at her, were warm. "I do not know that I warrant such a defense, my lady, but I am grateful for it nonetheless."

Jenevra would have disclaimed all the praise, for she knew she did not deserve it. She had acted out of temper, not out of thought and right judgment. But she could not deny Conoc's proud smile as he looked at her.

LATER, she and Conoc talked in his room. Sess had brushed her hair out and left it down in deference to the evening visits, and Jenevra twisted one lock around her finger as she spoke. "I fear what tomorrow will bring."

Conoc did not pace, and she didn't know where he found the control, for he must be as nervous as she. But he remained calm as he straightened arms and armor. "I know you do, and I would take that from you if I could. But nothing I say will calm you."

"Because we know, you and I, that this is not finished. Why does it not bother you the more?"

"Because..." He stopped to look at her. "Because it is done now. We do not need to wonder what will happen; the die is already thrown. Now we must be prepared to meet it, and in that, we have done all we can. What happens tomorrow, we will meet with our heads high."

CHAPTER TWENTY-THREE

The next morning, Sir Wyeth, again with guard escort and trumpeter, rode up to the castle and was granted admittance. Conoc did not wish to, nor did Jenevra, but Conoc equally had no desire to antagonize the king as blatantly as that would. Besides, though he came as messenger, Sir Wyeth had himself done nothing to them to warrant such ill treatment.

Sir Wyeth looked ill at ease as he rode through the gates, and though the guards had increased and every one stood at attention, he barely noticed them. The trumpeter, on his left hand, held his head up, as if he believed himself above all present. The two guards merely sneered at the men on duty. Sir Wyeth kept his eyes fixed on Conoc and, even more, on Jenevra.

She stood beside Conoc, a slim tall figure in dark green, a lighter green beneath, with her hair plaited in a single long braid twisted up and held in a caul. Her spine straight, the delicate face composed, her bearing as regal as the queen's and twice as fair, she stood out among the folk of Ravensmere and the villagers who had joined them. Conoc had granted himself an indulgence to admire her before he'd joined her, and to wonder when she'd grown so tall. No trace of the girl remained in the woman beside him.

Sir Wyeth approached them, but his eyes never left Jenevra. "My lady," he said, too softly for anyone but them to hear. "I would ask your pardon in advance for what I must do. The king has gone too far with this."

Her lips shaped into a fraction of a smile. "My pardon you freely have, Sir Wyeth. Now, I bid you, for all our sakes, be about your charge."

He nodded and unrolled the scroll he carried and began reading it in a loud, clear voice. So clear was his voice that if Conoc had not seen the sick look in Wyeth's eyes, he would have thought the man took pleasure in what he read.

Be it known by all that we, by our gracious majesty, have no desire to punish our kinswoman, Lady Jenevra Louvet, sometime of Allandale and now styled as Lady of Ravensmere, for the alleged deplorable and sacrilegious actions of her husband, and, as evidence has been presented that her marriage to Sir Conoc Torval, Lord of Ravensmere, was never consummated and is therefore not valid -

The castle had never been so silent. Conoc did not think so many men and women *could* be silent, but not a sound could be heard in the bailey. No one moved nor even breathed.

Jenevra stilled and her face paled by degrees as Wyeth kept reading, until she might have been a marble statue standing there. Only Conoc could see her fingers, clenched together and still shaking.

- we extend a hand of grace and offer her a place at court and a marriage of our own devising if she will repudiate her false husband.

She held out her hand, no longer shaking, for the scroll, which Sir Wyeth handed her gravely. Her eyes went to it, as if she read the words again, but nothing changed in her expression for a long moment, then half a smile appeared. "That is the king's word? Here, then, is mine." And she tore the scroll in two.

She hadn't shaken from upset, she'd shaken from anger, and she was glorious with the light of fury in her eyes. Conoc understood Lorent's words the night before about never wishing to anger her.

In a voice that carried across the entire silent area, she added, "I reject that offer and its lies. Let the king punish me if he will; I will not betray my husband." For a moment, she met his eyes then she whirled around and walked, regal dignity and fury in her carriage, up the steps and back into the keep.

Conoc picked up the discard halves of the scroll and handed them to Sir Wyeth. "I would leave quickly," he said lowly. "The king will not appreciate her response, and no one in the castle will appreciate your continued presence."

"Lord Conoc, you know -"

He waved it off. "I hope we meet again in happier times, Sir Wyeth."

Conoc intended to find Jenevra immediately. He suspected he would find her working and trying to hide her hurt or hidden in the solar. She was a private woman, his lady, and to have word of their marriage made so public, both here and in the camp below, would hurt her modesty and her pride.

All of that stood under his protection, and he intended to do whatever in his power would help her.

Despite his intentions, men needed his instructions on the ordering of the castle, and the plan for its defense. He knew, as did everyone else, that the king's offer to Jenevra, however sincere, was a prelude to more. A prelude to his condemnation of Conoc, in fact.

He put the castle defenses in the hands of Kenan and Lorent

and trusted their judgment to be as good as his own. Better, since they had fewer distractions.

The inside of the keep, when he had dispatched his chores and could enter in search of his lady, had a quiet unlike the bustle of the outdoors. Faintly he could hear the bustle of conversation and work being done, but not as clearly as he had heard on other days. He'd expected more noise, not less, with the villagers in the keep as well as the castlefolk.

He started to turn in that direction, as Jenevra oversaw the keep personally, but her voice would stand out clearly over others: the pitch carried, and so did her clear noble accent. He heard neither. Even Sess's less noble but equally crisp voice didn't reach him.

Instead, he headed for the stairs. The solar, then, where she could be alone and still see what went on in the bailey.

"Conoc?"

He turned at the female voice, deeper and richer than his wife's, a slight roll that gave away her origins.

Eseld stood there, the dark blue gown the same color as her eyes, though her turned back sleeves revealed a softer blue underneath. Her black hair, plaited in two plaits that hung down to the middle of her back, worn the way his mother and hers had always worn theirs. She looked foreign and familiar, making him think of another turn his life could have taken.

Her expression was cautious, but not hesitant. Eseld had never had a moment of hesitation in her life. "Are you well?" she asked.

"As well as could be expected," he said. "Given all that has gone on..."

"That is what I would speak to you on," Eseld said as he paused for breath. Eagerness in her expression puzzled him; he could not think what she could find so urgent.

"I do not have much time," he said. "I have other people to find."

He saw the faint narrowing of eyes that indicated Eseld's irritation. That had always been the telltale sign of her temper, even as a child, and he didn't know what had sparked it this time. She could not believe him to have nothing to do but wait for her appearance.

"Come with me," he said, ushering her down the hall to the small room he used for private meetings during the day.

This room was his for working, and as he had grown into his role as Lord of Ravensmere, he had come to use it more often. The table had stacked documents regarding the workings of the castle and the land around it. The few shelves held more of the same.

On either side of the wooden table sat chairs, one larger and measured for his height, that he could sit easily. Jenevra had ordered it made for him, as a gift, that he might be comfortable. The other chair, intended for those who came to see him, had not been made so grand.

A fire burned, freshly made by the sight of it, and a fur-lined blanket lay draped over the back of his chair. A faint hint of Jenevra's floral scent in the air told him that she had been there and made sure the room was ready for him when he needed it. She would never make her handiwork known, but in such small ways she let him - and others in the keep - know that she cared.

He sat down, feeling very much like the Lord of Ravensmere as he did and wondered how much longer he would have either title or feeling. "What is it you need of me, Eseld?"

She remained standing, but any trace of caution or temper disappeared. Instead, her lips curled into a sensuous smile. "The question should be, what need have you for me? The entire castle knows now that your wife is no such thing. She will soon return to her own people to make some new marriage with some witless lordling. You will be left alone to make a new choice."

Conoc frowned. "Were you outside for Sir Wyeth's message? I did not see you."

"I was not. I did not need to be." She shrugged, the movement meant to draw his eyes. "The state of your marriage is no secret."

"And yet no one has said a word in near two years?" He did not believe that possible, in such a small place as Ravensmere, that a secret like that could be kept from himself, from Jenevra, from Kenan and Lorent, and from Sess. One of them would have heard something.

"Who would say such a thing to you? But because no one spoke of it, it does not follow that no one *knew*."

"How did you know?"

"One of her maids is hardly discreet. Only a small amount of coin bought the knowledge that she sleeps alone in her bed every night, and even the wedding night had no evidence." Eseld relished sharing this, her smile made it clear.

His heart hurt for Jenevra, who would be mortified at such being gossiped about. He could not place the maid in question, but she would know and that woman would no longer have a place in this castle if he had anything to say on the matter.

He also remembered Jenevra's concerns of Eseld, her dislike of the other woman, which he had dismissed as he dismissed all of her concerns in the beginning. She had not been wrong.

"What is it you wish, Eseld?"

She perched herself on the edge of the table nearest him. "I wish to be to you what I have always wished: your wife, in more than name. When she is gone, we shall have our chance." Eseld reached out to touch his cheek, her smile warm and gentle. "I understood why you chose her, but it was a poor choice. She knows nothing of our people, our way of life. Now the king has turned his back on you, and you have no wife. It is time to make new choices."

The door that he hadn't realized Eseld had shut opened, and

Jenevra stood there. "Conoc -" Then she froze, and he watched the color drain from her face the second time this day. But she didn't speak, didn't change expression, just backed up and whirled away, the movement as fast as skirts would allow.

He stood up but Eseld blocked his way. "She is gone, you need not think of her again."

Conoc looked at her. "You have a low opinion of me, if you think I would dishonor my vows to set her aside and encourage you to break yours. You would have been better served to listen to her speak outside, for she rejected the king's offer and determined to stay my wife; I will give her nothing less than she has given me."

Her eyes narrowed again, and she pursed her lips. "I did not think she had that in her. She is such a milksop. But will she hold to her resolve when Altyrans storm the castle and attack the king, confirming that you have been conspiring? I think not."

"This was your plan, Eseld? You sent this to court, to someone who would pass it on, perhaps even phrasing it to sound more than it was. Meanwhile you gave information to the Northerners."

"Altyrans, not Northerners!" she spat out. "Remember, you are half of that as well."

"I am the king's man first."

"The king's man! A king who would abandon you so willingly! Why would you give your loyalty to him?" She glared at him, her face passionate and wild, eyes lit, showing her true self for the first time. "You should have married me! We would have held this castle for our own people, kept them safe against any more attacks from greedy kings. Our children would have been Altyrans, not king's men."

"Then you do not know me at all, nor ever did." He took her upper arm in his hand and pulled her from the room, shutting the door behind him. He didn't hide his anger, nor his disappointment. Eseld's betrayal cut deep, and if Kenan shared her feelings, that would cut even deeper.

"Go back to your husband, Eseld." He let go of her, so she could leave. "I will not throw you from the castle, but if you go near my wife again or cause her any hurt, I will not vouch for what I will do."

DESPITE HIS WISHES and his concern for his wife, Conoc did not go straight to her. The castle's need came first always, and he had a few words to pass, discretely, to Lorent and to Jorin, Eseld's husband. He could not guarantee that all would be well for her, but she would be watched.

Every time he tried to go to her, something - or someone - prevented him. Had he not known that every person who wanted him did so for true and legitimate reasons, he would have believed it a conspiracy; no matter which way he went, he was needed.

Of course, some people only wished to discuss Jenevra. Most wanted to discuss her confidence; none mentioned the accusation against their marriage. He didn't know if Eseld was correct, that everyone knew and no one dared say anything, or if they hadn't known and now didn't believe. Either way, he sensed nothing but true concern for his wife and righteous anger against the king for spreading something so publicly.

Jenevra did not come down for the evening meal, which she so rarely missed. He felt her absence as he sat at the head table without her beside him and without Sess in her place on Jenevra's other side. If anyone in all of Ravensmere had missed her upset, they could not any longer.

He signaled to a servitor and asked for a meal to be sent up to Jenevra, but was informed that the Lady Cecilie had already asked for one and that the cook had sent up some of her favorites to please her. Conoc felt unbalanced and foolish. Others had his lady's care well in hand.

When he did go upstairs after dinner, the outside of Jenevra's room was guarded by the ever-faithful Sess. Her blank expression told him that he needn't bother asking; she had chosen her side and would protect Jenevra with everything she had. On any other day, he would encourage this. Tonight he wanted to see his wife, to hold her in his arms and stroke her hair until she felt safe again.

He slipped into his room. Jenevra had been in since the morning, for the room had been set to rights after he left. But she must have done it much earlier, for no trace of her scent lingered, and though a new fire had been laid, it had not been lit, which she would normally have seen to in the evening.

He knelt to light the fire himself and glanced over his shoulder at the closed door between their rooms. She always came in when she heard his footsteps; she had not missed a night in nearly a year. But no silent figure stood there; no sounds came from her room.

Conoc rose and crossed to the door, but did not try to open it or touch it in any way. Never had she barred the door against him. He could not bear to try it and find that she had tonight.

CHAPTER TWENTY-FOUR

Jenevra slept fitfully and woke in a quarrelsome mood, except that only Sess was present to be quarreled with, and Sess had done nothing to deserve it. Nor would she have quarreled; Sess remained even-tempered no matter the provocation.

Though Jenevra defied even Sess to stay calm when the doings of her marriage bed had been made so public a thing as yesterday. Except that to herself, Jenevra would admit that her ill temper had more to do with what happened after the king's mockery of a gracious proclamation. That had been an anger she rarely felt, spurred on by embarrassment that something so personal had been put forward before everyone.

Finding Eseld in Conoc's study had been another thing entirely. Bad enough that she was there, with him, alone and with the door closed. But to find her with her hands on his face, a posture so intimate that Jenevra would never had dared it with him, had cut her to the quick. She had not given the matter any thought, she had only fled for the safety of her room and the one person she knew beyond any doubt loved her completely.

Sess had listened as she'd cried herself half-sick, passing no judgment. Not even when Jenevra had dropped the bar into place to block the door between her room and Conoc's. She had not expected Conoc to try it until much later, and by then she had recovered enough to remove it so that he could enter if he wished. He had not, and she had fallen asleep finally, wondering if he were with Eseld and that was why he had not tried the door.

With the morning light, Jenevra knew that Conoc would never do such a thing. He held his honor and his sworn word in too high a regard to break it. Eseld might have tried, but Conoc would not have accepted more.

Still, it had hurt to see. She would have to face Eseld, her head held high, knowing that what she had suspected for some time was true and the other woman sought Conoc for her own.

She dragged herself from her bed and to the window. The sun rose later these autumn days, so less was lit of the lake. Her garden lay completely in shadow still.

A last few curlews called as they searched the lakeshore for food. Soon they would go too, and she would be alone. She tucked her knees to her chest and laid her head down, too tired even to weep.

He had not come last night.

She had believed, she had been certain that he would. That he would wish to know she was well. That no matter what else happened with the castle and the king, he would count her among his cares and see her.

And he had not.

Sess found her there some time later, as the sun crept in the open window, still curled in the same position but stiff and chilled now, for the early morning air was cold. Without a word, she took a blanket off the bed and draped it over Jenevra, then wrapped her arm around her and rested her head against hers.

For a long time they sat together, both silent, one watching out the window, the other watching her friend, until the sun climbed high enough that it could no longer be ignored.

Sess rose first. "It is time to get up," she said, lifting the blanket. "There will be word from the king, and you will be wanted."

Jenevra rose, but her body felt heavy and difficult to move. She offered no resistance as Sess helped her into kirtle and gown and laced them up. Sess spoke little, except for directions as needed, which relieved Jenevra. Her throat felt thick, and the words didn't want to come out.

Which Sess had finished with her hair, a knock on the door drew both their attentions.

Father Andreu stood there, holding out a hand for Jenevra. "I thought perhaps I might escort the Lady of Ravensmere down. I have not spent much time with her of late."

The gentle warmth in the old priest's eyes nearly broke Jenevra. Instead, she took his hand, and he drew it through his arm. "There now," he said softly, as they began to walk. "Is it comfort you need, lady, or counsel? I am here for you either way."

She burst into tears, exhausted, uncontrolled sobs, her words incoherent even to herself. Andreu just petted her hair as her tears soaked into his cassock until she stopped of her own accord.

Then he offered her a kerchief to dry her eyes. "Does that feel better, lass?"

Surprisingly, it did. The release of tears had also released the heavy, weighed down feeling. She nodded.

"Good. Then perhaps I should take you to your husband. I do not think I am breaking any confidences when I tell you that he has not slept any more than you, and, though he did not handle yesterday well, he needs you desperately. He expects news from the king this morning."

It would not be good news. Jenevra knew that and knew

Conoc understood that too. She did not understand the king's motives, but his actions had become very clear.

Conoc waited for them at the bottom of the steps, relief etched so sharply on his face that Jenevra felt a pang of guilt for keeping him waiting. Andreu was correct; Conoc had circles under his eyes, and the normally faint lines marked his face more strongly. The black surcoat over his armor, unrelieved but for his crest in blue, emphasized those lines as well.

He drew her close and kissed her forehead, then rested his face on her hair. "A messenger from the king has already been spotted. Not Sir Wyeth today."

"No, it would not be." The king had sent Sir Wyeth for a purpose. That was done.

They walked outside together, Jenevra on Conoc's arm, Andreu behind them. Silence held across the bailey, a deep respectful silence, and people bowed their heads to Jenevra in a gesture of respect that made her blush. The people of Ravensmere usually accorded her all the respect to which she was entitled; this was more.

"I have a great deal to say to you, my lady," Conoc said softly. "This is not the time, nor the place, to make the apologies I owe you, nor to tell you the rest, but I will say it. I am sorry."

She shook her head once, her throat too tight to speak again. "Not now," she managed. She could not lose control of her emotions now, and she feared if Conoc spoke too much, she would not be able to hold herself in check.

Conoc assisted her up the stone steps to the top of the wall, a place she had never been and only seen from a distance. Several guardsmen moved to make a place for them where they could watch the approaching messenger. She nodded her thanks and received silent nods in return.

The wall, despite being the same gray stone that made up the castle, felt warm under her fingers, warmed by the sun rather than hidden in shadows as the keep was.

All around her wore grim expressions. No one believed that the king would send them good news, especially with a new messenger. They just didn't know how bad it could be.

Jenevra knew.

Not for certain or exactly what he would do. But the king had banished his own son for a crime he did not speak of. He could do a great deal more to one of his liegemen, who had no strong backing from other lords, no influence with the Council. In her heart, Jenevra feared the worst and knew her fears were not groundless.

The messenger, a burly man whose yellow surcoat bore a device worked in gray that Jenevra could not identify, reined in his horse before the closed gate. He wore no helmet, so the sneer upon his face was clearly visible, nor did he care.

"Will you grant me admittance?" he called up. "I come bearing word on the king's behalf."

"No," Conoc called backed. "You may deliver your message from here. The king's messengers are not welcome in this castle until they bring an apology to my lady for the scurrilous lies in yesterday's message."

The messenger's eyes flicked to Jenevra, and if anything, his sneer grew a little more pronounced. "If that is your wish." He pulled out a scroll and, after unrolling it, began to read.

Be it known that we have judged Conoc Torval, sometime knight under us and Lord of Ravensmere, guilty of conspiring against our throne. He is ordered to relinquish possession of Ravensmere and to surrender himself, and those knights under him, to our justice. He has until nightfall, else we shall bring our might against him.

Jenevra's heart twisted inside her breast; she held herself still and expressionless and didn't know how she managed either. Treason. The king accused Conoc of treason.

The messenger looked up at Conoc. "Is it clear?"

"Go. Tell the king you have delivered his message." No expression crossed Conoc's stony face.

The messenger waited, expecting some other word or action, then he kicked his horse so fiercely that the big bay jumped.

Conoc took Jenevra's arm and led her back down the stairs to the bailey, ignoring the people pushing round him trying to get answers. His face changed not one whit, he spoke no word, just kept his eyes forward.

When they reached the bottom of the steps, Jenevra could wait no longer. She pulled away from him that she could see his face and he hers. "You will not!" Her voice rose in pitch and volume, and though people could see her, she did not stop. "I will not allow you to turn yourself over to the king for execution! I will not have it!"

Conoc's smile, though it didn't reach his eyes, spoke more of amusement than any joy. "I have no intention of doing so. But my lady need not make a scene to convince me."

"If I must, I will. You went to the king once, how am I to know that you will not do such a thing again?"

"Because I have a wife and people to care for." He kept his voice low, between them only. "The king has broken his oath to me now, I can act as I must for everyone's good. Trust me, lady; I have no wish to be executed."

For a long moment, she stared at him. He told the truth, Conoc always told the truth, and yet she questioned if his honor would let him act against the king's command. Then she shook her head, because it did not matter.

"Excuse me, my lord. There is a great deal to do, and too little time to do it in."

He stopped her with a hand to her arm. "The solar, my lady, in one hour. As you say, we have a great deal to do."

CONOC HAD BARELY REACHED the inside of the keep - Jenevra had covered the distance far more quickly, despite the gown that hampered a full stride, and no one had stopped her with questions - when Kenan caught up to him.

"Conoc, I need to speak to you."

He raised an eyebrow, but did not say anything. He'd expected Kenan to come to him about Eseld, but he hadn't thought it would take so long, nor did he think this was the moment for it. But their friendship went too far back to deny his friend the chance to speak.

"I have a confession to make," Kenan said, voice low. "Eseld told me what... she did."

"You didn't know?"

"No! And I would never had approved of such a thing." He took a deep breath. "I won't deny I wanted you to marry Eseld; you know that. But to smear your name and Lady Jenevra's... No. Not ever.

"But..." Kenan paused, then the words came slowly, dragged out of him almost against his will. "I did tell someone how important she was to you. An Altyran warleader. That first attack, when she was out in the woods... That happened by my information."

Conoc stared speechless, cut by a betrayal far worse than Eseld's and by someone who meant far more. Kenan was more than friend, he was brother in all but name. Never had they been far apart. "You told them to kidnap my wife?"

"No... Yes... I told them that she mattered to you, that you would do anything to get her back. She would never have been harmed, and I thought... if she was scared, she might leave."

Kenan didn't raise his eyes from where he stared at his own shoes.

"Why?" Conoc whispered.

"Because... Because she ties you to the king, and I thought, with the right push, you could be brought to our side."

For a moment, Conoc was silent. Then, quietly, he said, "I thought we were on the same side."

"Always." Kenan met his eyes unflinchingly for that. "You are my lord and my friend, as dear as a brother could be. I will never be on a different side than yours."

"Can you be loyal to me and not to the king I serve?"

Kenan did not answer, though he did not lower his eyes either, and Conoc didn't expect him to. Divided loyalties, all of them. Choosing sides for love or honor, not for rightness. But Kenan, the brother of his heart all of their lives together.

"The attack on the castle, when they came looking for her?" He spoke more calmly than he felt, his thoughts shrieking at him but he did not have time to listen to them.

"No. By then... I knew her. She'd become one of us. And then she saved your life. I'm sorry." He waited, but Conoc didn't speak, and after a moment, Kenan bowed to leave.

"Wait," Conoc said. "Are you the one who trained them to fight better then?"

"No." Kenan shook his head once. "That wasn't me. I'm as baffled by that as you. I didn't help them that much. I tried to tip the scales a little, but I would never fight against you."

Though he attended to all the matters that needed attending before the hour was up and he went to meet with Jenevra, his mind remained most often on Kenan, though no resolution presented itself.

He could, he did, understand Kenan's desire for him to wed Eseld and turn to the Northerners' side. Kenan had always lived his life as an exile from the home he wanted, and he had stayed at least in part for Conoc. To return the castle to Northern hands and to bring at least a few knights would have ensured his welcome.

He even understood trying to frighten Jenevra away, making her want to leave before they were married. Though it might not have turned him fully, it might have soured the relationship between himself and the king, a relationship that had not needed much to break it.

But to bring harm to a girl-child by kidnapping her - and he did not believe, whatever Kenan said, that she would have remained unharmed - that he could not fathom. Especially because she was his wife by that time.

His brain rejected Kenan's reasons and excuses, but his heart whispered of the long years of their friendship. No matter how often he turned the matter over in his mind, he could not decide whether to condemn or forgive.

When he entered the solar and found Jenevra standing there with Kenan at her side, he knew that Kenan had gone to her and begged her forgiveness. She had forgiven him by the way she smiled at him.

Relief surged through him, that Jenevra had taken the choice out of his hands. He couldn't choose; she could see clearer than he today.

Lorent entered behind him, escorting Sess, then Father Andreu shut the door.

"We are all here. Good. Let me explain my plan."

JENEVRA DID NOT like the plan originally. At least, one part of her did not. The rest of her thought it a reasonable, if dangerous, undertaking. But the risk, almost in its entirety, would be borne by the six of them. Nor could she devise a better plan, as all four men would be executed if the king had them in his power. Sess would be safe, but Jenevra did not think the king would deal well with her after her dramatic refusal of his terms.

"I think it can work," she said finally. Conoc had waited for her opinion, and Lorent and Andreu had waited because of him. Kenan, who stayed behind and to her right, did not speak. She didn't blame him. Conoc avoided looking at him, with reason, and he did not want to draw attention to himself.

"The king will not care about the ordinary people, the villagers, the guardsmen, the castlefolk. If they are not here when he arrives, they will be forgotten. But we cannot delay. They must move now."

Conoc nodded in agreement. He took a piece of chalk and sketched a rough map of the castle. "The villagers can leave through the main gate. Even if they're spotted, and I hope they will be, they'll be ignored. From there, they can fade back into the woods if it becomes necessary.

"The guardsmen will leave by the postern gate as soon as the sun sets. They can skirt the lake and enter the woods along the foot of the mountains. Then they can slip around the king's army on that side. From there, I don't know."

She saw the answer immediately. "They can go to Caermor. The levies will know the way, and if they go under those colors, no one will suspect them of being Ravensmere's men. The king may not even realize that land was part of my dowry."

For a moment, Conoc, Lorent and Andreu stared at her. Then Andreu smiled and nodded, and Lorent grinned. "That will do, my lady. I do not envy the king: he expected only to thwart warriors; he did not intend to outthink you."

Jenevra blushed at the praise and even more at Kenan's approving hand to her shoulder.

Sess cleared her throat. "All well and good, but we cannot run with the guardsmen, nor fade into the woods with villagers, especially if you want them seen. The king will want you all. Where will we go, and how?"

"We're going out the passage under the lake, then we're going to follow the mountains north." Conoc looked at Kenan. "We're going to seek sanctuary with Northerners."

Neither man looked away from that, and a tension ebbed out of Kenan. "Aye, they'd shelter us. If they give us a chance to ask."

"We'll take our chances." He went on to parcel out duties, dismissing each person as they were assigned, until only he and Jenevra stood there, staring at each other.

She looked away first, not certain what she felt. "I ought..."

"Please, my lady, hear me out first. I owe you an apology, an explanation for yesterday." Conoc reached out a hand to catch hers and pull her closer.

"You do not need to apologize to me. I understand..."

"No, you do not. I did not want to be with Eseld. But she chose that moment to enact the final part of her plan. She was the traitor; she is the one whose words reached the king. She plotted to force a break with the king so that you would leave and I would join the Northerners."

"A plethora of people who wanted that," Jenevra said. "I wonder that you still want me here. No one else has."

"You are my wife, and if that were the only reason, I would want you here." He brushed a loose lock of hair back from her face. "But I care for you, and I do not want you to leave. I want you with me, as I promised."

A few tears filled her eyes, and he rested his forehead against hers. "You are mine, lady, and I am yours. I will not let you go."

JENEVRA HAD no time to think on Conoc's words. No sooner had he said them then Sess had come back, looking for her on a matter that could not wait. From there, she spent the day hurrying from one task to another, living several days in the span of hours. No one thing held her attention; while she argued with Symme about leaving, her mind worried over the packing of provisions. She wrote letters while eating a hastily prepared noon meal. Yet the sun's never-ending march across the sky assured her that time passed as it ought.

The villagers were first on their way, each carrying as much food as they could. Jenevra knew they would not be threatened; no noble would even think to harm commoners, if they thought of them at all. The food would help them manage through the winter, which, as a north wind blew down on her, drew increasingly close.

She shivered in that wind. In Allandale, summer would just be giving way to autumn. Here winter attempted to steal time from autumn. Farther north, early winter had already arrived.

She pushed those thought aside to squeeze the hand of the blacksmith and his wife. His wife said nothing, but the blacksmith lifted up their two littlest children and Jenevra brushed each child's hair back and shook their hands as well.

"Lady," the blacksmith began. "We don't know what's goin' to happen, but we hope you and the lord will be back here soon."

"So do we all," Jenevra said. "You must keep safe, all of you. We look to you to celebrate with us when that day comes." She smiled, projecting a confidence she in no way felt. For them to believe, she must convince them.

He nodded and offered an awkward bow before escorting his family out. Jenevra then turned to the next family and repeated the process. No member of Ravensmere, no matter how high or low, would leave without their lady's farewells in person.

After the villagers, the free holders left. Most of them left on horseback or in wagons, taking their own share of supplies. Many of the women of the castle went with them for protection.

Eseld and her husband were among the last to leave. Conoc

did not see them off; he had his own tasks. Jenevra would have forgone this one herself if she'd been able.

Jorin nodded once, but said nothing. Jenevra gave little thought to him; he was a freeholder under Ravensmere's aegis; to his discredit in her eyes, he sided neither with nor against Conoc. She wondered if he knew what Eseld had plotted. But his manners showed no change towards his wife.

Eseld stopped her horse beside Jenevra. "You think you've won, but you did it hiding behind him." Nothing in her face betrayed her, but a note underneath the words caught Jenevra's ear.

Men did not, could not, understand what passed between women sometimes. Though Jenevra had not been taught to play such games, for her mother and godmother held to a higher standard, she was not stupid. She could hear as well as any.

"I do not need to hide behind anyone, Eseld." A lifted chin. Let Eseld challenge her. She had no temper for it today of all days. For a long moment, they stared at each other, Jenevra's blue eyes meeting Eseld's darker ones.

Eseld looked away first. Then she nudged her horse after her husband's without another word.

As soon as the last freeholders left, she joined Conoc with the guardsmen. All of them, whether Conoc's men or Ravensmere men or levies from Caermor, wore armbands of sky blue and wheaten yellow, her father's colors, still flown at Caermor. If the god and goddess were kind, they would be away from the king's army and into safe lands and never need the protection of those colors.

She presented her letters to the most senior man among the levies. "As soon as you reach safety, send this to my father. He must know what has happened here; it cannot be delayed. This other is for the steward."

Jenevra had no hope that her father would act on what she had written. More likely, he would not, at least openly. She and Conoc would receive nothing certainly. But a word or two in the right ear might prevent another lord from suffering what Conoc did. If her father acted. He might decide his interests were better served by siding with the king; such an action would be in character.

She bade each guardsman farewell with as much attention as she had given the villagers. Those she knew more personally received extra smiles and words, though they remained silent. The guardsmen, as a whole, had not wanted to leave. Their loyalty was to Conoc personally or to her.

Like Kenan.

He stood, along with Lorent to one side, making sure each man had his pack and that none was overburdened.

One by one the guardsmen slipped out of the postern gate. In the deepening dusk, they would be less obvious in small groups until they reached the mountain trail.

Finn was the last out, and he hesitated before the gate.

"I won't go, my lady. I'm your guard and I should be with you."

Jenevra laid one hand on her heart, a sad smile on her face. "You have almost died twice in my service. You ought to give your allegiance to someone who will not ask that of you."

"I haven't died yet, my lady, and, until I do, I'm your man, wherever I am." With an equally sad smile in response, he bowed over her hand, then disappeared through the gate."

She watched him go, her heart and her throat too full for words.

THE SIX OF them stood alone in the empty bailey. Inside the keep, their own belongings, carefully packed by Sess and Andreu, waited for them.

But first, in the deepening dark, the castle had to be prepared. No trace could be left behind of where they or anyone else had gone.

Conoc and Lorent went to the main gates, and each of them pushed one of the heavy doors closed. They did not drop the bar - they wanted the king's men to gain entrance on the morrow, but the doors being closed would give everyone pause. They could not be pulled closed from the outside, only pushed from the inside. If the gates were closed, then someone inside must have closed them.

Jenevra and Kenan took the postern gate. She stood for a moment at the open gate, listening for one last lonely curlew, and when its call came, she nodded at Kenan, who pushed the gate closed. Then she lowered the wooden bar, too heavy for her to lift, to prevent it being opened again, at least from the outside.

Sess and Andreu waited inside the doors of the keep, where the doors would again be shut and not barred. These also could not be pulled shut from the outside. If any luck ran with them, the king's men would scour the keep from top to bottom looking for them and giving them time to make good their escape. Perhaps no one would suspect where they had gone for days.

Sess helped her with her bundle, containing a few kirtles and gowns, two books, a bit of embroidery, and, wrapped up in the very center of it, a few jewels that she could not part with. They would serve no practical purpose, but the thought of the king's men rummaging through her belongings and taking the jewels for themselves or giving them to the queen made her ill. She could not take everything, but she carried the pieces that mattered most to her.

She wore already her warmest gown and a cloak lined with fur. Her boots were the best she had, but she envied the men for their far sturdier ones. They wore mail over their warm clothes, and surcoat and capes over the mail. Only Father Andreu did not, and he wore two layers of cassock.

Together they walked down the stairs to the storerooms and the room with the secret passage, Conoc leading the way with Jenevra's hand held tightly in his. Then came Lorent and Sess, then Father Andreu, with Kenan bringing the rear.

The entrance to the passage stood open, waiting for them. As Conoc entered, still holding Jenevra's hand, Lorent dropped to the back to close the door securely.

"Mind your step," Conoc directed.

Jenevra tried, but she caught her foot on something, though she remembered the tunnel being smooth and obstructionless. "What is it?"

"The chests carrying your dowry and the jewels you could not carry." He kept his voice pitched low to reach only her.

She would have stopped, but he did not give her the opportunity. "You moved it all in here?"

"Sess told Lorent your concerns, so we moved everything." For a moment, his teeth flashed in the dim light. "I cannot fix everything, but I can fix that. No one will take what is yours."

Jenevra quickened her pace to keep up with him. "It is not, strictly speaking, mine. It is yours, and I objected as much to you losing it as I."

"I know that. But I did not think of it that way, because I do not know that we will ever come back to Ravensmere. I considered it all lost."

"We will come back. I believe that."

His fingers tightened on hers, but he said nothing, and she let the silence go as they walked the last uphill part of the tunnel to the door that led out into the hills. The north wind whistled down, blowing her cloak out and wrapping around her as she stepped from the protection of the tunnel. Full dark had finally come, and the only light came from the thin moon rising early in the evening.

Sess came out behind her, and the two of them stood together while Conoc, Kenan and Lorent piled first rocks, then bracken against the tunnel door until no one could have seen it.

"No one will find it now," Lorent said with satisfaction.

"And we will return," Kenan added, setting a hand on Conoc's shoulder.

Conoc said nothing, but turned and began walking up the hill. Jenevra hurried after him, a quick glance at the other men to reassure them that she too saw the expression of hurt and loss in Conoc's eyes.

As they crested the hill, Jenevra paused and looked back at Ravensmere. No lights shone; the castle lay in total darkness, empty, alone. Her eyes filled with tears, but she blinked them away.

Then she turned and followed her lord into the North.

ACKNOWLEDGMENTS

I could not have done this without a great deal of help, and there aren't words enough to thank the people who provided that help.

The indie writers from whom I've learned so much: DWS, KKR, the many writers of the Author Support Group and the Vellum support group among others.

Marisa, who has been my best friend for... well, lots of years, who never fails to remind me that I *can* do this. I'm a better writer because of you, lady.

My husband, who regularly asks me how it's going and has to listen to lengthy conversations about naming fictional countries, and who believes in me utterly. I love you.

And my children, who put up with Mommy's occasional distractions while she worked on her book. I hope they're satisfied with the results.